Alfred Blomfield

A Memoir of Charles James Blomfield

Bishop of London, with selection from his correspondence. In two volumes. Vol. 1

SALZWASSER
VERLAG

Alfred Blomfield

A Memoir of Charles James Blomfield

Bishop of London, with selection from his correspondence. In two volumes. Vol. 1

Reprint of the original, first published in 1863.

1st Edition 2022 | ISBN: 978-3-37500-747-8

Verlag (Publisher): Salzwasser Verlag GmbH, Zeilweg 44, 60439 Frankfurt, Deutschland
Vertretungsberechtigt (Authorized to represent): E. Roepke, Zeilweg 44, 60439 Frankfurt, Deutschland
Druck (Print): Books on Demand GmbH, In de Tarpen 42, 22848 Norderstedt, Deutschland

A MEMOIR

OF

CHARLES JAMES BLOMFIELD, D.D.

VOL. I.

A MEMOIR

OF

CHARLES JAMES BLOMFIELD, D.D.

BISHOP OF LONDON,

WITH SELECTIONS FROM HIS CORRESPONDENCE.

EDITED BY HIS SON,

ALFRED BLOMFIELD, M.A.

IN TWO VOLUMES.—VOL. I.

WITH A PORTRAIT.

LONDON

1863.

PREFACE.

It has long been desired by the friends of Bishop Blomfield that some authentic record of his life should be presented to the public. There was so little of egotism, and even of self-consciousness, in the Bishop's character, that he has left behind him fewer records of his inner life and feelings than are generally found in modern biographies. It has been truly said of him that his peculiarity, in writing as in action, was the absence of all pretension, which made him often unintelligible to those who could not understand the simple-minded greatness which went straight to its object; and this peculiarity made not only his conversation, but even his private diaries and letters, rather records of the outer life than revelations of the inner character. Hence, in those minute traits which go to make up the complete picture of a good man's life, this work may, perhaps, be found deficient.

But Bishop Blomfield's character is written in his actions; and these it has been attempted to set forth as simply and truthfully as possible. The Bishop has been allowed on all occasions to speak for himself. And such a life, so far as the desire to tell the story of it faithfully and intelligibly has been accomplished, will, it may be hoped, be instructive, in its occasional failures as well as in its successes, and in its consistent zeal and honesty, to all faithful sons of the Church of England: while even to those who owe her no allegiance, the record of such labours in the cause of our common Master, and of such a character moulded by His grace, may not be without its lesson of example and encouragement. To all it is commended, with the assurance that in no part of it has truth been knowingly sacrificed, even to a pardonable partiality, nor facts distorted in order to place the subject of the biography in a favourable light.

The Editor desires to express his acknowledgments to those friends who have aided his labours by the contribution of letters and other documents, or by the recollection of incidents in the Bishop's life; particularly to the Rev. W. G. Humphry, who had himself intended to write the life of Bishop Blomfield, an intention which he was compelled to abandon; to the

Venerable Archdeacon Sinclair; to his brother, the Rev. F. G. Blomfield, who has contributed the greater portions of the chapters on the Bishop's private and domestic life; to his brother-in-law, the Rev. C. B. Dalton; and to the Rev. Dr. Biber, whose work, published in 1857, and entitled "Bishop Blomfield and his Times," contains an able sketch of the Bishop's public career.

CONTENTS.

VOL. I.

CHAPTER I.

[1786.]

CHAPTER II.

[1811.]

CHAPTER III.

[1810.]

CHAPTER IV.

[1823.]

CHAPTER V.

[1825.]

CHAPTER VI.

[1829.]

CHAPTER XI.

[1841.]

A MEMOIR

OF

BISHOP BLOMFIELD.

CHAPTER I.

BIRTH AND PARENTAGE OF CHARLES JAMES BLOMFIELD—HIS SCHOOL-LIFE AT BURY AND EARLY RECOLLECTIONS—GOES TO TRINITY COLLEGE, CAMBRIDGE—SEVERITY OF HIS STUDIES THERE—HIS COLLEGE FRIENDS—BISHOP MONK—CHIEF-BARON POLLOCK—HIS ACADEMICAL DISTINCTIONS—TAKES HIS PLACE AMONG CLASSICAL SCHOLARS—HIS REVIEW OF BUTLER'S "ÆSCHYLUS"—HIS ORDINATION AND PROSPECTS AFTER IT—HIS MARRIAGE AND FIRST CURACY.

CHARLES JAMES BLOMFIELD was born on the anniversary of the Restoration, May 29th, 1786, at Bury St. Edmund's. In this ancient and then flourishing town, his father, Charles Blomfield, kept a school, which had previously been conducted by *his* father, James Blomfield, who removed to Bury from his native place, Ousden, in the same county, about 1760, and died in 1783.

Among the pupils of James, and contemporaries of Charles, though five or six years his junior, was the late Marquis of Bristol, then Mr. Hervey, who formed there a friendship for the father, which he afterwards continued to the more distinguished son.

In his father's school the future Bishop learnt the rudiments of Latin, and at the age of eight he was removed to the Grammar School of Bury, which already enjoyed a high reputation, under its master, Mr. Becher, an accurate and elegant, though not profound scholar. A delicate boy at first, and subject to affections of the chest, for which the air of Bury was too keen, Charles James used to climb up the stairs by the help of the banisters, and on account of his diminutive size was nicknamed by his schoolfellows *Tit* Blomfield. But he gave early promise of the ability and industry which marked his whole subsequent life. During the ten years which he spent at the Grammar School, he would often rise at four or five in the morning, in order to study modern languages, botany, and chemistry, in addition to his regular school-work. His verses and school exercises acquired him a reputation among his compeers; and those more serious compositions were diversified by vernacular poems on the incidents of school life; a kind of amusement in which he continued to indulge occasionally to the last.

Classical study was already his passion, and the possibility of attaining to high station in the Church was even then present to his mind; for when asked what profession he intended to follow, he answered, "I mean to be a Bishop." Later in life he attributed the origin of his literary tastes to an old nurse, who used to take him into the fields and tell him stories. To this person he allowed a pension till her death.

Among his fellow-pupils at Bury, were the late Baron Alderson, and the present Lord Cranworth.

In his own home he was an affectionate and lively

companion to a large family of brothers and sisters, all younger than himself. An electrical machine of his own making—poetry also of his own making, highly admired by the home audience—plays acted with schoolfellows of his own age, and music, were among the diversions of his holidays.

Thus, among the ordinary interests and occupations of a clever school-boy, Charles James Blomfield grew up in his quiet home, while the world was ringing with the crash of falling kingdoms, and the din of mighty battles. The first public event which he recollected was the illumination with which his native town celebrated the recovery of George III. in 1789 (though this must have been impressed upon him rather by hearing of it from others than by his own remembrance); the next, the execution of Louis XVI. in January, 1793, the news of which filled his young mind with horror, and produced for a time, as it did in many older minds, a strong abhorrence of the French nation.

In 1799 he was nearly being removed to a more famous school than that of Bury; he was examined and actually admitted as a King's Scholar at Eton, but his father, not liking what he saw of the place, never sent him there.

At the age of eighteen, in 1804, he experienced the first great change in a school-boy's life, by beginning his residence at Cambridge, as a pensioner of Trinity College, where he gained a scholarship in the following year. He found here several of his old schoolfellows, who formed a "Bury Club," which used to hold its meetings in the rooms of its different members. The Master of the College (Dr. Mansel, afterwards Bishop of

Bristol), received him kindly at his first coming up, and said that he would be a father to him; but he never saw anything more of him, as it was not the custom in those days for the Head of a College to take any notice of the undergraduates, save when for some delinquency they were summoned to appear before him, in what Hustler of Trinity used to call the "Commination Room."

In the wider sphere to which college life introduced him, he soon found that if he were to retain the reputation which he had gained at school, he must study even harder than before. The boys of Charterhouse and Eton were more than a match for the best scholar of Bury in some important parts of scholarship. Accordingly he began a system of reading which overtasked his bodily, though not his mental powers, and the bad effects of which lasted perhaps throughout his life. During the first four months of his residence at Cambridge, he read through Aristophanes, all the Greek tragedians, Herodotus, Thucydides, and a great part of Cicero, spending sometimes sixteen or even eighteen hours out of the twenty-four over his books. He wrote every day a piece of Greek or Latin composition, and a translation from a Greek or Latin author, which latter he translated back again some days after, and then compared his version with the original. He had no private tutor, but at the end of his first academical year he was fortunately introduced to Mr., afterwards Bishop Maltby, who was then residing at Buckden in Huntingdonshire, and taking pupils. Maltby, with much kindness, seeing in his young friend the promise of much classical eminence, took him into his house as one of his pupils, for six weeks, without payment, and gave him some good advice as to the method of reading he should pursue; his previous work had been too rapid; he had neglected commentators, and had not written notes of his own.

When he first came to Cambridge, he had lodgings in the town, at the house of a tailor in Trinity-street; and he used to describe how he had been annoyed, while reading, by the sounds from the cutting-room, which was under his own sitting-room, and by the noises of a girls' school, kept by the tailor's wife; while, his bedroom being over an archway, beneath which three coaches rumbled every night into the yard behind, he was as much disturbed by night as by day. But when he was promoted to rooms in college, he was enabled to pursue his studies without interruption. He often observed a light burning very late in the rooms of the undergraduate who lived opposite to him; and he was determined that he would not be outdone in devotion to study. Sometime afterwards, he discovered that his neighbour sat up not to read, but to play chess.

In the year 1805 he gained Browne's Prize for a Latin Ode, "In Obitum mœstissimum Ducis d'Enghien"—an event which was still fresh in the English mind. He now recommenced reading on the improved plan recommended by Mr. Maltby. His day was generally thus divided. Rising in time for the early chapel service, which he never missed during his undergraduate life, except when prevented by illness, he began reading at nine; at twelve, allowed himself two hours recreation, walking, or rowing, or occasionally a game of billiards; dined at two, the college dinner hour; and, returning to his books at three, read without intermission till twelve at night, and occasionally till three in the morning. Sometimes he alternated his work, one week sitting up till three, and the next rising at four. The remonstrances of friends or physicians, who warned him that he read too hard, were in vain; the objects which he had set before him must be gained at whatever cost of ease, time, and health. Of his industry at this period some proofs still remain in the shape of very elaborate note-books, written with that calligraphy which scholars had not yet learnt to despise. A Bury friend meeting him in the streets of Cambridge in a long vacation, exclaimed, "Why, Charles Blomfield, I believe if you were to drop from the sky, you would be found with a book in your hand."

It will be readily understood that a life of such severe and unremitting study left far less time for social enjoyment than even a diligent undergraduate commonly finds. Nor was Blomfield's at this, or indeed at any period of his life, one of those impulsive characters which invite familiarity, and are equally genial with every companion. But in the small circle of fellow-students among whom he spent whatever leisure he allowed himself, his talents were readily acknowledged, and his character warmly appreciated. Among these was James Henry Monk, afterwards Professor of Greek, and subsequently Bishop of Gloucester; Baron Alderson, Sharpe, and Hustler of Trinity; Frederick Pollock, now Chief Baron; and, in the latter part of his course, his own brother Edward Valentine Blomfield, and the younger Rennell. Monk was senior by four years to Charles Blomfield, but was from the first his intimate friend; and being entirely free from any jealousy of his somewhat more brilliant classical achievements, lost no opportunity of doing him a good turn.

Blomfield found at Cambridge, what he had not found at Bury, fellow-students who were his equals in ability; and this tended to check the self-appreciation which might otherwise have degenerated into self-conceit. It was at Cambridge too that he first saw anything of what is called "good society;" and this fitted him for his introduction into the world, of which he had seen so little. Yet a certain shyness, which might be observed in him occasionally in after life, is perhaps attributable to the fact, that it was not till he was passing the period of boyhood that he was thrown into any society but that of a country town.

But whatever there might be in the social tone of Cambridge at that time to contaminate rather than to improve—and there is no doubt that a great change for the better in this respect has taken place in the last half century—Blomfield himself was quite unharmed by the contact. A contemporary bears this testimony to his character as an undergraduate:—"Few persons were equal to him in the point and liveliness of his talk; yet I never heard him originate or repeat an expression which, as a Bishop, he could wish unsaid; and though he largely contributed to the vivacity of every party where he was present, and was the author of many witty and smart sayings, which were handed about, he never forgot the decorum that belonged to the path of life he had already chosen."[1] By the tutors of Trinity —Tavell, a man of great kindness of heart, and Dealtry, afterwards Archdeacon of Surrey—he was treated with

[1] From a letter of Chief-Baron Pollock's.

much consideration, and looked upon as a scholar of great promise.

In 1806 he added to his academical laurels the Craven University Scholarship, for which he was examined by Porson. Having to translate a difficult and corrupt chorus in Æschylus, he added from memory Porson's own emendations of the text, and drew from the Professor the acknowledgment that he was "a very pretty scholar." He gained also this year Browne's Prize for a Greek Ode on the Death of Lord Nelson. But the highest distinctions at Cambridge then, as now, were not to be gained without considerable attainments in mathematics. To mathematics, therefore, towards the close of 1806, he devoted himself almost entirely, until his examination at the beginning of 1808. He had not indeed neglected this branch of study at school, having advanced as far as conic sections; though this was without the encouragement, and even contrary to the wishes of Mr. Becher, who regarded mathematics as the root of all evil; and who, when he heard that Blomfield was reading for his degree, sent him a message expressing a hope that he would obtain "a gentlemanly Senior Optime."

It was at this part of his college life that he saw most of the present Lord Chief Baron, who was about to stand for a Trinity Fellowship; Blomfield's superiority in classics, and Pollock's in mathematics, making it a convenient arrangement that each in turn should assist the other in his studies. In this way the two spent together the greater part of a long vacation, sharing one another's recreations as well as studies, and enlivening their more serious pursuits by an occasional game at piquet. The Bishop used to say in after life that he had never known anyone construe Thucydides better than the Chief Baron. Blomfield now became so fond of mathematics that at one time he had serious thoughts of abandoning in their favour his classical studies; but on taking up his Greek books again before the examination for the Chancellor's Medal, the love for them returned with renewed force. The result, however, gave some grounds for this temporary preference; for though he missed the highest place in the tripos, owing to his unacquaintance with the analytical mathematics, then recently introduced from France, he obtained the great honour of the third place among the wranglers; the first being gained by Bickersteth of Caius, afterwards Lord Langdale, who had the advantage of four or five years in age; and the second by Bland of St. John's, who had been trained to mathematical studies from his infancy; both men of a very superior stamp. Next to Blomfield was the present Professor Sedgwick, who, the Bishop used to say, was a much better mathematician than he. In the problem paper he was first; it was in the book-work that he was beaten. Fresh from this trial, and refusing to compete for the Smith's Mathematical Prize, he went on to win in the more congenial field of scholarship, the highest honour which, in those days when there was no classical tripos, the University had to bestow—the Chancellor's Classical Medal.[1] The Members' Prize for a Latin dissertation, gained in 1809, completes the list of his academical honours.[2]

[1] In this examination Blomfield happened to ask one of the candidates, "Have you finished your Elegiacs?" "Yes," replied he, "I have done *all the Pentameters*."

[2] The scholarships and prizes which he had gained had enabled him, almost from the first, to support himself at Cambridge with but little assistance from his father.

After the strain and stimulus of his undergraduate life, he began to feel the effects of his over exertions. One day, while walking in the gardens of St. John's College, he was seized with violent spasms; and this attack left him for years with an impaired digestion, and so weakened his nervous system for the time, that he could not ride on horseback without having to dismount at the slightest alarm, and cling for support to a tree or railing, until the nervous tremor had passed off.

C. J. Blomfield to his Sister.

"Trinity College, *Nov.* 5, 1808.

". . . . I delivered my speech[1] in chapel yesterday, and was highly complimented by several of the Fellows upon it. As soon as I can spare it I will send it home for my father to read. I received the ten pounds from the Bursar for the prize. I supped again on Thursday with Dr. Davy, who expressed himself in the most friendly manner both towards me and Edward. Last night I supped at Mr. Tavell's for the third time this term, and to-night I am going to Professor Smyth's, so that you see I am figuring away quite amongst the sublimer order of Academicians. The Vice-Chancellor, in his Latin speech upon quitting his office, gave his reasons for adjudging a second prize,[2] and called Edward 'an elegant and learned young man,' and his composition a delightful poem; and certainly with his new

[1] A declamation on William III. which gained a College prize.

[2] A second prize was this year given for a Greek Ode to E. V. Blomfield. The Vice-Chancellor was Dr. Barnes, of Peterhouse.

gown he is much more elegant than he used to be. I am a man of so much business, and am so anxious to get a walk before dinner, that I cannot possibly protract this letter further than the top of the next side, although I have a thousand things to say. . . ."

Any one acquainted either personally or by reputation with Charles James Blomfield, at the time of his taking his degree of B.A. in 1808, would probably have predicted that whatever distinction he was to achieve in after life, he would gain entirely or mainly as a scholar; so thoroughly did he appear to be devoted to those studies, in which Bentley and Porson before him had thrown lustre on his University and his College. Though often urged by members of his college to go to the Bar, he always, as has been seen, looked to the clerical profession as his destination; but at this time he probably regarded it rather as affording means and leisure for literary pursuits, than as offering in its own peculiar duties that wide field of usefulness which ere long opened upon him. In the Latin letter which he addressed to one of the senior fellows of Trinity, when a candidate for a Fellowship in that Society, in October 1809, he describes himself as one "qui jamdudum litterarum amore ita sim incensus, ut inter eas omne ævum transigere decreverim," and counts as the greatest advantages which he would enjoy if elected, "ut domicilium mihi inter doctissimos viros comparatum esse videam, bibliothecasque ditissima librorum supellectili instructas." Accordingly he was no sooner elected, than he began to devote himself for the benefit of others to the same studies which he had hitherto pursued for his own. The idea of an edition of Æschylus, with notes and glossaries, must have been formed in his mind at latest, early in 1809, since his 'Prometheus Vinctus' was published in 1810.

This is not the place to attempt a general review of the state of Greek scholarship at the time at which Blomfield began to be known as an editor. Every one is aware that the progress made in this department of literature in the last half century is very great; and every scholar is aware that that progress owed no inconsiderable impulse to Bishop Blomfield. In 1809–15 there was no Englishman who held undisputed sway as master of Greek; for the great Porson was recently dead. "There are about ten men in England" (wrote Elmsley to Blomfield in 1813) "who really study the *minutiæ* of Greek, and of these ten, four or five do not write." Intercourse with foreign scholars was suspended by the disturbed state of the Continent; and the name of Godfrey Hermann was as yet rather odious to the Græcists of England, in consequence of his literary quarrel with Porson.

Samuel Parr, Charles Burney, and Butler of Shrewsbury, were probably the most distinguished scholars then living; but the first seldom applied his vast reading to any purpose which could benefit the world in general; the second, though a man of taste and information, was deficient in critical acumen; and the last, though lacking neither skill nor industry, belonged to a school of critics who encumbered Greek authors quite as much by accumulating the lumber of former commentaries, as they illustrated them by the acuteness of their own. On the other hand, among the younger school, who professed themselves the disciples of Porson, while they laboured to obtain not only correctness of *text*, which was the object of that great scholar, but clear explanations of the author's *meaning*, which he had unfortunately neglected—were found, besides Blomfield himself and his brother Edward, Monk, who had succeeded Porson as Regius Professor of Greek in 1808, Kaye, Dobree, Elmsley, and Maltby: Gaisford standing rather apart in solitary dignity. A third party, distinguished rather for miscellaneous industry than for taste, knowledge or judgment, was represented by the contributors to the "Classical Journal," and found its appropriate head in Mr. Valpy, the adoptive parent of the Digamma.

A letter of Blomfield's to his sister will show his success and his hopes at this time.

"TRINITY COLLEGE, *March* 3, 1810.

".... Before long you will have to direct to me, as the Rev.; for the Bishop of Bristol has promised to ordain me in the course of the present month. I began to fear that I should be obliged to go to Norwich or Buckden, the former of which has no particular attraction for me just now; and I do not wish to be examined by the Bishop of Lincoln.[1]

"I had a letter the other day, directed to (the Rev.) C. J. Blomfield (Esq). It was from Mr. Jeffrey, the editor of the Edinburgh Review, to thank me for my favours. He apologized for the oddness of the direction, as he did not know whether I was in orders; but the most satisfactory apology was the contents of the letter, a draft for twenty guineas, for my critique on Æschylus,

[1] Pretyman.

of which a second number will appear in the review which is just coming out. The long review,[1] which I was writing when at home, will not appear till next number about May; for that I shall probably have fifteen guineas more, and they are very desirous of my future communications.[2]"

The articles in the Edinburgh Review, here alluded to, upon the edition of Æschylus which had been undertaken by Butler of Shrewsbury, at the expense of the University of Cambridge, were looked upon as a kind of challenge from the younger to the older scholars, the criticisms contained in them being only partially favourable. The articles provoked a reply from Butler, in the shape of an angry pamphlet, addressed "To the Rev. C. J. Blomfield, one of the Junior Fellows of Trinity College, Cambridge," in which he speaks of the pretentious arrogance of the Porsonian party, and twits Blomfield with his youth. Dr. Parr was so indignant at Blomfield's reviews, though he had previously shown him kindness, that he became for a time quite estranged. "What!" he exclaimed, "a young man dare to write against Sam Butler! I'll crush him." This displeasure did not, however, last long. Parr again became his friend, and sent him many letters full of complimentary expressions, but, unless written by an amanuensis, nearly illegible; the doctor's own handwriting being of the worst

[1] On Gaisford's edition of Hephæstion.

[2] "Has a Mr. Blomfield, of Trinity College, Cambridge, offered you any classical articles? Do you want any, and will you accept any from Dr. Maltby?" "Blomfield is an admirable scholar. Publish his review, and Payne Knight will write you something else."—*Sydney Smith to Jeffrey*, 1809, *March* 7 and *Nov.* 4.

imaginable. The warmth of the controversy between the Æschylean critics extended even to Butler's school at Shrewsbury, where, although of course the majority of the boys supported their master, *one* was found bold enough to take the side of Blomfield, and to support his claims in a stand-up fight with the stoutest champion of the opposite party.

Six and thirty years afterwards this anecdote was communicated to Bishop Blomfield by his solitary defender, the Rev. George Matthews, who added that he still bore the marks of the contest in a scar on his lip. Mr. Matthews having asked him to help in restoring his church, the Bishop replied:—

"FULHAM, 23*d* *Nov.* 1846.

"REV. SIR,—Such an appeal as you have made to me it is impossible to resist. It has revived many recollections of an interesting period of my life. I have often wished that I had never written the review of Butler's Æschylus, although the criticism was generally true. It caused an excellent man to regard me for several years with suspicion and dislike, besides the lesser evil of inflaming the wrath of the press. However, I had the happiness of being cordially reconciled to Dr. Butler some time afterwards, and of becoming intimate with him. He was a really learned as well as amiable man, but his forte did not lie in verbal criticism. I am much amused by your account of the πυγμαχίη: you do not say who conquered; but I hope that as *I* was fortunate enough to beat my friend Thomas Smart Hughes in various academic contests, so *you* triumphed over his brother at fisticuffs, and were the Epeus, not the Euryalus, of the fight, although it might be said of him—

ἐπὶ δ' ὤρνυτο δῖος Ὑησος
Κόπτε δὲ παπτήναντα παρῆιον.[1]

I enclose a cheque for 10*l*., of which I request your acceptance, not so much, however, for a *μνήμη ἀντί-μισθος*, as an expression of my good wishes for the success of your pious endeavours to restore the house of God to a due degree of seemliness."

Thus the young Fellow of Trinity was fairly launched into the turbid sea of classical controversy, and received his due share of the *odium philologicum.*

Two important changes in his life, ordination and marriage, occurred in 1810, but they did not affect at first the nature of his principal pursuits. He was ordained deacon in March, and priest in June of that year, by Dr. Mansel, Bishop of Bristol, and Master of Trinity College; and declining an offer to become private tutor to the sons of Bishop Pretyman, with a salary of 400*l*., and the promise of a living, he took the curacy of Chesterford, a parish of which he was afterwards rector. The then incumbent being non-resident, he lived in the rectory house, and received pupils whom he prepared for the universities. In October, he was an unsuccessful candidate for the living of Ovington, in the gift of the university, but was immediately afterwards presented to that of Quarrington in Lincolnshire, by Lord Bristol, the warm friend and patron of his father and himself; and, in November, he was married to Anna Maria, daughter of W. Heath, Esq. of Hemblington, Norfolk.

[1] See Hom. Il. xxiii. 689.

The Rev. C. J. Blomfield to his Father.

"TRINITY COLLEGE, *Aug.* 20, 1810.

[Describing an interview with Lord Bristol at Tunbridge Wells.] ".... His Lordship stated that he had been for some time anxious to have a personal interview with me, and to know my wishes and plans of life, as he had felt a degree of embarrassment whilst considering the means of providing for me, from a want of information on this head. He considered me in every point of view, both from the regard which he had long felt towards you, and for my own sake, as entitled to the *best preferment* in his disposal; and he was in some uncertainty, when Mr. Macklin's illness rendered the falling in of Chesterford a probable event, whether it would be consonant with my wishes to be fixed there; this he considered as the best piece of preferment in his gift, and therefore I was the first person whom he thought of. He thinks that, if at the end of a year and a half, or two years, no preferment should have fallen, such as he would wish to offer me, it would be a good plan to take a limited number of pupils at not less than 150*l.* per annum; and he thinks that in this way, or in many other ways, he could settle me so as to have a comfortable income, and the literary leisure which is a principal object to me. Lord Hervey is going to Eton, but he expressed a wish to have me in some way connected with his family, in order that, if it should be in his power to present me with a living only of two or three hundred a year *at first*, he might procure another from Government, to be added to it. On this head, however, he did not explain himself quite so fully. At all events, whenever I should be inclined to settle in life, there were many ways in which it would be in his power to make me comfortable at first. He particularly mentioned that a living of the value just mentioned was not such as he should consider himself bound to offer me; but that *I was entitled to choose of the best in his disposal.* We had a good deal of conversation on literary and general subjects, and I was very much pleased by his turn of thinking and expression."

The Earl of Bristol to C. Blomfield, Esq.

"ROTTINGDEAN, *Sept.* 1810.

". . . . It was a very sincere pleasure to me to make your son's acquaintance, and to learn from himself all his plans and all his wishes. It will be a much greater pleasure, and one which will last as long as I shall, to promote them by every means in my power. Valuable as he is from conduct, from qualities, and from acquirements, and interesting as he is to me personally, from his being your son, you may rest well assured that I experience a real anxiety to make him comfortable, which approaches very nearly to a parental feeling. . . ."

The Rev. C. J. Blomfield to Professor Monk.

"CHESTERFORD, WALDEN, *Nov.* 15, 1810.

"MY DEAR MONK,—I thank you sincerely for your kind congratulations,[1] and I have every reason to believe that the occasion justly calls for them. I am comfortably settled here with my *wife*, and I need not say that we shall be most happy to see you, when a hearty

[1] On his marriage.

welcome must supply the want of splendid accommodations. I will not say that I am *quite* settled or quite accustomed to the new feelings and associations which this change of life brings with it, but as a proof that I am not quite altered, I have really been reading some Greek. . . .

"I am curious to see Tate's Diatribe.[1] 'O Tate tute, what canst thou have said? With club of Greek I'll break Tate's tête or head.'"

Mr. Tate does not seem to have anticipated this attack on his literary character. We find him writing to Monk soon afterwards:

"RICHMOND SCHOOL, YORKSHIRE,
Jan. 15, 1811.

". . . . The greater wealth, with the greater demand for the very best education in what we Yorkshiremen call the *south,* will supply, I hope, to Mr. Blomfield and his rising progeny—that I predict without the gift of prophecy—comfort and competence. My *fellow*-feelings and *matrimonial* feelings also sympathise cordially with his case. I married in 1796, before I had got a farthing from my fellowship at Sidney; and on this day week I hope to see and enjoy the christening of my eighth child, who is better than a year old already. How Mr. Blomfield and I are to meet Mr. Malthus, I know not. We must overpower him at first attack with our wives and children, standing aloof from the combat ourselves."

There being no parsonage house at Quarrington, he was not required to reside upon his benefice, but continued to live at Chesterford. He thus became, and

[1] On Greek Metres.

remained till 1828, one of a class which in later life he was bent on exterminating; that of non-resident Incumbents. His was a case which, if any, might be sheltered by the authority of Hooker, who defends pluralities and licences of non-residence as privileges to be conferred on men of learning and ability, for the furtherance of their studies; but, as Hooker goes on to observe, "as it fareth in such cases, the gap, which for just considerations be open to some, letteth in others through corrupt practices, to whom such favours were neither meant nor should be communicated."

Among his neighbours at Chesterford, was Mr. Eustace, a priest of the Roman Catholic Church, and author of the "Classical Tour," who, like himself, was engaged as private tutor to the sons of noble families of his own persuasion. He was a kind-hearted man, of refined taste, considerable knowledge, and great candour; and Mr. Blomfield was a good deal in his society, when classical and even theological subjects would be freely but amicably discussed.

Mr. Eustace was indeed by no means a bigoted Romanist, and was looked upon with some disfavour by his co-religionists, especially by Dr. Milner, the Vicar Apostolic. When Mr. Blomfield returned to Chesterford in 1817, Eustace was absent on a second tour in Italy, where he died soon after.

CHAPTER II.

BLOMFIELD AS RECTOR OF DUNTON, AND HIS CHARACTER AS A PRIVATE TUTOR—HIS EDITIONS OF ÆSCHYLUS—SCHEME OF THE MUSEUM CRITICUM—LITERARY POLEMICS—STEPHENS'S THESAURUS AND THE "ARISTARCHUS ANTI-BLOMFIELDIANUS"—LETTERS TO MONK, AND FROM ELMSLEY AND G. HERMANN—CEASES TO CONTRIBUTE TO THE EDINBURGH REVIEW—HIS WORK AT DUNTON AS A PASTOR AND A MAGISTRATE—THE SOCIETY FOR PROMOTING CHRISTIAN KNOWLEDGE—VISITATION SERMON—PAMPHLET ON CHURCH REFORM—LECTURES ON JEWISH TRADITION—DEATH OF HIS BROTHER EDWARD—IS PRESENTED TO THE LIVING OF CHESTERFORD—DEATH OF HIS WIFE—CHESTERFORD AND THE NEWMARKET RACES.

In December, 1811, Mr. Blomfield was presented by the second Earl Spencer—himself an elegant scholar and judicious friend of classical literature—to the Rectory of Dunton, in Buckinghamshire; and resigning the curacy of Chesterford, but retaining Quarrington, he removed to Dunton, where he continued to reside till the summer of 1817. In this remote village, which, seated upon the edge of an elevated table-land, looks across the slopes that skirt the vale of Aylesbury to the hills of Tring and Chiltern, he was in complete seclusion. His parishioners were seventy-two in number; his clerk was an old *woman* between seventy and eighty, who could not read, and who, when she stole the Communion plate of the church, took it to the nearest pawnbroker, in ignorance that the name of the parish was engraved in conspicuous letters upon it. The neighbours were few and far between, though hospitable, and the roads, when he first went there, almost impassable. There was however a tolerable parsonage, in which he could accommodate his pupils; and his reputation as a scholar being now pretty widely known, many noblemen were anxious to place their sons under his care—among them, Earl Spencer, Lords Ashburnham, Colchester, and Lilford, the Duke of Beaufort, and the second Marquis, afterwards Duke, of Buckingham. "I cannot satisfy myself," writes a parent of his son, "with any arrangement for him which promises inferior advantages, so long as I can entertain the hope of placing him with you." Indeed, his character as a private tutor had now become so established, that he was enabled to raise his terms, which had at first been only £150 or £200, to £300, or even £400 a year. The moral influence which he exercised over his pupils, and the standard which he set before them, may be illustrated by letters which will be appended to subsequent chapters, and by the following extract from one addressed to the mother of a pupil, who had hinted that the principles which he was impressing upon her son were somewhat overstrained and unnecessarily strict:—

"…. My general notions are, undoubtedly, strict compared with those which are most current in the world, and I lose no opportunity of enforcing and explaining to those under my care the grounds upon which they are built, because I am most intimately convinced, that there is no motive whatever of sufficient power to preserve a young man in those trials which to many are ruinous, and to all that are not fortified, pernicious, except an habitual sense of religious duty. This conviction has arisen not only from what I have read, but from my uniform observation of those of whose principles and practice I have had any means of judging; and with regard to the University, I am sure that no young man can pass through its ordeal unhurt, whose religious principles have not been strengthened and confirmed beforehand. Some may be less incorrect than others in their conduct; but it is impossible to say how far any one may go, who has nothing to restrain him but a vague and indefinite notion of what is *gentlemanly* or respectable, and does not regulate his conduct by the clear and unerring light of religion, and by the broad and conspicuous line which discriminates *right* from *wrong*.

. . . I believe that from the constitution of society in modern times, in many cases a regard for appearances, and a consideration for their own interests, with a natural refinement of mind, form among *females* a sort of substitute for religious principles, which, as far as their comfort and character in life are concerned, sufficiently answer their end; but with *men* the case is very different, as you must perceive; and be assured, if you trust to *refinement of mind* to preserve *them* from gross and unreasonable conduct, you will in no instance find it a sufficient safeguard. . . ."

Here, also, he continued his editorial labours on Æschylus. The 'Prometheus Vinctus' had appeared in 1810, and was favourably received. The good sense and diligence displayed in the notes, the comparative purity of the text,[1] and the addition of a glossary, which

[1] The Glasgow edition of Æschylus, then in general use, bore the name of Porson, but had received but little emendation from him.

was a novel feature, combined to make this a good specimen of the new scholarship. It was favourably noticed in the Edinburgh Review by Elmsley, and the Quarterly added its meed of praise:—"We congratulate our readers, not only upon the acquisition of this very useful volume, but upon the appearance of a scholar, who, at a very early period of life, has displayed so great a share of judgment, ability, and learning as to justify the most sanguine expectations of his future excellence." The 'Septem contra Thebas,' on the same plan, followed in 1812; the 'Persæ,' in 1814; the 'Agamemnon,' in 1820; the 'Choephori,' in 1824; and in 1815 he edited the remains of Callimachus, with a dedication to Earl Spencer.

The labours of subsequent editors have since then rendered Blomfield's Æschylus a book of comparatively small value, but it remained for a considerable time the most generally useful edition published in England; and had the Bishop possessed in more mature life leisure to spend in such studies, his work might have been kept up to the level of the age.

Another classical scheme which occupied his attention at this time was that of a new critical magazine, or periodical, for the miscellaneous contributions of scholars. This design, originally started by himself and Monk (now Professor of Greek), took shape under the title of the 'Museum Criticum,' of which the first number appeared in 1813; and was favourably entertained by Parr, Elmsley, Dobree, James Tate, John H. Frere, Kaye, Maltby, and others. Its editor was Monk; its object to bring to notice fragments, and less-known authors, and whatever had hitherto escaped the industry of critics; to furnish essays on Greek and Roman history, antiquities, arts, manners, and customs; to give notices of eminent scholars, and to contribute towards the history of classical literature.

Dr. Maltby wrote thus when asked to contribute to the work:—

"*Nov.* 27, 1812.

". . . . I believe I have lamented to you the want of such a publication as you propose to set on foot; and if my cerebellum when more disengaged can produce anything worthy your acceptance, my effusions shall be readily contributed, feeble though they may be. John Frere was lamenting that no such work could be furnished from Cambridge, and would, I am sure, make some curious contributions to it. When your plan is matured, and the secret ripe, I will write to him. . . . "

Blomfield's own views of what the Museum Criticum ought to be, are thus expressed in a letter to Monk:—

"DUNTON, *November* 25 [1812].

". . . . I forgot to say when I wrote to my brother, that I continue most decidedly adverse to the notion of printing any juvenile poetry. The prize compositions in Greek and Latin are frequently creditable to young men; but as they are generally centos from ancient authors, and are at best but the exercises of seventh-form boys, I cannot think that the admission of them into our journal will be judicious. By all means leave them to Valpy and Mr. Deighton, who prints correct editions of them "ad calcem Kalendarii." I would have our book severely chaste—merum sal—savouring only of the true χνοῦς ἀρχαιοπινῆς. . . . My omission of Dr. Parr's name in the list of contributors, which I hastily sketched out, was accidental, and not arising from disrespect. Whatever he may furnish relative to learning will be valuable. As an 'Umbratic Doctor' I look up to him—τἄλλα σιγῶ. . . . Gifford gives a laughable account of the articles for this number of the Quarterly, many of which have been travelling over half the bogs in Ireland in pursuit of Goodman Croker, who has had to stand two contested elections."

In this periodical (which was finally brought to a close in 1822) Blomfield wrote many articles on classical subjects: and we may here anticipate a somewhat later period of his life than properly belongs to this chapter, by mentioning two literary contests in which his connexion with the Museum Criticum involved him. Its publication was regarded by Valpy and his adherents in Tooke's Court as an act of hostility to the 'Classical Journal,' to which they were the principal contributors. Among these gentlemen was Mr. G. Burges, the now almost forgotten editor of certain plays of Æschylus and Euripides. He took occasion to charge Blomfield, in no measured terms, with plagiarism from Porson, Butler, Burney, and others; a charge which is fully refuted by the accused in the seventh number of the Museum Criticum, published in 1821 or 1822. Many years afterwards, when Bishop of London, he accidentally met his former literary opponent, and spoke so kindly that Burges wrote to him and told him of his necessities. The Bishop set on foot a subscription for him, and afterwards procured for him from Lord Melbourne a pension of £100 a year.

Another of Valpy's coadjutors was a Mr. E. H. Barker, O. T. N.[1] He was on several occasions rather severely handled in the Museum Criticum; but the special occasion which drew forth his wrath was the publication of an article by Blomfield in the Quarterly Review of January, 1820, on Valpy's edition of Stephens's 'Greek Thesaurus,' in which Barker had a principal hand. This work, for which Valpy procured 1,100 subscribers, had enveloped the original Stephens (himself of no meagre bulk) in such a mass of ill-digested and irrelevant commentation,[2] that the Reviewer calculated, that if it were continued on the plan on which it had been begun, it would fill fifty volumes, consume seventy years in publication, and cost 400 guineas to the large-paper and 200 guineas to the small-paper contributors; and as the *vitæ summa brevis* forbade the hope of outliving this Nestor of Lexicons, their interest in its unborn numbers might be an appropriate subject of testamentary dispositions. For this article Mr. Murray, the publisher of the Quarterly, sent him 100 guineas; and Lord Stowell told him that the subscribers to the Thesaurus ought to have presented him with a piece of plate, for having brought the work to an abrupt termination, and thereby saved their pockets. From the gigantic beginning and rapid ending of the publication, another subscriber said it was a *tadpole* book. Mr. Barker took

[1] *I. e. of Thetford, Norfolk.* This gentleman practised the art of writing criticisms *upon himself*, in periodicals, disguised under the initials of other scholars, in order to have the satisfaction of answering them in his own name. (This at least Elmsley thought he did.)

[2] The article on the single word Ἄγαλμα filled 139 columns.

his revenge in a pamphlet, entitled 'Aristarchus Anti-Blomfieldianus;'[1] in which he showers upon the Reviewer such flowers of rhetoric as "utter disregard of truth—egregious and disgusting hypocrisy—foul, secret, and desperate malignity—an understanding crooked—a heart envenomed—a pen full of gall;" and on the supposed evidence of style attributes to Blomfield articles in the Quarterly Review and Museum Criticum which were *not his.* This pamphlet Barker had the audacity to dedicate to Earl Spencer; who wrote, in reply, to say that he was astonished at his presumption, as Dr. Blomfield was his "intimate and particular friend." An answer appeared in the Quarterly of January, 1821, by Monk, which was rendered almost necessary by the fact that Valpy had published a defence of his own share in the work among the advertisements which formed the fly-leaves of the *Quarterly itself;* and from that time Bishop Blomfield was never again engaged in any literary polemics.

The Rev. P. Elmsley to the Rev. C. J. Blomfield.

"ST. MARY CRAY, *Feb.* 8, 1813.

"... . I propose the following scheme to you. Should the communication with the North of Germany be opened in the spring, let us collect all the classical labours of English scholars for the last five or six years, and send them as a present to Hermann, who, I believe, lives at Jena. I mean Greek plays out of number, 'Burney's Tentamen,' 'Gaisford's Hephæstion,' 'Por-

[1] So called after the 'Aristarchus Anti-Bentleianus' of Richard Johnson, master of Nottingham School, published in 1717-8.

soniana,' &c. The present to be made by Gaisford and Monk (the two Professors), Burney, you, and me. I looked the other day into a volume of 'Erfurdt's Sophocles.' The German scholars appear to be entirely unacquainted with our labours for several years past. . . ."

The Rev. C. J. Blomfield to Professor Monk.

"DUNTON, *Feb.* 20, 1813.

". . . . With regard to Barker, it strikes me that a good motto for Valpy's journal[1] would be, 'Hylax in limine latrat.' Lucky would it be for the readers of that work were it only *in limine;* but it is also in the hall, in the parlour, upstairs, on the roof, Mungo here, Mungo there, Mungo everywhere. I have not time for anything elaborate for this cur, but I propose throwing him an occasional morsel in the Gentleman's Magazine. It is quite clear that Valpy is in a stew (*i.e.* in *hot water*, not *sensu nequiori*). Tooke's Court will be in an uproar. Barker and Burges will be summoned to town, and a consultation of physicians held in the sick room of the expiring journal. Sick, indeed, she must long have been with such a load of nauseous stuff upon her stomach, and I am afraid the doctors will only give her more, and so kill her with their medicines. Rest her soul! . ."

The same to the same.

"DUNTON, *April* 30 [1813].

". . . . With regard to the Chemical Professorship, I think you know me too well to suppose that I should vote for Cumming, because he is *of Trinity*, in opposition to a candidate whose merits are so eminently and decidedly superior.[2] It is this spirit which has already

[1] The Classical Journal. [2] Tennant of Emmanuel.

done the University so much harm. If there be an office in our body which ought to be given to the worthiest, *i.e.* to the best qualified, surely it must be a lecturing Professorship. Much as I am attached to our College, I will never sacrifice to it the least particle of what I think to be my public duty. I consider myself individually indebted to Cumming for his support in the Ovington business,[1] but that has nothing to do with his chemical merits, and I cannot help feeling that the Chemical Professorship ought, *in justice*, to be given to him who is decidedly the most scientific man, and a *tried* lecturer. I feel, however, that my obligation to Cumming, though it cannot sanction my *supporting* him in opposition to a more deserving candidate, justifies me in my resolution not to oppose him, and therefore I shall not give any vote on this occasion. . . ."

The Rev. P. Elmsley to the Rev. C. J. Blomfield.

ST. MARY CRAY, *May* 18, 1813.

". . . . There certainly must be some connexion between Greek and Popery. Besides Messieurs Blomfield and Elmsley, there are Doctors Parr, Butler, Maltby, Raine—all men conversant in the subjunctive mood, and all supporters of the Catholic claims, as they are called. . . . . I have just received a letter from Dr. Butler, in which you are mentioned in a way that is creditable to his good-nature, after the review of his 'Seven against Thebes' and 'Agamemnon.' It is plain to me that he wishes a reconciliation with you. I think it would be creditable to both of you to shake hands, if your arms are long enough to reach from Shrewsbury to Aylesbury. The Doctor has lately passed through a good deal of δυσφημία in his theological

[1] See p. 16.

character, on account of his Commencement Sermon. A neighbour of mine, who has something of an evangelical turn, takes in the Christian Observer, in which Dr. Butler 'points a moral' almost every month. . . ."

The Rev. C. J. Blomfield to Professor Monk.

"DUNTON, *July* 8, 1813.

"MY DEAR MONK,—I am glad that you are pleased with Elmsley, and that he is pleased with me, and I think I may add with you. The good opinion of such a scholar is more than ἰσόῤῥοπος to the abuse of a myriad of Barkers. . . . I have not heard from my brother [Edward], except through the medium of my friends at Bury. When he wrote to them he was at Gottenburg, highly pleased with all around. . . . I commissioned him to lay out £100 for me in books, but I think it probable that he will not see ten pounds' worth during the whole of his journey."

The same to the same.

"DUNTON, *Sept.* 26 [1814].

". . . . I rejoice in common with you, and all friends τοῦ πρέποντος, at Kaye's elevation;[1] the cause of literature begins to gain ground. I begin to look forward to the time when a man may mention a Greek or Latin author in a company of Cambridge seniors without exciting a general thrill of horror and surprise. . . . Dr. Parr proposed my health the other day at Emmanuel! Ἄπολλον ἀποτροπαῖε καὶ Σαβάζιε! . . ."

---

[1] To the Mastership of Christ's College.

Hermann's opinion on the disagreement between German and English scholars at this time, may be read with interest:—

Professor G. Hermann to the Rev. C. J. Blomfield.

"…. Litteras tuas, præstantissime Blomfieldi, accepi d. ix. Martii, eoque ipso die has dedi, quibus tibi responderem. Tanto minus enim committendum putabam, quin quam primum tibi ostenderem, eum me esse, quem tu ipse velles, quod et aliis rebus, et ipsis illis litteris tuis insignem erga me benevolentiam, prætereaque injuriam ego tibi viderer fecisse. Volo vero ita de me existimes, me boni justique viri laudem omnium primum putare, nihilque ducere turpius, quam injustitiam et malevolentiam. Atque ut nemo est eorum, qui me norunt, quin me in omni vita talem esse testetur, ita te quoque, quem virum probum esse vel illud ostendit, quod mihi ipse, quid sentires, scribere voluisti, adductum iri confido, ut me ab injuria facienda alienissimum esse intelligas. …

Unde vero ista in Germanos ferocia et superbia? Nempe contenditis nobiscum de principatu. At utri utris præstent, judicare neutros decet. Neque vero arbitros habemus alios; quum Gallos Italosque ambo recusemus; Batavi propemodum conticuerint; Helvetii et Dani Suevique nobis adnumerentur; cætera autem barbara sint. Est autem contentio illa quidem honestissima; sed nos securi arbitrium posteris permittimus, vos autem (ignosce, vir humanissime, si dicam, quod vellem non esset dicendum) vestro ipsorum judicio principes agitis, et insultatis nobis. . . . Et quid est quo freti ita feroces estis? Porsonum uno ore omnes nominatis. Quod nobis perinde videtur esse, ut quum Galli, quod Napoleonem habebant, sese primos omnium hominum esse existimabant. Non ego mehercule ita inique de vobis, ut vosmet ipsi, sentio, sed plures esse apud vos puto, qui Porsonum vel ingenio æquent, aut etiam superent, vel doctrina, si velint, possint æquare: miror autem, et nequeo satis mirari, quod superstitione quadam præpediti nec sui memores sint plerique, et in hoc viro omnem patriæ suæ gloriam periclitare velint. Sed id qui factum sit, video. Bentleius, æternum gentis vestræ decus, qui ingenio multum antecelluit Porsonum, adversarios habuit plurimos, admirationem autem est maximam post mortem adeptus. Nam aquilam rapido volatu sublimia petentem qui sectari nequeunt, indignantur, irascuntur, obtrectant, lædunt. Sublata autem per mortem caussa invidiæ, tum demum debitos honores concedunt. Porsonum qui ingenti doctrina, summaque circumspectione ubique solum, cui firmiter insisti posset, explorabat, nec sequi difficile erat, et ubi ipse constitisset, tuto adiri posse apparebat. Hinc admiratores vivus consequutus est, et merito; idemque quum præ se alios omnes contemneret, tantum omnibus terrorem incussit, ut non nisi sub hujus clipeo tutos se esse arbitrarentur.

Non bonum est, gentes et populos in litteris bella gerere, nec fuit ita apud majores nostros, apud quos homines litterati litteras ipsas communem sibi patriam esse putabant, et quamvis locorum longinquitate disjuncti, tamen studiis mutuoque commercio conjunctissimi erant. Vellem desinerent tandem aliquando simultates istæ parum lætabiles: quod efficere vestrum est, non nostrum, qui non lædimus vos, sed monemus ne lædatis, nec metu tacemus, sed quia, quos Porsoni vultus non terruerit, multo minus persona ejus, quam qui non sunt Porsoni induerunt, terrere potest. . . . Cæterum tu, vir humanissime, non recte fecisti, quum, quod me tibi iratum putares, intermisisti facere, quod facturum te fuisse scribis, ut sententiam meam de quibusdam locis

Agamemnonis requireres. Oportebat enim, si me virum bonum esse existimares, etiam si iratum tibi crederes, tamen interrogare. Invenisses autem promptum et paratum, atque ab omni simultate alienum. . . .

Vale, et fac, ut per te, et quantum in te erit, etiam per alios cessent illa odia vestra nec decora vobis, et, si abutendo patientia nostra aliquem, qualem non unum habemus, asperum tactu leonem lacessant, etiam insontibus vestrum periculosa. D. Lipsiæ a. MDCCCXVII."

The next two letters are on the controversy between Blomfield and Barker:—

The Rev. C. J. Blomfield to Professor Monk.

"LONDON, *April* 10, 1821.

"MY DEAR MONK,—I have been going to write to you from day to day; but the half-hour which I had set apart for that purpose has been always swallowed up in some other occupation. I am much pleased with the article in the Quarterly,[1] which will, in my opinion, produce the greater effect from its being written in a tone of moderation; and yet it is strong, though not abusive. It seems to me (who, to be sure, am not an impartial judge) to embrace all material points, and to set the question fairly at rest. Not that the controversy will terminate here; for it seems, from a letter to Barker, in the last number of Blackwood's Edinburgh Magazine, that the second part of 'Aristarchus' is forthcoming, in which, I doubt not, that both you and Lloyd[2] will be cruelly cudgelled, and exalted respectively to a 'bad eminence.' My brother George writes word that he hears the article attributed to you. It will be soon known; for amusing to relate, it turns out that Roworth, the printer of the Quarterly, married a relation of

[1] On Barker's 'Aristarchus Anti-Blomfieldianus.'

[2] Charles Lloyd, afterwards Bishop of Oxford.

Vealpye's, so that, doubtless, the modern Curll and the modern Dennis have a right to all articles relating to the Thesaurus in manuscript. . . . I don't know whether I told you that I was proposed by Lord Spencer, seconded by Lord Liverpool, as a member of the Club at the Thatched House, originally instituted by Dr. Johnson and Sir Joshua Reynolds. I have been to one meeting, and found it very agreeable; the number of members is limited to thirty-five; the only ecclesiastics, the Bishop of London and myself.

Believe me, dear M.,
Ever your's affectionately,
C. J. BLOMFIELD.

P. S. My father writes word that he is quite satisfied with the article on Barker, which is a great deal for *him* to say, who thinks nothing short of flagellation at the cart's tail meet for that worthy."

C. J. Blomfieldio viro reverendo S.D.
G. Hermannus.

"Periniqua mea conditio est, Blomfieldi, vir reverende, in altercatione illa, quæ tibi est cum Barkero. Nam et Barkero amicus sum, nec tibi, ut tu putas, inimicus. Nam te virum bonum esse, et Elmsleius, cujus magna apud me fides est, mihi asseveravit, et nunc, qui mihi litteras tuas reddidit, confirmavit Bohtius. Quibus tanto lubentius credo, quod non modo bene quam male de te sentire malo, sed ne causam quidem habeo, cur malum in te animum esse suspicer. Poteris id ipse ex eo intelligere, quod jam a longo tempore Barkerum sæpius et graviter cohortatus sum, ut iram componeret, ac potius in gratiam tecum rediret. Non dissimulabo tamen, habere illum, quod tibi succenseat. Neque enim, ut spero, infitias ibis censuram illam Thesauri sic a te scriptam esse, ut iniquus in Barkerum fueris. In universum eadem de Thesauro illo dixisti, quæ ego: sed dixisti cum contemptu quodam et gravi reprehensione. At quod consilium illud edendi Thesauri non recte initum est, ea vereor ut Barkeri culpa sit. In exsequendo autem eo consilio si quid ille minus commode fecit, cogita, quam magnus, quam molestus, quam plenus tædii sit labor iste, ut non modo ignoscendum sit, si aliquid minus apte institutum repereris, sed laudanda potius multa illa, quæ sedulo congesta et diligenter adnotata videas. Facile mihi persuadeo, non esse ista malo animo a te scripta: sed non est mirum, si secus videtur ei, quem illa lædunt. Itaque ut te apud Barkerum malitiæ suspicione liberarem, scripsi ei, videri te mihi non malignitate quadam ita scripsisse, sed quod eum morem tuum esse putarem, ut asperius notares, quæ tibi displicerent. Nemo enim mihi quidquam mali de te in aures, ut sentis, insusurravit, sed ipse ex scriptis tuis hanc opinionem concepi.... Ego quum per hanc æstatem in scholis meis Bacchas interpretaturus sim, paratas habebo sub initium hiemis adnotationes in hanc fabulam. Eas animus erat Valpio mittere, ut Diario Classico insereret. Deterruit me vero incredibilis incuria, qua typothetæ Valpiani multa corrumpunt. Itaque tibi, Blomfieldi, adnotationes illas offero, si quidem rationes vestræ sinunt, ut etiam exterorum commentationes in Museum Criticum recipiatis; sin minus, aliæ sunt opportunitates, quibus, si visum fuerit, uti possim. Tibi obtuli, ut intelligeres, me a simultate longe esse alienum. Quod si, ut et ipse significas, et Bohtius ait, mihi bene cupis, scias velim, me mutuum facere. Opto autem et rogo te, ut studeas etiam cum Barkero in gratiam redire. Litteris vivimus, quibus ut libere dissentiendo consulitur, ita nocetur cupiditate et odiis. Vale.

D. Lipsiæ d. XV. Maii, a. MDCCCXXII."

In 1815 Blomfield had ceased to contribute to the Edinburgh Review. He may have been partly influenced in withdrawing from it by the dilatoriness and irregularity in payment, for which Jeffrey, the editor, was remarkable. But the immediate cause of his severing the connexion was the appearance in the Review of some article which he appears to have considered injurious either to religion or morality, although it is not easy to discover, among the articles published at this time, any which deserves such a censure. His letter to the editor has not been preserved; but the following is Jeffrey's reply:—

F. Jeffrey, Esq. to the Rev. C. J. Blomfield.

"EDINBURGH, *Feb.* 19, 1815.

"....I am afraid our offences are too great in your eyes to leave me any hope of again profiting by your occasional contributions. I feel it, however, a duty to myself to add, that no one could be more sensible than I was of the impropriety which produced your alienation; and no one less likely, I hope, to commit in his own person the offence which, in a period of much hurry and personal anxiety, he inadvertently allowed to be committed by another. I flatter myself accordingly that, if ever you cast your eye on the pages of our Review, you will admit that you have not since met with anything that deserved equal reprobation.

However this may be, it will always be a matter of pride to have had you among my associates; and it will certainly lessen the regret I must feel at losing your assistance to learn from yourself that you have indulgence enough to forgive the irregularities into which I have unfortunately fallen in my correspondence with you, and that we part as good friends as we met."

It must not be supposed that the Rector of Dunton had none but literary occupations and interests. Besides his unremitting attention to his pupils, it was at Dunton that he laid the foundation of his solid theological acquirements. Patristic divinity was not at that time very much studied: he read, however, to a considerable extent in that department; and with the writings of the masters of English theology, and of the principal commentators on Holy Scripture, he made himself thoroughly acquainted. His little flock, too, among whom there was no Dissenter, and only one adult male who was not a communicant, was visited and relieved. It was the custom for the Rectors of Dunton to append a text to the entry of their names on the first leaf of the Register, which, with the names of many of them, is repeated on the gallery of the church. The text chosen by Mr. Blomfield is one which expresses the mutual relation and duties of a pastor and his flock:—"We are labourers together with God; ye are God's husbandry, ye are God's building." His farewell sermon, of which he gave a copy to a parishioner, still living in her eighty-eighth year, is remembered as having filled the little church of Dunton with strangers from the neighbouring villages, attracted by the reputation of the retiring Incumbent.

In 1813 he was made a magistrate, and used to ride to the petty sessions at the neighbouring town of Wing, equipped in yellow overalls to protect him from the mud of the Buckinghamshire lanes. He writes to Professor Monk:—

"DUNTON, *June* 7 [1813].

".... My time will be somewhat more occupied than formerly, as I am now a Commissioner of Turnpikes (there's for you), and a Justice of the Peace; and the county business will never get on without me. I must study Burn with diligence before I can *indifferently* minister justice. (By the way, that's a very awkward expression in the Liturgy.) I shall, moreover, probably be a Commissioner of the Property Tax—all which offices will a little interfere with Greek."

He was looked upon with some disfavour by the neighbouring squires and clergymen, not only as a man of learning, but as a Liberal; for he supported the claims of the Roman Catholics, opposed county jobbery, and took in the Morning Chronicle. Indeed, it now began to be surmised that he must have been christened Charles James, after the great Whig leader. The farmers of his parish long remembered how his union of magisterial and ministerial authority had kept them in order. In later years, as a Bishop, he disapproved of such a union, saying that the secular duties would be likely to interfere too much with the spiritual. He found, even at this time, that the Game Laws pressed so harshly upon the poor that he could hardly bring himself to be instrumental in enforcing them.

He took an active part, also, while at Dunton, in whatever Church work was as yet stirring in the neighbourhood. In 1815 he was the means of founding a district depôt of the Society for Promoting Christian Knowledge, at Aylesbury; and the sermon[1] which he preached on the occasion of its opening was thought to explain the objects of the Society so well, that he

[1] 'The Peculiar Claims which the Society for Promoting Christian Knowledge has upon the Liberality of Churchmen.' Cambridge. 1815.

was requested to publish it. A letter to his friend Hustler, who was now a Tutor of Trinity, shows the way in which he maintained the claims of the Society, as pre-eminently a *Church* Society.

The Rev. C. J. Blomfield to the Rev. J. D. Hustler.

"DUNTON, *Jan.* 23, 1815.

"MY DEAR HUSTLER,—I take it for granted that you have read my last Sermon, because you tell me so in the beginning of your letter, otherwise your observations might have led me to suppose that you had not, for you set me to maintain a position which I have nowhere, even by insinuation, advanced—viz.: that the Bible Society is hostile to the interests of the Established Church. Whatever may be my own opinion on this question, I have carefully avoided any discussion of it in my Sermon, which is addressed exclusively to Churchmen, and in which I have laboured to establish these points alone:—1. That on general grounds the old Society is calculated to produce more real benefit than its rival. 2. That *as far as Churchmen are concerned*, where two associations are formed for the propagation of Christianity, one of which proposes to teach it *as received and understood by our Church*, and the other *does not*, there can be no question to which of the two *we* are bound to contribute our support. . . . Of the mischief likely to be produced by the co-operation of sectaries I have said nothing; the question, as far as it relates to members of the Establishment, may be debated on a much wider and less disputable position; but even here I have seen great reason to agree with those who contend that the weight which is thrown into the dissenting scale by the character and purses of Churchmen, has no counterpoise in the increased influence of the latter. . . . When I resided at Chesterford I subscribed liberally to an auxiliary Bible Society, of which I was a vice-president; but before *I* was able to procure a single Bible, my parish had been inundated with them by a brace of Anabaptist preachers. . . . Excuse the freedom which I use in begging that you will give these reasons, and many others which will easily suggest themselves to you, a proper consideration, because the question, whatever it was originally, is now become one of such essential importance to the Establishment, that it is our *duty* to follow Solon's maxim, "That no man should stand neuter." We act from interested motives, it is said; undoubtedly we do—if we are not interested, and very deeply too, in the welfare and pre-eminence of our Established Church, we are unworthy ministers of it—if we contribute to weaken it, we are like the *κυνὲς ἐν τριόδοισι*, the dogs who eat up the cates of the goddess, and then bark at her when she approaches. . . ."

At the Visitation of the Bishop of the diocese (Pretyman, of Lincoln), in the same year, Mr. Blomfield was requested to preach the sermon. We find him asking his old friend, Mr. Hasted, of Bury, what subject he should choose for the occasion.

To the Rev. H. Hasted.

"DUNTON, *April* 20, 1815.

"MY DEAR SIR,—I stand in need of your advice. The Bishop has desired me to preach the Visitation Sermon, at Aylesbury, on the first of June, and I am at a loss for a subject. You are experienced in this species of composition, and can recommend me a topic fit for a discourse *ad Clerum*. I was thinking of discussing the utility of learning to the clerical profession, but the mention of this might give offence to my worthy brethren in the Archdeaconry of Bucks; as it would be unpolite to hold forth in praise of a fair complexion to a party of Negresses. I shall really be much obliged for your advice..... I am glad you have got the 'Persæ;' it has had an extraordinary sale. My two publishers, at London and Cambridge, have disposed of above 700 in a few weeks; and of the last play very few copies are left....."

Eventually he chose for his subject "The Responsibleness of the Pastoral Office," and delivered a calm and temperate address on the mutual duties of clergy and people.

The Rev. C. J. Blomfield to the Rev. H. Hasted.

"DUNTON, *May* 8, 1815.

".... I am much obliged to you for your advice about my Sermon, which very nearly falls in with the plan which, upon considering the matter, I had sketched out for myself. Taking for my text Heb. xiii. 17, I shortly consider the divine appointment of the ministry, and dwell upon the pastoral *responsibility* mentioned in the above passage, as a strong argument in favour of the office being confined to those who are regularly entrusted with it, and on the correlative duties of obedience and adherence to the regular ministry, and of a faithful discharge of the pastoral duties; of forbearing to distract people's faith by preaching doctrines of dubious foundation and ambiguous tendency, whether inclining to Socinianism or Calvinism, and the danger of departing from the line of doctrine laid down in the ordinances of the Church. The necessity of learning to qualify a person to explain many parts of Scripture, particularly the Epistles of St. Paul; but, at the same time, the duty of candour and charity in our hearers, in looking to the nature of the truths delivered rather than to the manner of expounding them; finally, the great good which would result to religion in general, if both those who teach and those who are taught would avoid all causes of offence, whether doctrinal or personal, and the Christian duty of making any sacrifice, short of our principles, to preserve unbroken the bond of unity. . . ."

In this sermon, as Dr. Biber[1] observes, "the Scholar predominates over the Churchman;" the advantages of learning in the clergy are dwelt upon by one who had some right to speak on this subject; and it is urged that "enthusiasm, without learning and judgment, is a fire which burns but to delude." But that the duties of a clergyman were not lightly regarded by him, is shown by the earnest exhortations with which he concludes:—"Whatever be the measure of obedience which may be paid to us in our spiritual capacity, may the Almighty give *us* grace and wisdom, on our part, to use such endeavours that not a single soul shall, by the fault of its ministers, wander from the pale of our Church. . . . We may still hope, if not to build up the breach which has been made in the unity of the Church, at least to stop the further progress of disunion. It is not yet too late for us to

[1] 'Bishop Blomfield and his Times,' p. 29.

put fresh incense in our censers, and to stand between the dead and the living. If," he adds, "there be any circumstance calculated to give additional importance to these considerations, it is the awful complexion of the times in which we live. A spirit of religious unity and fraternal concord is rendered more than ever desirable by the storms which are again gathering over the hemisphere of civilized society. It well becomes us, who are of one household, to be all of one mind and spirit, and to cultivate that peaceable and conciliating disposition, which is too apt to be forgotten when 'the days of vengeance' come upon the earth with 'distress of nations and perplexity.'"

A very similar line of argument is pursued in two sermons, published in 1820, which he preached respectively at the Visitation of the Bishop of Norwich ('The Qualifications necessary for a Preacher and Hearer of the Word,') and at the Cambridge Commencement ('The Importance of Learning to the Clergy').

In 1816 he published anonymously a pamphlet[1] upon the residence and duties of the clergy, and the salaries of curates; subjects dealt with in a Bill which was then before Parliament, but which did not pass into law. This pamphlet gives evidence that he was already a Church Reformer, in the best sense of the term. He

[1] 'A Letter to a Clergyman of the Diocese of Bath and Wells, upon Certain Clauses said to be contained in the proposed Bill to consolidate the Laws concerning Spiritual Persons; and upon certain Resolutions relating to these Clauses lately adopted and published by the Clergy of the Rural Deanery of Cary in the said Diocese. From a Beneficed Clergyman in the Diocese of Lincoln.'

did not consider, as many of the clergy appeared to do, that benefices with cure of souls were freehold property, independent of all conditions. The clause in the proposed Bill which limited the power of the clergy to farm land, he regarded as a wholesome enactment; and he reminded his brethren that the mere celebration of Divine Service being by no means the whole of a clergyman's duty, his abstraction in agricultural or other secular pursuits must needs impair, if not destroy, his efficiency; "let it not be said that while his time and thoughts are occupied in the ox-stall or the fold, in his own flock, which looks up to him for spiritual comfort and instruction,

"The hungry sheep look up and are not fed."

The Hon. W. H. Lyttelton to the Rev. C. J. Blomfield.

"Saville Row, *Feb.* 5, 1817.

".... I have read your pamphlet, which is as conclusive in argument (in my humble opinion) as it is liberal in principle. To be sure you had no very formidable antagonists in those shallow, passionate and presumptuous gentlemen of the rural deanery; but it is fit that arrogance and presumption should be exposed, and prevented from laying their rash hands on matters of great importance, and I think you have done a good service to the Church and the State by exposing them in the present instance. . . . I have no news of any importance for you. You see the Ministry talk already of following the precedents of 1795. Extreme remedies —the knife and cautery in the first instance. The practice of quacks. I can only say, God help us! and in the meanwhile let each man put his shoulder to the wheel..."

The allusion here is to the suspension of the *Habeas Corpus* by Lord Liverpool's Ministry, as a precaution against seditious societies.

Early in 1817 he published a Sermon, preached before the University at Cambridge, on the importance of a knowledge of Jewish Tradition to the interpreter of Scripture; a subject which he handled more fully in a 'Dissertation[1] upon the Traditional Knowledge of a promised Redeemer,' published two years later. The line of argument followed out in this work was one comparatively new to English theologians; and the sense and learning with which the subject was treated elicited the praise of such judges as Dr. Parr, Bishop Kaye, and Bishop Howley, as may be seen by the following letters:—

Dr. Kaye to the Rev. C. J. Blomfield.

"CAMBRIDGE, *April* 15, 1817.

".... You have reminded our Cambridge divines of a principle of interpretation to which too little attention has been paid; but the truth is that our pious theologians dislike all principles, the application of which is to cost them any trouble; they prefer the short cut, and would persuade us that human industry is not only unnecessary but prejudicial to the right understanding of the Scriptures. You must not, therefore, expect their approbation...."

Dr. Parr to the Rev. C. J. Blomfield.

"HATTON, *Oct.* 28, 1819.

"DEAR, EXCELLENT, LEARNED, AND DEEPLY RESPECTED MR. BLOMFIELD,—Your 'Dissertation on the Traditional

[1] The substance of this dissertation had also been preached before the University.

Knowledge of a promised Redeemer' reached me about ten days before I left home. I read it twice; I read it most attentively; and though I am not a convert to your opinion, yet I consider the work as an additional proof of your diligence in research, and your acuteness in reasoning. Very particularly was I pleased with your correct statement of the question itself, and with the exact method in which you have arranged your arguments. Every enlightened believer will acknowledge his obligations to you, and most earnest is my hope that our ecclesiastical superiors may bestow upon you the rewards to which you are substantially and pre-eminently entitled. Among the effects produced by your book, I felt an increased desire to live near you, and to converse with you frequently, unreservedly, and seriously. . . . Mr. Blomfield, you told me some time ago that you were in possession of the 'Fax Artium,' by Gruter. Well, dear sir, as you did not want the copy I intended for you, I determined to look out for some other book not unworthy your acceptance. Yesterday morning I selected a series of the 'Acta Eruditorum Lipsiensium.' It begins in 1682 and goes to 1703 inclusive. It is accompanied by an Index in one volume, and Supplement in two. Will you accept these books as a mark of my profound respect and sincere friendship, even though you should have duplicates? In the course of a month I shall send some other books to Cambridge, and if you permit me, I will put into the same box the little present which I now offer you. From the bottom of my soul I wish you health, prosperity, and fame.

And I am, dear Sir, most truly,

Your admirer and your friend,

S. Parr."

The Rev. C. J. Blomfield to Dr. Parr.

[*November*, 1819.]

"DEAR SIR,—I need scarcely say with what pleasure I received so flattering a testimony of your good opinion. If the approbation of one real scholar and critic has been at all times considered by me an ample recompense for the labour I have bestowed on the investigation of truth, whether in theology or classical literature, I must, of course, experience a more than ordinary degree of satisfaction in receiving so honourable and so cordial an expression of praise from the profoundest scholar, and most sagacious critic of the age. With regard to my 'Dissertation,' I aimed at no other praise than that of setting the question in a clear point of view, and bringing some arguments to bear upon it, which had been altogether passed over, or but cursorily noticed by other writers. Where so much of the discussion must necessarily depend upon inductive reasoning, I would neither lay too much stress upon the position itself, nor upon the arguments by which I have endeavoured to maintain it; especially as the decision does not involve the great doctrine of our Lord's Divinity, which must stand or fall by the testimony of the Christian Scriptures. . . . Be assured, my dear sir, that I shall on all occasions be proud to receive your friendly and impartial criticisms. No person, I believe, is more open to conviction than myself, or more prompt to acknowledge an error, being well aware, that as it is not the lot of humanity to be exempt from failings, so it is not the part of real wisdom proudly to deny or pertinaciously to defend them. Every succeeding year makes me more sensible how very little progress I have made in any department of learning, compared with the ground which still remains to be traversed; and this conviction, strengthened as it is by a deep and awful sense of the truth that our sufficiency is not of ourselves, renders me less confident in my own resources, and more accessible to the advice and instruction of others. But you will, I trust, do me the justice to believe, that there has never been a period of my life, in which I was not ready to pay the humble tribute of my respect to the profound and varied erudition, the sagacious discrimination and classical eloquence of Dr. Parr. . . . ."

The last event which remains to be recorded in Bishop Blomfield's life at Dunton is a melancholy one —the death of his brother Edward, which happened in October, 1816, on his return from a continental tour, which he had taken as tutor to a son of the Duke of Atholl. Gifted with singular talents, accomplished, amiable, and religious, and of a disposition somewhat softer than that of his elder brother, Edward Valentine Blomfield left a blank in a wide circle of friends which was not readily filled up, and by his early death cut off the promise of much distinction and usefulness.

"I know of no event," writes his friend Rennell, then Vicar of Kensington, "out of my own immediate family that could have distressed me more. Your poor brother was the best and most innocent of human creatures. What a Marcellus in letters have we lost!"

Similarity of pursuits and interests, combined with brotherly affection, to make this loss very acutely felt by his elder brother. He writes to his father five or six weeks after the event:—"I have not known an hour's comfortable sleep since I left Bury;" and even at the close of his life he said that the death of his brother was the greatest grief he had ever known.

Edward Blomfield had begun a Greek-English Lexicon: this was necessarily abandoned after his death; but a translation of "Matthiæ's Greek Grammar," which he had nearly finished, was completed by his brother, and brought out in 1819. He was buried in the chapel of Emmanuel College, of which Society he had been a Fellow; and a Latin inscription by his brother, upon the monumental tablet erected to his memory, records his virtues, his talents, and his early death.

On this sad occasion the elder writes thus to his father:—

"DUNTON, *Oct.* 21, 1816.

"MY DEAREST FATHER,—I have scarcely recovered my spirits sufficiently to write as I could wish, yet I am unwilling to delay any longer what must be for some time a melancholy task. I am glad to learn that you are as much recovered as could be expected. Indeed I was sure that your own piety and virtues were such that God would not leave you comfortless under this great trial of your patience. I regret very much that I could not remain with you and my dear mother a longer time, to share with your other children the office of alleviating your grief; but I trust you will not suppose, because I am obliged to be absent, that I feel the less sensibly both the severity of our loss and the desire of affording you consolation. At present I am quite unable to return to my own studies and pursuits, which would continually remind me of poor dear Edward. I shall be more comfortable after I have seen you again at Christmas. . . ."

From Monk he received the following, among other letters of sympathy:—

"CAMBRIDGE, *Nov.* 12, 1816.

".... What you must feel on your own account in the loss of such a brother I can imagine from what I have myself suffered in being deprived of one of the best and kindest friends that I ever possessed. It may be some melancholy gratification to the relations of your dear brother to know how many people sympathize with their feelings at his loss. Never have I known a person so much regretted; and this regret will not hastily subside, for it is the tribute to his virtues and his various merits. The election to the Divinity chair you are apprized of. On the morning after, the new Professor (Dr. Kaye), in resigning the office of vice-chancellor, paid a feeling tribute to the memory of your dear brother."

In the summer of 1817 the Rector of Dunton was presented by Lord Bristol to the more valuable benefices of Great and Little Chesterford, at that time in the diocese of London, and Tuddenham in Suffolk. About the same time he was appointed by Bishop Howley one of his chaplains, and from this time till his resignation, in 1856, his connexion with the diocese of London was unbroken.

Chesterford is an agricultural parish, on the borders of Essex and Cambridgeshire, stretching for some distance over the low undulating hills, beneath which the Cam winds slowly towards Cambridge. The population of the straggling irregular village, with its white-washed and gabled houses, and substantial church of late Gothic, was about five hundred when Mr. Blomfield was appointed to the living. The smaller parish of Little Chesterford lies about a mile to the south-east.

It has already been mentioned that Mr. Blomfield served the curacy of this parish when he first took orders. Since then there had been one incumbent who had resided in the parish, and was chiefly remembered for having set up a carriage and four on a sudden accession of fortune; and a second, who was non-resident, and had for his curate Mr. Davys, now Bishop of Peterborough. The new incumbent prepared to enter energetically upon his new duties, and as a first measure he laid out a considerable sum on improving the parsonage-house, which was small and inconvenient.

It was while these alterations were going on, and while he was living at the neighbouring village of Hildersham, that he lost his wife, who was a person of delicate constitution, and of whose six children only one lived beyond infancy. He writes thus to his friend Monk on the occasion :—

"HILDERSHAM [*Feb.* 1818].

"MY DEAR FRIEND,—You have heard of the heavy visitation with which God has afflicted me. I have lost her, of whom I was not worthy. It is my particular wish that, by attending the funeral, you should mark your friendship for me, and pay the last tribute of respect to one who entertained for you the most sincere regard and esteem. I cannot write any more; the bearer of this will tell you the rest.

Your afflicted friend,

C. J. BLOMFIELD."

She was buried at Chesterford—a melancholy beginning of his new life.

Bishop Blomfield is still remembered at Chesterford for his activity and benevolence. He took a more prominent part in parochial business, and in the administration of local charities, than was then usual among the clergy; so that one of his parishioners described his energy in a farmer's simile, "I call him Mr. Snap-trace." He visited the poor, one of whom described him afterwards as "a wonderful forgiving gentleman;" he superintended the schools, which had been improved by Mr. Davys; he saw that the public-houses were closed in good time at night; he improved the vicarage grounds by planting, and buying up the adjoining slips of land; and he continued, as before, to devote much of his time to study, and to the pupils whom he received into his parsonage.

One circumstance which at that time tended to mar a clergyman's usefulness in the parish of Chesterford, and to lower the moral tone of its inhabitants, was this. The village lay upon the high road between London and Newmarket, and the frequenters of the Races at the latter place always stopped to change horses and refresh themselves at the large inn near the church. This in itself was undesirable; but to make matters worse, at that time the first day of the Newmarket Spring Meeting was Easter Monday, and those who were to be present passed through Chesterford on Easter Day. The country people from the neighbouring villages flocked in to see the gentlefolks pass in their carriages, and a regular fair, with its apparatus of booths, was held on the open space in front of the inn: and while the vicar was celebrating the Eucharist in the adjoining church, on the most sacred day of the Christian year, the aristocratic sportsmen would drive up to the inn in open carriages, playing at whist, and throwing out their cards, would call to the waiters for fresh packs. To quote the words which Bishop Blomfield himself used some years later,[1] "More than forty pairs of horses have sometimes been changed there on Easter Day, a great proportion of them while I was celebrating Divine Service. Not only all the servants and dependents of the inn, but a great number of the young men of the parish, were taken away from their own Sabbath duties, to assist in this flagrant violation of them by others; not to mention that hundreds were engaged in observing their betters thus ostentatiously setting at nought the ordinances of religion; some urging with bribes, and others with execrations, the drivers of those poor jaded animals, for whom the merciful provision of a Sabbath seemed almost to have been made in vain; while others were seen engaged in gambling, and scattering the implements of their unholy pastime about the road."

He had endeavoured, though unsuccessfully, when curate of the parish, to remove or mitigate this scandal; and when he returned as vicar he renewed his remonstrances to the Jockey Club, which were now backed by his neighbour, the then Lord Braybrooke. The influential patrons of the turf were at first very unwilling to make any change. Bishop Howley addressed the Duke of York on the subject; but the Duke declined to alter his practice, and said, that though it was true he travelled to the races on Sunday, he always had a Bible and Prayer Book in the carriage. Eventually, however,

[1] 'Letter on the Present Neglect of the Lord's Day.' 1830.

the first day of the races was changed from Monday to Tuesday.

Of his life at Chesterford, Bishop Blomfield used often to relate the following anecdote:—Walking over one Sunday to his duty at Little Chesterford, he found on his arrival that he had forgotten to bring his sermon with him. It was too late to return: so, for the first and only time in his life, he preached *ex tempore*, taking for his text the first verse of the fifty-third Psalm, "The fool hath said in his heart, there is no God." Being anxious to know how he had seemed to succeed in an unaccustomed effort, he asked one of the congregation on coming out, how he had liked the sermon. "Well, Mr. Blomfield," replied the man, "I liked the sermon well enough; but I can't say I agree with you; *I* think there *be* a God."

Another Chesterford reminiscence was the answer of a school-boy, being asked what was meant in the Catechism by *succouring* his father and mother, replied promptly, "Giving on 'em milk."

CHAPTER III.

CHANGE IN THE CHARACTER OF THE ENGLISH CLERGY SINCE 1810—LOW STANDARD OF CLERICAL CHARACTER—LAXITY OF BISHOPS—MR. BLOMFIELD TAKES HIS DEGREE OF B.D.—HIS SECOND MARRIAGE—SERMON ON RITUAL—IS PRESENTED TO THE LIVING OF BISHOPSGATE—HIS CHARACTER AS A CITY INCUMBENT—HIS LIBERALITY—HIS SERMONS—IS APPOINTED ARCHDEACON OF COLCHESTER—ANECDOTE OF THE ARCHIDIACONAL OFFICE—HIS ANSWER TO THE EDINBURGH REVIEW—HIS 'FAMILY PRAYERS.'

HAVING reached that period of the life of Bishop Blomfield at which he entered upon a wider sphere of clerical usefulness than any which he had yet filled, it may be well to remind the reader of the change which has taken place in the condition and character of the English clergy since the time at which he first became one of them; for after the lapse of half a century it is only by an effort that we can appreciate how great that change has been. In character, habits, attainments, social position, and general reputation, the ordinary clergyman of 1860 is a very different being from the clergyman of 1810. Exceptions, of course, occur in every rule; and in some instances the type of the later epoch may be anticipated in the earlier, or the type of the earlier reproduced in the later; but, speaking generally, the remark of Mr. Thomas Grenville, who died in 1846, at the age of ninety-one, may be taken as true, that no change which had taken place in his lifetime was so great as the change in the clergy of the Church of

England. Even where we differ for the worse, we still differ; as our faults are not the faults, so our virtues are not the virtues of our predecessors.

The most obvious difference is the low standard of character and duties which then prevailed among clergymen compared to what is now generally expected of them. Fifty years ago, a decent and regular performance of Divine Service on Sundays was almost all that any one looked for in a clergyman: if this were found, most people were satisfied. The clergyman might be non-resident, a sportsman, a farmer, neglectful of all study, a violent politician, a *bon vivant*, or a courtier; but if he performed in person, or by deputy, that which now usurped the name of his "duty," that was enough. We find Bishops of this period, in their Charges, insisting upon duties and qualifications which are now taken for granted, and deprecating practices which are now almost unheard of.

What were the causes which produced this low standard of clerical character? They appear to have been mainly these:—First, the general laxity of the eighteenth century, not much improved by the external irritation of Methodism, and extending into the nineteenth. Secondly, the strong Conservative feeling engendered in England by the French Revolution, which clung to things as they were because they were so; upheld the rights, while it repudiated the duties of property, and stigmatized reform as sedition, and earnestness as enthusiasm. Dr. Copleston wrote in 1814, "The leading partisans who assume that title (High-Churchmen) appear to me to be only occupied with the thought of converting the property of the Church to their private advantage, leaving the duties of it to be performed how they can."[1] Thirdly, that legacy of the Reformation which had never been substantially altered—a system of benefices most inadequately endowed in the great majority of cases, but richly in a few, entailing all the evils of non-residence, pluralities, and proprietary chapels, and by the unequal distribution of revenues, inflicting upon the Church at once the discomfort of being extremely poor, and the discredit of being extremely rich.[2]

These evils, indeed, had not been altogether overlooked by the statesmen of the day. The residence of the clergy, and the payment of curates, frequently formed the subject of legislation in the first ten or twelve years of the century; and in 1809, Mr. Perceval proposed to raise £100,000 a year towards augmenting the salaries of curates, which was actually done for ten successive years; but the results so obtained were quite inadequate to counteract the magnitude of the evils complained of. Meanwhile, the shortcomings of the Church were a scandal to those who wished her well, and furnished a handle to all who were in principle opposed to her, or who, under the name of Reform, sought her destruction; thus slowly, but surely, preparing the way for the great convulsions which, twenty years later, shook the ecclesiastical institutions of the country to their base, simultaneously with the introduction of important changes in its political institutions.

And if the duties required from, or performed by, the clergy were small, and the character of many of them of

[1] 'Memoir of Bishop Copleston,' p. 47.

[2] In 1802 there were 5,557 benefices in England, or about half the entire number, worth less than £50 a-year each: in 1812, of 10,261 incumbents, 5,840, or considerably more than half, were non-resident.

an inferior type, their social position was proportionately low. Some, indeed, by birth, wealth, talents, or dignity of preferment, ranked high in the world's estimation; but when a large proportion of the clergy consisted of curates to non-resident incumbents, who "served" two or more churches at miserable stipends, it was not possible that the profession, as a body, should take that social position which belongs to it under more favourable circumstances. In Miss Austen's novel of 'Mansfield Park,' the fashionable young lady who meets a clerical admirer at a dinner party is thankful to reflect afterwards that the uniformity of modern dress would not have betrayed to the company the profession to which he belonged.

Patronage was often exercised with little regard to fitness for the clerical office, and orders were conferred by Bishops with a fatal facility. On the subject of ordinations at this period such anecdotes as the following are told, of which it may be said that, even though they are not true in every particular, it does not speak well for the Episcopal Bench that it should have been possible for them to obtain currency. The chaplain and son-in-law of Bishop North (1781—1820) examined two candidates for orders in a tent on a cricket-field, he himself being engaged as one of the players. Bishop Pelham (1807—1827) performed the same duty on one occasion by sending a message by his butler to the candidate to write an essay;[1] the chaplain of Bishop Douglas (1787—1807) did it while shaving, and stopped the examination when the examinee had construed two words. The laxity of Bishop Bathurst, of Norwich

[1] It is right, however, to add that the Bishop is said to have afterwards repented the carelessness of this act.

(1805—1837), known to his Whig admirers as "the good bishop," with regard to ordinations, is well known, and involved him in a misunderstanding with Dr. Blomfield when Bishop of Chester. The natural consequence of this state of things was a very low standard of theological acquirements among the country clergy. When they were useful and well-informed they busied themselves generally with matters foreign to their own profession. They were eager politicians, or amateur farmers; they were "constant readers of the Gentleman's Magazine, deep in the antiquities of the signs of inns, speculations as to what becomes of swallows in winter, and whether hedgehogs, or other urchins, are most justly accused of sucking milch cows dry at night."[1]

Bishop Blomfield, in a pamphlet already alluded to, notices the following announcement in a provincial newspaper: "——, Esq. has presented the Rev. —— to the living of ——; at the same time acknowledging, in a very handsome manner, the obligation he felt to that gentleman for his exertions in the cause of *agriculture*, particularly by the service he has rendered him in the execution of the office of Secretary to the —— Agricultural Society, which he has now held thirteen years without any emolument."

The Bishops, though numbering some men of superior stamp among them, and as a body decorous in private character, were often either politically subservient, avaricious, courtiers, domineering, or neglectful of their dioceses. Indeed, measured by the standard of our own days, even the best would be considered as deficient in

[1] Rev. H. H. Norris, in Churton's 'Life of Joshua Watson,' vol. i. p. 277.

some parts of his office. Bishop Porteus (1776—1809) was justly honoured as an amiable and conscientious prelate; yet, when asked by a neighbouring clergyman to preach a charity sermon for him, he could reply, "I only give one in a year, and *the next year is promised.*" Bishop Watson, of Llandaff (1782—1816), was by no means the least distinguished member of the Episcopal Bench, and his 'Apology for Christianity' was considered a masterly performance. Yet Bishop Watson never resided in his diocese, during an Episcopate of thirty-four years, and, says the Annual Register, "passed the evening of his life chiefly at his seat of Calgarth, in Westmoreland, where he actively employed himself in rural decorations and agricultural improvements." This account is confirmed by the Bishop himself:—"I pursued my intention of *retiring, in a great measure, from public life,* and laid, in the summer of 1789, the foundation of my house on the banks of the Windermere. I have now spent above twenty years in this delightful country, but my time has not been spent in field diversions, in idle visitings, in county bickerings, in indolence, or intemperance; no, it has been spent partly in supporting the religion and constitution of the country by seasonable publications, and principally in building farm-houses, blasting rocks, enclosing wastes, in making bad land good, in planting larches, and in planting in the hearts of my children principles of piety, of benevolence, and self-government."[1]

It must not however be forgotten, that in the midst of this general laxity there existed within the English Church, at the beginning of the present century, a body

[1] 'Life of Bishop Watson,' vol. i. p. 388.

of men whose piety and usefulness would have done honour to any age and any Church. These belonged generally to one of two sections of the Church, influential rather from character than numbers. On one side the Evangelical party, numbering in its ranks such laymen as Wilberforce, and his allies in the abolition of the Slave-trade, and such clergymen as Richard Cecil and Bishop Wilson of Calcutta; on the other the old High-Church party (in the good sense of that term), which inherited, through Jones of Nayland and William Stevens, the traditions of Robert Nelson, and Bishop Bull, and of which the representative man is Joshua Watson. Each party has left substantial memorials of its labours at this period: the one in the Church Missionary Society, founded in 1799; the other in the National and Church-building Societies, which date respectively from 1811 and 1818. Bishop Blomfield was not in the beginning of his clerical life brought into immediate contact with either of these two parties; the circumstances which afterwards made him, to a great extent, an ally of the latter will be presently related.

We now return to the events of Bishop Blomfield's life. At the Cambridge Commencement of 1818 he took his degree of B.D., and the circumstances which took place at his public disputation for this degree, held in the Schools, have been thus described by an eye-witness[1]:—

"I had known Blomfield, and his equally gifted brother Edward, from their earliest years; I had observed with delight their triumphant progress through

[1] Gunning's 'Reminiscences of Cambridge,' vol. ii. p. 297.

the University; and I had been in the habit of congratulating their excellent father, when he made his annual visits at the Commencement, upon the unexampled success of his sons. Notwithstanding my long and intimate acquaintance, Charles James Blomfield was not *exactly* the opponent I should have wished to meet in any of the schools.

When the day arrived for the keeping of the act, the schools were crowded to excess, from the well-known fame of the respondent. His Thesis was such a one as only himself could have written. The disputation commenced; and whether it was that Beverley's[1] arguments were ill chosen, or his mode of defending them particularly infelicitous, very certain it is that Blomfield kept the schools in a continual laugh at Beverley's expense, during the whole of this usually solemn, not to say gloomy exhibition. Beverley was not at all disconcerted, but defended each argument with unyielding obstinacy, until the *probes aliter* of the Professor obliged him to produce a fresh argument."

The result was that Beverley was desired by the Regius Professor of Divinity to discontinue keeping exercises in the schools.

In the same year Mr. Blomfield published a sermon preached at Saffron Walden at the Visitation of Bishop Howley, 'On the Duty of a canonical adherence to the Ritual of the Church.' This sermon is remarkable as enunciating the same principles which he afterwards repeated in his Charges at Chester in 1825, and at London in 1842. The Church, he argues, must have a certain external splendour corresponding to her inward holiness, and men must be religiously affected partly through their senses. And since our own Church has

[1] The Esquire Bedell.

made ample provision for these objects, we shall best do our duty by obeying her rules, observing the decent solemnity of her ritual, and imitating her reverent language.

In the Notes to the sermon he calls the attention of his brother clergymen, with strong expressions of reprobation, to two practices sanctioned by some of them. The one is "the habit of holding those anomalous assemblies called 'Prayer Meetings,' which must tend directly to weaken, in the minds of their flock, the sense of the utility and importance of public worship." The other is, "the irregular practice, to call it by no harsher name, which prevails amongst some of the clergy, who embrace the peculiar tenets of Calvin—the custom of curtailing and mutilating the Service of Baptism, so as to bring it somewhat nearer to their own notions of regeneration. I mention the subject here," he adds, "chiefly as affording a satisfactory proof, that some who impugn the doctrine of baptismal regeneration, find the language of our Church, in this solemn service, too plain to be misunderstood, too strong to be eluded. Their only resource, therefore, is to blot out so much of it as they cannot digest; although it is difficult to say what is too hard for *their* digestion, who can wilfully alter and deprave the prescribed form of administering a Sacrament, to which they have declared their unfeigned assent and consent. To those who think themselves authorised by a spiritual illumination thus to deviate from that line of public duty which they have solemnly bound themselves to observe, we may recommend the just and sensible caution of the Fathers of our Church: "It is not the part of a Christian, under pretence of the Holy Ghost, to bring his own dreams and phantasies into the Church." (Homily for Whitsunday, Part II).

The reader will not fail to observe that there is in these remarks something of that "predominant desire to marshal and put in order all the rest," which could find its appropriate sphere of action only in the third and highest order of the ministry.

In December, 1819, he married Dorothy, daughter of Charles William Cox, Esq., and widow of Thomas Kent, Esq., barrister; a union which was the source of unmixed happiness and comfort to him to the latest hour of his life. By her he was the father of eleven children, one of whom died in his infancy.

The time was now come when the reputation and character of Charles James Blomfield were to be recognised by those who had the bestowal of the public patronage of the Church; who were at this time of the Tory party, under the premiership of Lord Liverpool. The disappointed ambition of Sydney Smith represented this administration (1812–1827) as a period of profound corruption in Church as well as State—"a long and hopeless career in your profession, the chuckling grin of noodles, the sarcastic leer of the genuine political rogue—prebendaries, deans, and bishops made over your head—reverend renegadoes advanced to the highest dignities of the Church for helping to rivet the chains of Catholic and Protestant Dissenters, and no more chance of a Whig administration than of a thaw in Zembla!"[1]

Those who remember that among the dignitaries who owed part or the whole of their promotion to Lord

[1] Preface to his Works, p. v.

Liverpool, besides the name of Blomfield himself, are to be found those of the present Bishop of Winchester—Bishops Howley, Ryder, Bethell, Van Mildert, Kaye, Monk, Copleston, Heber, Mant, and Jebb, and Dr. Wordsworth, Master of Trinity, will probably admit that this minister's use of ecclesiastical patronage was such as to make the postponement of a Whig administration a very tolerable misfortune for the Church.

On the cardinal point of Roman Catholic emancipation the opinions of Mr. Blomfield, so far as they had yet been expressed, had been opposed to those of the existing ministry. But his views on this subject had been for some time undergoing a change, founded upon a more careful study of what he considered to be the necessary political effects of the Roman system; although he was not called upon to give expression to this change till after he became Bishop of Chester.

In the year 1819, Lord Bristol took occasion, before going on the Continent, to call the attention of his brother-in-law, Lord Liverpool, to Mr. Blomfield; and while abstaining from a request for any preferment for him, he begged the minister to make inquiries about him.

Accordingly, when, in the following year, the promotion of Dr. Mant to an Irish bishopric rendered vacant the valuable benefice of St. Botolph, Bishopsgate, Lord Liverpool wrote to Bishop Howley, to inform him that he intended to appoint Mr. Blomfield. The Bishop wrote in reply, that as no one can be appointed to an *Irish* see, until he has actually *resigned* all his English preferment, the appointment, in this case, would not fall to the Crown: but he added that, in fact, no better person could be found than Mr. Blomfield, whom, indeed, he had some time before appointed one of his chaplains, and that he would gladly collate him. The appointment was communicated to Mr. Blomfield, in a letter from Lord Liverpool to Lord Hervey (the present Marquis of Bristol), who was then residing as a guest and pupil at Chesterford Rectory, the rest of his family being abroad at the time.

The preferment thus conferred upon Mr. Blomfield, as it were, from two different quarters at once, marks an important epoch in his life. The income of the living being large (something over £2,000 a year in the gross), and the Bishop allowing him to retain Chesterford with it, he was enabled, for the first time in his life, to enjoy a comfortable independence without the labour of tuition, and thus to devote his time more fully to the duties of his profession. By removing his principal residence to London, his new position brought him before the eye of the metropolitan public, accustomed him to habits of business, and quickened his natural promptitude in dealing with men; while the pastoral superintendence of a populous and crowded parish enlarged his sympathies, extended his knowledge of human nature, and gave him that particular kind of experience which afterwards, as the head of the London clergy, he found of such great and permanent value.

At the request of his parishioners, who said they had always had a Doctor for their rector, he proceeded, in July, 1820, to the degree of D.D., at Cambridge, by Royal letter.

He still continued to reside at Chesterford, for about three months in the year; and when absent his curate, an active and amiable representative, used to send him a weekly account of the parochial history "in the vegetable basket."

The Rev. C. J. Blomfield to Professor Monk.

"LONDON, *April* 19, 1820.

".... The value of my new living has been overrated, as I supposed: it is about 2,100*l.* per annum. The clear annual income, after cu-rates, poor-rates, and other rates have been paid, will be about 1,600*l.* But even this is too good a thing to refuse, seeing that it is tenable with Chesterford, and that the Bishop does not object to my passing some months in the year at the latter place. The house is bad, but the Bishop thinks I may be able to exchange it for a better; or he will allow me to let it, and hire a better. I met with a most kind reception from Lord Liverpool...."

To the same.

"CHESTERFORD, *June* 28, 1820.

".... I have written to Lord Liverpool by this day's post, saying all that I thought might be conducive to your success.[1] I need not tell you how sincerely I shall rejoice, for the sake of the University and the College, even more than your own, if you should be appointed. Till I got Bishopsgate, I confess that the Mastership of Trinity was always the highest object of my ambition. But my notions are now considerably modified; and although it might be in some respects

[1] Mr. Monk was at this time a candidate for the Presidency of Queens' College.

suited to my tastes, yet in many substantial advantages it would be inferior. I shall hail your elevation with feelings of unmixed satisfaction and delight, and so will every friend of sound learning and honourable conduct. Lose no time in communicating me the result. I confess I am sanguine about it, because I firmly believe that Lord Liverpool's decision will be a conscientious one. . . . ."

The parish of Bishopsgate contained, in 1821, a population of 10,140. These were principally of the poorer class; but the resident parishioners at this time also comprised many wealthy tradesmen and merchants, whose families or successors have since migrated to the suburbs. One of these influential inhabitants was Sir William Rawlins, the City knight, who has sometimes been claimed as the author of the celebrated "Three R's," and who is known to have said at a City dinner that he hoped he might live to see the day which had been prophesied, "When every man should do that which was right in his own eyes." With this class the new Rector of Bishopsgate made himself very popular. He mixed in their society freely when invited to do so; and he managed their parish meetings with tact and good-nature. It is related that he once overcame an obstinate Quaker, who had refused to take off his hat at a vestry-meeting held in the church, by proposing to the meeting a resolution, "That the beadle be directed to take off Mr. ——'s hat;" which was accordingly done, and the Nonconformist, having saved his conscience, submitted.

The tithes of Bishopsgate, as is the case with some other City parishes, rested upon a special Act of Parliament, known as the "Two and Ninepenny Act," the strict enforcement of which would have produced an immense income. Dr. Blomfield, when he had been Rector three or four years, procured the settlement of the question by a compromise, on terms exceedingly favourable to the parishioners. The income, £2,000 a year, was to be raised as a Church-rate, which was then thought as secure as the Consolidated Fund, so little had the abolition of Church-rates as yet been dreamt of. At the same time he alienated a portion of the tithes for the endowment of a chapel of ease, which, after some difficulty, was built, but not consecrated till after his translation to the see of London.

In pastoral visitation among the poor and ignorant, Dr. Blomfield was, as he had always been, active and unwearied. One of his curates, at this time, was the Rev. Richard Harvey, now Rector of Hornsey, and Canon of Gloucester, who has kindly communicated the following particulars:—

"He was exceedingly kind and friendly, and most candid both in telling me of my faults and commending what he approved. He had a kindliness of manner and winning smile, which were perfectly irresistible. His activity was marvellous, and the number of things which he did hardly credible. . . . I used to see him nearly every morning, and tell him about the sick and poor, and what was going on in the parish; also as to any particular cases which it was desirable that he should visit himself. He was very attentive to all, and used to visit the sick without reference to their being members of the Church; and he took me with him generally, that I might learn how to proceed when by myself. He had a singularly quick eye, and often told me of seeing me at a distance, when I had gone into some house, and had no idea that he knew it. Just before I came, during the severity of the winter (of 1822-3), I was told that he was going round to relieve the distressed with other gentlemen. The people were relieved partly according to the number of their families. The Bishop thought he detected the same children in different rooms, and at last discovered that, as he went up and down stairs, the people let down children by the window from one storey to another. . . . Soon after I came he established a Society for the Promotion of Christian Knowledge Committee, for which he drew up admirable rules, and shortly afterwards he allowed me to collect for the Society for the Propagation of the Gospel. He did not then like to use tracts not on the Society for the Promotion of Christian Knowledge list, but said, 'Show me any good tracts, and I will get them on the list;' and accordingly he got many on, by Mrs. More, Mrs. S. Hoare, Mr. Davys, now Bishop of Peterborough, and others."

A curious testimony to his diligence in visitation while at Bishopsgate was accidentally elicited some thirty years afterwards by a Scripture reader employed under the Rev. T. Saulez, Incumbent of All Saints', Islington. He has in his diary the following entry:—

"Mrs. Y——, Brandon Road, York Road.

"When her husband was an apprentice in Angel Alley, Bishopsgate, Dr. Blomfield was Rector of the parish. He used to go round from street to street, court to court, and house to house, with his Bible, and visit the families, 'like the city missionaries or Scripture readers do now.' The neighbourhood was disreputable, and teachers attending the Sunday school in it were pelted with refuse by the people. Mrs. Y—— was one of these teachers, and frequently observed the Rector on his rounds. She mentioned it to me with great pleasure. He and Mr. Tagg (father of the Incumbent of St. John's, Bethnal Green) succeeded in inducing many unmarried couples to become married. Y——'s master was a bad man, and used him so as to make him wretched; although he was but young, yet he was rendered so miserable that he cannot call to mind much of the pastoral visits of the reverend Scripture reader. He used to call about once a week on his master, to read and advise him to a better course of life. He was received civilly, which was not the case at many houses. But it is to be feared that the Rector never saw the man turn from his evil ways. The Y——s are pious people."

Another parishioner thus writes of Dr. Blomfield, as Rector of Bishopsgate:—

"He was never idle, for it was well known in how many public works, connected with moral and religious objects, he was taking part beyond the limits of his parish. For the poor he not only had kind words, but an open purse. He visited among the middle class of his parishioners as a neighbour and friend. His frank and kindly manner made him acceptable to the Dissenters in his parish, with whom he was always on good terms. While he never flinched from upholding the truth, he respected the conscientious feelings of all. He was constitutionally of a warm and impetuous temperament, but it was an impetuosity fired by an uncontrollable desire to advance the glory of God, and the good of his fellow-men."

He was remarkable, indeed, at this time, for a certain liberality towards Nonconformists. He maintained friendly relations with his neighbour, Mr. Clayton, the respected minister of the Poultry Chapel; and his parochial schools, as he stated some years afterwards in the House of Lords, were attended by the children even of Jews, of whom there was a large population in Houndsditch, under the shadow of his church. The consequence was that when, some time after his coming to Bishopsgate, some of his influential parishioners determined to summon a public meeting to testify their approbation of what he had done in the parish, the meeting was attended by many Dissenters, who united with Churchmen in bearing testimony to the services of the Rector. But with a tolerant and conciliatory spirit towards those who differed from him, he could unite, when necessary, a bold and uncompromising assertion of his own principles. In the third year of his incumbency he published a course of Lectures on the Gospel of St. John, with the avowed object of demonstrating from that evangelist the Divinity of Christ, in opposition to the Unitarians, then a more influential body than they are at present; and these lectures were immediately suggested by the popularity of Mr. W. J. Fox, now the representative of Oldham in the House of Commons, but then preacher at the Unitarian Chapel in Eldon Street, Finsbury. At an earlier date (1820), his Sermon "on Predestination, for the use of Country Congregations," is directed against the Calvinistic doctrines of reprobation and election, and insists upon the axiom, unpalatable to so many minds, that "where the Gospel is plain and precise, and the Epistles obscure and perplexing, the Epistles are to be interpreted according to the Gospels, not the Gospels according to the Epistles." His liberality, therefore, was the more valuable because it did not spring from a latitudinarian spirit, embracing indiscriminately heterogeneous opinions, but approached more nearly to the Apostolic ideal of "speaking the truth in love." His anti-Calvinistic tendencies had been shown still earlier than this. Speaking of a visitation sermon which he was to preach while at Dunton, he writes to his friend Mr. Hasted—"I don't think Socinianism has any footing hereabouts; and to attack Calvinism would be fighting with the Bishop's [Tomline] own sword; but I mean to give it a rap or two in the course of the sermon." And he appears to have written on the same subject to Dr. Maltby, whose reply has been preserved:—

".... You are most perfectly right in your judgment upon the effects of Calvinism, and indeed they may be applied to almost every species of religious enthusiasm; but particularly when the high merit of Faith, and the alluring doctrine of Election, are so praised and preached.

It was this, among other mischievous consequences of the prevailing enthusiasm, that made me take the side I did about the Bible Society,[1] which was certainly set on foot by the sects, although encouraged now by persons of a very different and more meritorious description. As you grow older and more conversant with the habits of the lower classes, I think you will find that they turn from the plain, practical parts of Scripture to dwell on mystical and doctrinal, and that the growth of Calvinism and of Methodism arises from the poring over the Epistles in the received version, as one of its causes. . . . ."

[1] Founded 1805.

Yet he was so far from failing to appreciate the merits of the so-called Evangelical party, that it was he who proposed Charles Simeon as a member of the Society for Promoting Christian Knowledge. Many letters, couched in very friendly terms, passed at different times between the Bishop and Mr. Simeon; who even presented to the episcopal library at Fulham his voluminous works, of which (in allusion to the "Skeleton Sermons") Bishop Mansel had maliciously asked "whether these dry bones could live?"

Among other proofs of the success of his ministry, that of large and attentive audiences in his church was not wanting. A volume of Sermons, selected from those which he preached while at Bishopsgate, has been published, and furnishes a fair specimen of his abilities as a preacher. The style of his sermons remained much the same throughout his life, though they gained something in what may be called affectionateness as he grew older. Perspicuity of argument, simplicity and correctness of language, and a happy application of Scripture, are the principal characteristics of his pulpit style. He sought to win attention by plainness, earnestness, and simplicity, rather than by elaborateness of illustration and flights of rhetoric; and even where he did not rise to eloquence, he never degenerated into platitude. Thus, with less natural talent for preaching perhaps than some of his contemporaries, yet the genuine worth of his sermons, and his habit of doing to the best of his power anything which he had to do, made him one of the best preachers of the day. The effect of his sermons was heightened by an impressive delivery, a clear and musical voice, and, while at Bishopsgate, by a pleasing though youthful countenance, of which a friend once remarked, 'She had never seen so *infantine* a face for a D.D." One who was his constant hearer at this time says of him, "No one could hear a sermon of his without feeling the depths of his heart stirred up by the enforcement of Christian truth, with an eloquence as chaste as it was practical."

The sermon, in the volume above mentioned, on St. Luke, xiii. 4—"Or those eighteen, on whom the tower in Siloam fell"—was occasioned by the fall of the Brunswick Theatre, by which many persons were killed; and was written to point out the true Christian interpretation of such disasters, in opposition to those who had not scrupled to assert, in handbills circulated through London, that the accident was a Divine judgment upon the particular sufferers. He had only seen these handbills on the day before that on which the sermon was preached, and had intended till then to preach on a different subject; but, on his return home, he happened to find that the passage from St. Luke occurred in the Sunday lesson; and this coincidence struck him so much, that he sat down, and, contrary to his custom, wrote off the sermon late on the Saturday evening. This sermon attracted considerable attention at the time, and is said to have been reproduced by a country clergyman many years afterwards, and applied to the visitation of the cholera. The plagiarism was detected by a friend of the Bishop's.

In the latter part of his incumbency at Bishopsgate, after he became a Bishop, his week-day lectures in Lent, on the Acts of the Apostles, were very largely attended. Bishop Daniel Wilson records in his diary, March, 1827, his going to hear one of them:—"I went at eleven o'clock this morning to hear the Bishop of Chester. It was a most excellent and spiritual sermon, on the Martyrdom of St. Stephen, tender and energetic;" and the next day, "There is a most curious list in to-day's paper of those present at the Bishop of Chester's sermon. It is strange that I did not see one of the many persons so named."[1] The sermon which Bishop Wilson heard was one of a course; and it was Bishop Blomfield's custom at Bishopsgate annually to preach one or more such courses—on the Liturgy, Evidences of Christianity, Prophecies, Divinity of Christ, or the Acts of the Apostles. When he was made Bishop, it was not the custom for bishops to preach at ordinations or the consecration of churches; but he began to do so at once. During his residence in London, while Bishop of Chester, he generally preached at least one charity sermon every Sunday. He never, except on an occasion which has been already mentioned, preached *ex tempore*, or from notes; although his readiness as a public speaker might have encouraged him to the attempt. Sermons of any importance were always taken in hand early, and finished some days before they were wanted.

He was fond of telling anecdotes of other preachers. He once said that he wished he had heard a perfectly good preacher; he never had: then, correcting himself, he excepted Rowland Hill. When a young man he once went with Dr. Maltby to hear this famous preacher at Leamington, and was much impressed by the sermon, which lasted an hour and a quarter, and was clear and earnest, without exaggeration or rhodomontade. The

[1] Bateman's Life of Bishop Wilson, vol. i. p. 256.

preacher, however, attempted two pieces of Greek criticism, which were both wrong; and at this Blomfield and Maltby winked at each other. Among Cambridge preachers, in his undergraduate days, he remembered particularly the clear style, dignified manner, and melodious voice of Dr. Moore, then Vicar of St. Pancras. Of Dean Andrewes, Rector of St. James's, Westminster, the Bishop's friend, Lady Spencer, gave him this account:—"He was generally liked as a preacher. He had the merit of not preaching his own sermons; he used to preach Paley, and seldom let two years pass without preaching the same sermons over again. It was his manner which took; of which he was himself so much aware, that when asked to publish his sermons (those, it must be supposed, which were not Paley's) he declined, saying, that he could not publish his manner with them. Yet his manner would not have been tolerated in later days; he used to preach with his spectacles on and his head down, and never raised his head from his book till he came to some marked passage, when he would raise his head, take off his spectacles, and looking round at his congregation, would repeat the passage with great emphasis." An instance, perhaps unique, of the rhetorical use of spectacles.

In Bishop Blomfield's boyhood, there was a clergyman at Bury of whom he used to relate, that when on one occasion Lord Bristol had given a number of scarlet cloaks to some poor old women, who all appeared in church on the following Sunday resplendent in their new array, the preacher pointed to them with a wave of his hand, and applied the words of the text, that "even Solomon in all his glory was not arrayed like one of these." On another occasion, when a dole of potatoes was being distributed, by the local authorities, to the poor, the same preacher chose for his text Exodus xvi. 15, "And when the children of Israel saw it, they said one to another, It is manna;" and warned his hearers, by the example of the Israelites, to beware of taking more than their share. A corpulent frame and pompous manner, and a habit of rolling from side to side in the pulpit, added to the effect of the oratory in this case.

Some other works in which Bishop Blomfield engaged, while Rector of Bishopsgate, still remain to be noticed. He was one of the earliest and most zealous promoters of infant schools, which had then only recently begun to be established. The school of this kind which he established in his own parish, was considered a model; and a Catechism for Infants which he drew up, and which was afterwards placed on the list of the Christian Knowledge Society, had for some time a large circulation, and was even translated into French.

Another scheme which engaged his attention at this time is thus described in his diary:—

"1821. *April* 10.—Met the Bishop of London (Howley), who proposed to me that I should undertake the editing of the Old Testament, part of the new Family Bible, for the use of the lower classes, Dr. Lloyd[1] taking the New (which I should have preferred). To this I assented; as I consider that the circumstance of my holding a lucrative benefice in the Church imposes upon me additional obligations to submit to any labour which may promote the cause of religion. I trust that God will enable me to do good in my vocation."

[1] Afterwards Bishop of Oxford.

This work, however, he was never enabled to carry out; and the undertaking, somewhat modified from the designs of its first promoters, was eventually committed by Archbishop Howley, after his translation to the primacy, to his two chaplains, Mr. D'Oyly and Mr. Mant.

He began also at this time to take an active share in the proceedings of the Societies for Promoting Christian Knowledge and for the Propagation of the Gospel, 'in both of which," he writes to Dr. Monk, "I am attempting to introduce considerable changes;" and also in those of the National Society, still almost in its infancy. He was thus brought into more immediate contact with the knot of zealous Churchmen who at that time were taking the leading part in the proceedings of these societies; and this connexion may, perhaps, have insensibly modified his views on some questions (especially on Roman Catholic Emancipation, and on the amount of exclusiveness desirable in Church of England schools), and may have made him more of a High Churchman than he was originally inclined to be. At all events it was with these men that he mainly acted for many years; although on some points, of expediency rather than of principle, he often differed widely from them. His was a mind which sought for the sphere of its activity, not in any peculiar and eccentric orbit, but rather in paths already beaten, and in which he would find fellow-travellers; and there was almost no opinion, on any speculative point, which he would not be ready to modify or hold in suspension, rather than lack that co-operation which was essential to his ideas of usefulness.

These occupations were momentarily interrupted, in 1822, by the loss of his eldest son by his second wife. Twice he had given his own name, Charles James, to a son; and twice death seemed to forbid its perpetuation in his family. He writes to Dr. Monk (who had recently been promoted to the Deanery of Peterborough):—

"CHESTERFORD, *August* 14, 1822.

"MY DEAR FRIEND,—You will, I am sure, sympathize with me under the additional calamity with which I have been visited in the loss of my only remaining little boy, who died last Friday, after a few days' illness, of the same fatal malady which has already deprived me of four of my children, water in the head. For my own part, I cannot but perceive that this is the particular kind of trial with which God is pleased to visit me, amid much prosperity. This loss revives the recollection of others, and especially of the last."

In the same year Dr. Blomfield received from his diocesan, Bishop Howley, a fresh mark of confidence, in the appointment to the Archdeaconry of Colchester, once held by the learned and pious Beveridge, and now vacant by the death of Archdeacon Jefferson. He held this office only a little more than two years; but he found time, in 1823, to make a general visitation of his archdeaconry, and to deliver a Charge to the Clergy. Ecclesiastical law was a subject to which he had for some time paid more attention than is always given to it even by the dignified clergy. Many years later he said, "When I was a young man, I used to fancy myself a pretty good ecclesiastical lawyer." When appointed Archdeacon, he made it his business to study the origin and the nature of that office, of which in his Charge he gives a historical sketch. "I have always been of opinion," he says, "that whatever post may be assigned to an individual, whether by the Church or the State, his only safe rule of proceeding is, to obtain a correct knowledge of the duties which the law has assigned to his province; and to perform them as nearly according to the letter as the circumstances of the case will permit." There are not wanting in this Charge indications of the same spirit which was noticed in his Sermon on the Ritual of the Church: and the clergy of Essex must have listened with mixed feelings to an Archdeacon who declared his intention of strictly enforcing the duties of non-resident incumbents in repairing their glebe-houses, and who laid particular stress upon that part of the Archidiaconal office which consists in "detecting unto the Bishop" all ecclesiastical irregularities.

The Bishop of Bristol, Dr. Kaye, thus congratulates him on his promotion :—

"CAMBRIDGE, *January* 16, 1822.

"DEAR MR. ARCHDEACON,—For by that title Monk informs me that you are now to be addressed—when I read the paragraph announcing Jefferson's death, I conjectured that you would be his successor, and I rejoice most sincerely, not only for your own sake, but also for that of the Church, that my conjecture has proved true. Dr. Copleston, I fear, would quarrel with me for this use of the word."

In allusion to Dr. Blomfield's article in the Quarterly Review, on 'Copleston on Predestination,' and Whately's edition of 'King on Predestination,' he adds—

"I need scarcely say that I read your review with great pleasure, particularly the concluding part. It must be productive of the most beneficial effects, by softening the asperities of the disputants on both sides, and showing them the peculiar propriety of speaking temperately and diffidently on subjects, on which men of the acutest understandings have been guilty of false reasoning."

The next letter, to his sister, gives an account of his first visitation to the Churchwardens of his Archdeaconry:

"CHESTERFORD, *April* 26, 1822.

". . . . I thought you would like to have a short account of my first Visitation, which has been only to the churchwardens. I have everywhere been received with great respect; and of the churchwardens of 154 parishes not one was absent, except in two cases of illness. On Monday I went to Chelmsford, where I dined at Colonel Vachell's, and slept at Mr. Parkes's, the registrar. The next day we went to Kelvedon, where I began my Visitation, and dined and slept at Mr. Dalton's, who had a party of the clergy to meet me. On Wednesday we proceeded to Colchester, where the bells were rung in honour of the new Archdeacon; and immediately upon my arrival I was waited upon by all the clergy of the town and neighbourhood. Yesterday I came to Chesterford, and this morning visited Saffron Walden. Upon the whole, I have been much pleased with the respectful manner in which I was received, and the readiness which was manifested to attend to my wishes in the only cases in which I was called upon to interfere officially."

On the subject of the Archidiaconal office a good story is told of Bishop Blomfield. Lord Althorp, when Chancellor of the Exchequer, having to propose to the House of Commons a vote of £400 a year for the salary of the Archdeacon of Bengal, was puzzled by a question from Mr. Hume, "What are the duties of an Archdeacon?" So he sent one of the subordinate occupants of the Treasury Bench to the other house, to obtain an answer to the question from one of the Bishops. The messenger met first with Archbishop Vernon Harcourt, who described an Archdeacon as "*aide-de-camp* to the Bishop;" and then with Bishop Copleston, of Llandaff, who said, "the Archdeacon is *oculus Episcopi.*" Lord Althorp, however, declared that neither of these explanations would satisfy the house. "Go," said he, "and ask the Bishop of London; he is a straight-forward man, and will give you a plain answer." To the Bishop of London accordingly the messenger went, and repeated the question, "What is an Archdeacon?" "An Archdeacon?" replied the Bishop in his quick way, "an Archdeacon is an ecclesiastical officer, who performs archidiaconal functions;" and with this reply Lord Althorp and the house were perfectly satisfied.

It ought to be added, however, that when this story was repeated to the Bishop himself, he said that he had no recollection of having made any such answer; but that if he had, it must have been suggested to him by a saying of old John White, a dentist, whom he had known in early days, who used to recommend the use of lavender-water to his patients, and when pressed for a reason for his recommendation, replied, "On account of its *lavendric* properties."

In 1823, Archdeacon Blomfield was the anonymous author of a pamphlet,[1] occasioned by the attacks to which the Church of England was at this time exposed on every side, "from the sophistry and misrepresentations of the Edinburgh Reviewers, down to the shameless and wilful falsehoods of the Morning Chronicle, and the ribaldry of Benbow and Carlile." It has already been mentioned that he had ceased writing for the Edinburgh Review about ten years before, and since that time the tone of this periodical towards the church had been one of unceasing bitterness. The pamphlet is a spirited remonstrance to Mr. Brougham, as one of the most powerful contributors to the Review, to use his influence in checking the rancour and unfairness of his coadjutors; and it contains incidentally a defence of the dignitaries of the church (who had recently been more than usually unpopular, owing to an ill-advised prosecution for libel against the clergy of Durham), and particularly of Bishop Howley, whom the Edinburgh Review had described as "the enemy upon principle of whatever informs and enlightens the poor." As Bishop Blomfield did not again appear in the character of an anonymous pamphleteer, the following paragraphs may be interesting, as a specimen of his style in this kind of composition.

"The reviewer asks, 'Who can pretend to doubt that religious instruction might be *afforded far cheaper* to the people than in either England or Ireland?' He seems to consider that religious instruction is a sort of staple commodity, of invariable goodness; and that

[1] 'A Remonstrance addressed to H. Brougham, Esq., by one of the "Working Clergy."' London: 1823.

by a judicious application of the principles of political economy, a bargain may be made with the ministers of religion, to *do* the people in theology at so much a head. But you, sir, know perfectly well, that if the instructor be meanly paid, the instruction will fall proportionably in goodness, although the subject matter of instruction may remain the same. I can with ease find a tailor who 'can afford me my clothes far cheaper' than I am accustomed to get them; but if my coat hangs loosely upon me, and the seams give way, and the nap wears off in a week or two, I shall not gain by the exchange. I have seen, not long since, an advertisement in one of the papers, of a classical tutor, professing to teach the Greek language 'according to the method of the late Professor Porson,' in six lessons, for one guinea. This is selling Greek at a much cheaper rate than that at which the public schools and universities can afford it; and upon the reviewer's principles, I suppose we should soon have a 'London Commercial Divinity Company,' who would favour the public with religious instruction unadulterated, at the lowest wholesale price."

".... But, perhaps, the secret of this inveterate rancour against the Establishment may be that which is well expressed in the Greek proverb—

Δρυὸς πεσούσης, πᾶς ἀνὴρ ξυλεύεται.

'When an oak falls, every man scuffles for a faggot.'

Some great proprietor of coal-mines may, perhaps, anticipate with conscious delight the auspicious day—

'When Troy shall fall,
And one prodigious ruin bury all;'

when of the slices, which shall be carved out of the patrimony of the See of Durham, no inconsiderable share shall be added to his own territories; while you, perhaps, may carry to your tent something ὀλίγον τε φίλον τε, an estate or two from some other northern diocese. But you, sir, well know, even if *he* has not the wit to perceive it, that the spirit of equalization will make but one step from the palace to the hall; and when Ucalegon shall be on fire at Durham, it must be a strong party wall which will protect *his* manors and his mines from conflagration. 'Haslerigg,' says Mr. Disraeli, 'whom Clarendon terms *an absurd bold man*, would have no bishops; but this was not from any want of reverence for Church lands, for he heaped for himself such wealth, as to have been nick-named "the Bishop of Durham."' Such are ever the disinterested statesmen who exclaim against the Church, 'Babylon shall be overthrown,' and who look to accomplish in their own persons the remainder of the prophecy, which declares that 'her palaces shall be inhabited only by owls and satyrs.'

"Spencer describes a certain *Kirkrapine*—

> 'Who was to weet a stout and sturdy thief,
> Wont to rub Churches of their ornaments,
> And poor men's boxes of their due relief,
> Which given was to them with good intents;
> The holy Saints of their rich vestiments
> He did disrobe, while all men careless slept.'

This worthy person was slain by *Una's* lion, who in turn was killed by the Paynim knight *Sans Loy*. I need not open the allegory, nor illustrate it by the transactions of the very next century after it was written; but let me ask of you, sir, in the words of your admired Cicero, *In vastitate omnium* TUAS *possessiones sacrosanctas futuras putas?*"

But the work of Bishop Blomfield, while Rector of Bishopsgate, by which he will be best remembered, is the publication, in 1824, of his "Manual of Family

Prayers," preceded by a sermon on the same subject. The general acceptance which this Manual has met with is the best proof that it has been found free from the faults which often disfigure books of this kind—diffuseness, familiarity, bombastic and exaggerated language, or the prominence of eccentric doctrines; and that it expresses with sufficient reverence and fulness the devotional sentiments which a Churchman, attached to his Prayer-book, would desire to embody in the worship of his household. The episcopal authorship of the book (for its appearance was rapidly followed by the promotion of Dr. Blomfield to the Bench) removed the dislike of many well-disposed persons, who before had looked upon the use of family prayers as somewhat "methodistical;" and the work obtained an immense circulation, in America as well as in England. A clergyman in Kent, having preached the Bishop's Sermon on Family Worship to his congregation, ended by telling them whose it was, and informing them that they might obtain copies of the Manual of Prayers in the vestry. The result was that about three hundred copies were taken on that day, and about four hundred more were sold in the parish in a few weeks.

It should not be forgotten that, although this Manual should cease to be used, it will not have been without its effects in reminding the upper and middle classes of the country of a duty too much neglected; and that too at a time when the Church did not offer nearly so many opportunities of *public* worship as she affords at present. It is said that the publication of the book elicited the fact, that there were many among the Bishop's parishioners at Bishopsgate, of the well-to-do class, who not only had never used family prayers, but who had never even heard of such a thing.

When it is remembered that, in addition to the occupations already mentioned, Dr. Blomfield continued, till 1824, to bring out his editions of Æschylus, and to contribute articles to the Quarterly Review, the British Critic, and the Museum Criticum (which had been suspended in 1816, chiefly in consequence of the death of Edward Blomfield, but was recommenced in 1821 or 1822); some idea may be formed of the "marvellous activity" which we have already seen attributed to him.

He writes to Dean Monk, March 22, 1823:—

"I have had on my hands six charity sermons, a course of Lent lectures, an anti-Catholic petition, the management of the tithe question against the citizens of London, a weekly committee at Bartlett's Buildings[1] in consequence of Dr. Gaskin's resignation, two articles in the British Critic, &c. &c., all of which I have got through in the last four or five weeks, and am now ready for the Museum Criticum, notwithstanding that I have still to write a 'Spital sermon, a sermon for the Magdalene, three more charity sermons, and my visitation charge, all within the next month."

And, again, about a year later—

"I am quite overpowered not only by parochial business, but by matters relating to my Archdeaconry, to the West India bishoprics, affairs at Bartlett's Buildings and the Society for the Propagation of the Gospel, in both of which I am attempting to introduce considerable changes. The Choephori is just finished. . . .

[1] Then the head-quarters of the Society for Promoting Christian Knowledge.

We are all highly delighted with Southey's Book of the Church, which will do a great deal of good, and is really a most interesting work."

It was amid these multifarious occupations that he perfected those business habits, and that promptitude of action, which he afterwards displayed so remarkably in administering the diocese of London. He acquired the power of holding in his hands a great number of separate threads without confusion or entanglement; so that he could turn the whole force of his mind at a moment's notice on any subject upon which he was engaged.

The next letter shows him in a moment of relaxation from these engrossing occupations. It is addressed to his wife, from the house of Lord Spencer:—

"ALTHORP, *Aug.* 23, 1823.

". . . . I propose going to see Mr. Sikes [the Rev. Thomas Sikes, brother-in-law to Joshua Watson,] on Monday or Tuesday. He is not in very good odour here on account of his very High Church notions. He is called in this neighbourhood *the Pope.* I rather expect to find the Norrises there . . . . Lord Spencer was introduced the other day to Mrs. ——, who accompanied the Bishop on his visitation. He found her sitting in a room at the George Inn at Northampton, clad in all the colours of the rainbow, and covered with diamonds. Never having seen her before, the sight of such a mass of splendour quite overpowered him, and he was struck 'all of a heap.' The Bishop has been breaking out into sallies of violence against his clergy during the visitation in a most extraordinary manner."

CHAPTER IV.

VACANCIES IN THE EPISCOPAL BENCH—DR. BLOMFIELD IS OFFERED THE SEE OF CHESTER—ACCEPTS THE OFFER—CONGRATULATIONS ON HIS PREFERMENT—THE EPISCOPAL WIG—LABOURS OF THE NEW BISHOP—DIFFICULTIES IN THE DIOCESE—CHARACTER OF THE CHESHIRE CLERGY—MR. BAYLEY'S ACCOUNT OF THE BISHOP—HIS OPINIONS ON DISPUTED POINTS—LETTERS—CHURCH DISCIPLINE—THE ATHANASIAN CREED—LETTERS ON SICKNESS.

THE promotion of Dr. Blomfield to the highest order of the ministry followed hard upon his acceptance of the office of Archdeacon. It seems to have been a favourite amusement with Churchmen about 1823-4, to hear or to tell a report that Bishop Bathurst of Norwich was dead; which, although not improbable, as he was already in his eightieth year, was so far from being true that he lived till 1837. Dr. Monk appears to have heard the rumour, and to have believed it, for Dr. Blomfield writes thus to him:—

"CHESTERFORD, *July* 23, [1823.]

" .... Your elevation of me to the Bench is somewhat premature, for two reasons—first, because it is not reasonable to expect that persons high in office will think of me as you think; and, in the second place, because there is no vacancy—the Bishop of Norwich being alive and well. When the see of Norwich shall be really vacant, it will be an awful charge for any man to undertake. I have been staying a fortnight at Bury, where I have heard enough of the state of ecclesiastical matters in that diocese, to convince me that a strong pair of shoulders, and a vigorous arm to wield the besom of purification, will be required in the new bishop."

Bishop Stanley could have told that the condition to which fourteen more years of the inert rule of Bishop Bathurst reduced the diocese of Norwich, fully justified the forebodings here expressed.

In the following letter to Dr. Monk, written early in 1824, when the death of the Earl of Cornwallis had left vacant the see of Lichfield, the mitre seems to be hourly impending:—

"MY DEAR DEAN,—Bethell goes to Gloucester, *vice* Ryder translated to Lichfield, to evangelize the collieries and potteries..... Bethell's is certainly a good appointment. I am glad that *I* was not sent to Gloucester on all accounts.

".... I have now a most distressing piece of intelligence to communicate—poor Rennell is so ill that no hopes are entertained of his recovery. His first attack, which seems to have been a bilious fever, reduced him to death's door. Several relapses from a seeming state of recovery during the last five weeks have deprived him of all strength, and now what his physicians apprehended has taken place, viz., the fixing of the irritation on the lungs. The prospect of his loss is really so afflicting that I know not how to contemplate it. The circumstance of his recent marriage renders it doubly distressing."

Rennell, the son of the Dean of Winchester, was a contemporary of Blomfield at Cambridge, but some two years his junior. After a brilliant career at the University, he was presented by Bishop Howley to the Vicarage of Kensington. He was for some time editor of the British Critic, and was the author of several theological publications. "His lively powers of conversation and brilliancy of remarks, ready on all subjects, made his society acceptable in many circles."[1]

In May, 1824, Bishop Beadon, of Bath and Wells, died. His place was filled by Bishop Law, translated from Chester; and Dr. Blomfield received a letter from Lord Liverpool, offering him the latter see. There were not wanting inducements to him to say *Nolo Episcopari* on the present occasion, and to wait for the next chance. The Bishopric of Chester was one of the most laborious, and probably, without exception, the worst paid among the dignities of the Church (its income being about £1400 a-year). Chester was then distant a long two days' journey from London, the episcopal residence was mean, the local associations were all strange to him. Moreover, he was still young; and there seemed no reason to doubt the stability of the existing Government, by which he had already been favourably viewed. Lady Spencer appears to have considered it probable that he would think fit to decline the offer:—

"My dear Doctor," she writes, "I hope I need not tell you that I trust I shall soon have to shake you by the hand as Bishop of Chester. Don't be so indiscreet as to refuse it because it is a sadly poor one—remember it is the step which you must tread on to a richer one. All the old twaddles have dropped—young ones don't depart so readily; and I am myself so old that I am

[1] Churton's Life of Joshua Watson, vol. i. p. 236.

impatient to see you seated on that bench, where you will be so admirably placed, and so usefully disposed of. If the Metropolitan is translated, which his looks portend, the Bishop of London replaces him; and who so likely as yourself, with all your London knowledge and experience, to be the Bishop of this diocese, if you *are* on the bench—but then you must be, or my plan can't take place. Seriously, Lord Spencer and I are all on tiptoe to hear of your acceptance; for, though it may be present ruin, yet it will be *soon* future affluence. And why should you not keep your St. Botolph? Indeed, pray, pray give me a line, and pray think, reflect, and ponder with all your powers, before you refuse; for, indeed, I do think it a very different thing to refuse now than it would have been to have refused some time ago. I am so hurried and so bothered with all sorts of perplexities, that I am sure I must have written nonsense, and I cannot now read it over to be sure I have done so. Excuse me, my excellent friend, and take the intention of this note in good part, although it may be so inadequately expressed.

Ever affectionately yours,

LAV. SPENCER."

Being allowed, however, to retain with his bishopric, *in commendam*, the living of Bishopsgate, as Lady Spencer had suggested, the main difficulty was removed; and the prospect of a laborious office in a remote province was to his mind only an additional reason for gladly accepting the position. He was consecrated June 20, 1824, by Archbishop Vernon Harcourt and the Bishops of London and Exeter, in Whitehall Chapel; the consecration sermon being preached by the Rev. John

Lonsdale, the present Bishop of Lichfield, then domestic chaplain to the Archbishop of Canterbury, and at all times the warm friend and admirer of Bishop Blomfield. In the autumn of the same year, the new Bishop began his residence in the gloomy palace of his see, under the shadow of the crumbling walls of the cathedral.

When the news of his promotion reached his native place, one of the boys of the Grammar-school produced the following epigram :—

> "Through Chester-ford to Bishops-gate
> Did Blomfield safely wade ;
> Then leaving ford and gate behind,
> He's Chester's Bishop made."

It is hardly too much to say that the elevation of Dr. Blomfield to the Bench was received with universal acclamation. Those who knew him well could predict with confidence the advantages which would accrue to the Church from such an episcopate; and those who knew him only by reputation, even the organs of the public press, admitted that in this appointment the Premier had been influenced by no unworthy considerations, whether of family or politics, but had been guided solely by the just claims of sound learning, conspicuous talents, unblemished character, and unusual pastoral activity.

The following letters will show the new Bishop's own feelings, and those of his friends, on his preferment :—

Dr. Parr to Archdeacon Blomfield.

"HATTON, *May* 3, 1824.

"DEAR, LEARNED, AND TRULY RESPECTABLE DOCTOR BLOMFIELD,—Though on many questions of Church and

State you and I may differ widely, yet I honour you as a great scholar and a well-informed theologian. Pardon me then for expressing my sincere and ardent hope that you may be raised to the mitre on the present vacancy. Not one of your friends will feel greater joy on your receiving the preferment which you eminently and pre-eminently deserve. I was at Margate [?] last year, when the Bishop of Norwich was said to be no more. Some learned friends agreed with me in pointing out Dr. Blomfield as the new Bishop, and we filled and emptied a bumper to his health. I will fill and empty *two* bumpers now, if my anticipation be realized.

With great and unfeigned respect, I am, dear Sir,

Your friend and obedient humble servant,

S. PARR."

From a former Pupil.

"*May* 7, 1824.

"....How should I not be pleased in every step you make, my best and most respected friend, towards greater dignity, and what attracts you more, towards greater usefulness? I have long been earnestly wishing for this event, and now I thank God that it is coming to pass not only for your sake, but for the Church, to which I pray most heartily that you may become both an ornament and a support for many years to come. I should like much to observe and be made acquainted with your feelings on occasion of rising to this new situation. High and arduous indeed are its duties, and great its responsibility; but the more difficult they are, the greater is the joy and reward of their due performance. May God direct and assist you through them all! and improve and strengthen you in all those sentiments and principles which I have so often listened to with pleasure, and I humbly hope not without benefit and improvement. Pray excuse me if I am too forward in my expressions; but I should not be doing justice to my own feelings if, on such an occasion as this, I did not indulge them...."

To his Wife.

"LONDON, *May* 10 [1824].

"....You would be pleased to hear the universal expression of joy, both in and out of the parish, at my advancement.....I am going to call on the new Bishop of Chichester [Dr. Carr] to see whether he will try and persuade his Majesty to dispense with our *wigs.* .... The Bishop of Ely[1] tells me that at his last visitation in the diocese of Chester, he confirmed 8,000 children at Manchester in one day—between eight in the morning and half-past eight in the evening.

....I preached yesterday at St. George's, Hanover Square. Present, Duke and Duchess of Gloucester, Princess Sophia, Duke of Grafton, Marquis Camden, Archbishop of York, Bishops of Norwich and Ely, and an immense congregation. Collection £115....."

The request to George IV. to permit the discontinuance of the episcopal wig, if preferred, was not acceded to; it was not till the reign of William IV. that the wig was dispensed with. On this subject the following anecdote has been communicated by Sir George Sinclair:—Soon after the accession of King William, Sir George happened to be at Fulham Palace

[1] Dr. Sparke, Bishop of Chester, 1810–12.

just before paying a visit to his Majesty at Brighton. He asked the Bishop whether he could deliver any message from him to the King. The weather was extremely hot, and the Bishop jocularly replied, "You may present my duty to his Majesty, and say that at this tropical season I find my episcopal wig a serious encumbrance, and that I hope he will not consider me guilty of a breach of Court etiquette, if I am induced to lay it aside." Sir George repeated this message for the amusement of the King, who, however, took it up seriously, and replied, "Tell the Bishop that he is not to wear a wig on my account; I dislike it as much as he does, and shall be glad to see the whole Bench wear their own hair." The result was that Bishop Blomfield took the hint; other bishops followed his example, and the episcopal wig was gradually discontinued.

A little before this, it would seem from the following letter of Mr. Lyttelton to Bishop Blomfield, that a rebellion against the tyranny of the wigs had been attempted by Bishop Bagot:—

"BLITHFIELD, *Aug.* 3, 1829.

"MY DEAR BISHOP,—A wig-question, in which your Lordship is concerned, and your name confidently appealed to, has fallen under my notice during my stay here with my friend, the newly-appointed, and yet wigless, Bishop of Oxford: and before I leave his house, I think I cannot do better than at once to refer the matter to you, and to beg you to acquaint me, or him (when you meet him, which I understand you will in a few weeks) with your opinion, which will be final, on the subject in debate. The enclosed document will at once show your Lordship the important nature of this capital controversy; and I will say no more upon it, than that as I wish heartily well to the heads of the Church, I sincerely hope it may be settled to their advantage and comfort."

Bishop Blomfield set himself to work in his new position with all his characteristic energy. The diocese of Chester then included not only the teeming population, manufacturing or agricultural, of Lancashire and Cheshire, but the scattered and primitive Westmoreland "statesmen," who tended their mountain-sheep along the slopes of Helvellyn and Loughrigg, or cultivated the small farms which nestle in the valleys of Grasmere and Langdale. To the different evils with which the Church has to contend in dealing with classes of people so distinct as these, must be added other discouraging circumstances, in reviewing the field which Bishop Blomfield saw before him when he first came to Chester. Most of these he enumerates in his first Episcopal Charge, delivered in the autumn of 1825; stating at the same time that one or two of them are not found to so great an extent in Chester as in some other dioceses. They are—the poverty of benefices, and the consequent non-residence of incumbents, neglect of churches and glebe-houses, and destitution of clerical families; the indifferent character and inadequate salaries of curates; infrequency in the celebration, and irregularity in the performance, of the sacred offices of the Church; the incapacity and negligence of churchwardens; the intrusive zeal of some of the more active clergy, and the prevalence of unclerical dress, pursuits, and amusements among others; the use of sham titles, and untrue or careless testimonials to candidates for orders; the short stay of bishops in the see, owing to its inadequate endowment; and lastly, as the natural consequence of all the rest, the general obloquy now heaped upon the Church, which was the more stinging because it was in part deserved, and which made every faithful one among her sons feel as though with one hand he must hold the sword, while with the other he repaired the breaches of the sanctuary. The prospect, indeed, was not an encouraging one, to any one whose heart was in his work, and Bishop Blomfield's letters show that he felt this; but whatever could be done, with the help of God, by his own industry and devotion, he determined should be done.

He writes in his diary on New Year's Day, 1826:—

"I thank God that it has pleased Him to carry me through the past year without any calamity or great disappointment; and I humbly hope that I have been, by the help of His grace, useful in the ministry of His word, and the government of His Church. But how inconsiderable and insufficient is all that I have done or can do, in comparison with that which He has a right to look for from one whom He hath redeemed with the blood of His Son. Lord! enable me, I pray Thee, to serve Thee with greater diligence, and a more perfect singleness of heart!"

It was no impossible ideal that he set before himself in his endeavours to give efficiency to the Church in the diocese of Chester. If the clergy could be persuaded or compelled to reside on their livings, or, if non-resident with a tolerable reason, to provide respectable substitutes, and keep their glebe-houses in habitable repair; if the crying wants of the large towns could be supplied by additional churches and clergymen; if the tone of clerical society could be raised a few degrees; if a stimulus could be given, through the Church Societies or by other means, to the education of the poor and the diffusion of religious knowledge; if this could be done, he would not indeed be contented, but would feel that something substantial had been effected. But even in accomplishing this much, he had many difficulties to contend with. He writes to Dean Monk:—

"PALACE, CHESTER, *Oct.* 25, 1824.

"....I have been busier for the last three months than ever I was before for any trimestral portion of my life; nor am I likely to be otherwise for some time to come. My first ordination is over—it was an anxious time for me: the *tone* and *character* of examinations must be raised here. I was forced to reject two out of thirty candidates. There are many sad evils in this diocese, which I have set myself in good earnest to redress, and in time I hope that much may be effected. Within the last ten days I have travelled 200 miles, and confirmed nearly 8,000 children, and have three more expeditions to make on this side Christmas, soon after which I shall probably *retire* to Bishopsgate..... You have probably seen in the papers some account, though an incorrect one, of my proceedings here in the way of re-invigorating our Diocesan Committee.[1] We have already raised £200, and are going on admirably. All the noblemen in the county have become vice-presidents, myself being president.

[1] Of the National Society.

And to Mr. Joshua Watson:—

"CHESTER, *Oct.* 26, 1824.

". . . . I am wading through business with my seven-league boots on, but there is a long dreary tract of country before me. Discipline is sadly relaxed here. The things which want rectifying are almost numberless—and it may very well be said, with reference to the average period of a bishop's continuance at Chester, 'Ars longa, vita brevis.' However, I hope to be able to effect something. I have already set the elements in agitation; and, from a well-conducted process of fermentation, I hope to extract some *highly rectified spirit of orthodoxy*. An explosion or two in the course of the process must be looked for; accidents will befal the most cautious operators. . . . "

Again, writing from Manchester in the same month he says:—

"There is a sad want of spirit here in matters connected with religion, which I fear I shall not do much towards supplying. There is no *personal* energy or activity."

One of his first acts was to raise the character of examinations for holy orders. He made it a rule to require three months' notice of the intention of candidates to present themselves, and to insist upon a personal interview with them; the latter regulation having been suggested to him by his chaplain, Mr. Hale, the present Archdeacon of London, though the Bishop at first disliked giving the young men so much trouble. He also took care "to inquire particularly whether the title is a *bonâ fide* title; whether the specified salary is to be paid in full, or whether any deductions are to be made; not to ordain any person who has been in the navy, army, or trade," nor any one who has not a University degree, except the students of St. Bees' College; and to discourage, if not in all cases actually to refuse, applications from Irish candidates, who, under a less vigilant episcopate, are certain to inundate a diocese so conveniently situated as that of Chester. The biographer of Bishop Jebb records of him in the year 1825, "From Winwick he went to Chester, to pass some days with his friend Bishop Blomfield; where he had the satisfaction of witnessing a strictness in ordination, and finding views of clerical duty and responsibility, corresponding with his own."[1]

This strictness in the matter of ordination naturally created an unfavourable feeling against the new Bishop among the less deserving clergy of his diocese. Nor were there wanting other causes which extended and deepened this feeling. He was diligent in enforcing compliance with recent acts affecting clerical duties, which some of the clergy habitually set at nought. He expressed his disapproval of the employment of clergymen in secular occupations of an engrossing kind; and when we find that at this time one clergyman was post-master in a large town, another was engaged in an extensive agency, and a third was, or hoped to become, Mayor of Macclesfield, the necessity of strictness in this respect is apparent. He also strongly deprecated in his clergy the pursuit of field-sports, and especially of fox-hunting—an amusement which was then almost a religion in Cheshire. To a curate whom he had

[1] Forster's Life of Bishop Jebb, vol. i. p. 307.

refused to license without a promise to abstain from hunting, he wrote thus:—

"I have had far better opportunities than you of forming an accurate opinion of the effect produced upon the minds of the laity by the practice in question. Independently of the disapprobation with which it is spoken of by every gentleman whom I have ever heard mention the subject, the light in which it is viewed by every religious person in the lower ranks of life, stamps it as an inconsistency most injurious to the ministerial character and to the credit of our Church—the only Church in Christendom the ministers of which would think of defending such a practice."

In speaking or writing on the subject of clerical duties, the Bishop would sometimes convey his admonitions with a certain sharpness of manner, which concealed the real kindness of his heart; nor was he careful to make that difference which the Cheshire clergy expected, in his treatment of the mere curate, of narrow means and no position, and of the independent squire-parson of good family. When some one remarked that his portrait, painted soon after he became a Bishop, represented him with a decided frown, "Yes," he replied, "that portrait ought to have been dedicated, without permission, to the non-resident clergy of the diocese of Chester."

He used to tell a story of one clergyman, whom he had reproved for certain irregularities of conduct which had been brought to his notice by his parishioners, and who had replied, "Your Lordship, as a classical scholar, knows that lying goes by districts; the Cretans were liars, the Cappadocians were liars; and I can assure you that the inhabitants of —— are liars too." Intoxication was the most frequent charge against the clergy. One was so drunk while waiting for a funeral, that he fell into the grave; another was conveyed away from a visitation dinner in a helpless state by the Bishop's own servants. A third, when rebuked for drunkenness, replied, "But, my Lord, I never was drunk on duty." "On duty!" exclaimed the Bishop; "when is a clergyman not on duty?" "True," said the other, "I never thought of that."

Such a Bishop could hardly fail to have enemies; and enemies he had. By some of his clergy his motives were misrepresented, his acts severely criticised, his authority defied; he was stigmatized as overbearing, tyrannical, meddlesome, hasty, inconsiderate: a puritanical austerity and dislike even of innocent amusements, totally foreign to his real character, was attributed to him. His detractors, however, were after all few in number; the great majority respected his zeal even when they did not imitate it. Out of numerous testimonies to his merits as Bishop of Chester, the following letter may be selected, addressed by the Rev. H. V. Bayley, afterwards Archdeacon of Stow, to his friend Joshua Watson, and preserved in Archdeacon Churton's life of the latter.[1]

"*January* 5, 1825.

"You will, perhaps, be glad to hear something of this diocese, which is my native one; from our Bishop himself you will have received tidings of his marvellous activity and success. But at the same time reports of

[1] Vol. i. p. 249.

his ultra-discipline, which are very widely circulated, may have reached you. Having known and heard much of his proceedings at Liverpool, &c., and having witnessed them at this most important place, I can assure you that he has made an impression on the public mind and feeling, such as I never saw, or could have believed possible. With the utmost firmness, openness, and decision, he joins a manner of conciliation and a tone of persuasion quite irresistible. Every one sees that his whole heart is in his duty; that he does not seek popularity, and that his object simply is to do good. He has gained the Dissenters, not by compromise, but by boldly and openly avowing his decided attachment to the Church, and his full belief that in her services and communion the best rules and means of Christian conduct are to be found. At the same time he judges liberally of all men, and imputes no bad motives to the less orthodox opinions of any person or sect. Really, all sorts of people seem to contend who shall speak most highly of him. The great secret of his popularity is manliness; speaking with authority, and trusting to the character of his office, and to the truth of his arguments, he convinces and influences all who hear him. In company he is delightful. In short, I cannot picture to myself a more perfect image of a Christian bishop. The only fault I can find is, that he will soon sacrifice his constitution, if he persists in working so outrageously both with mind and body. In addressing his ordinees on the subject of amusements, he has deprecated fox-hunting, the Cheshire idolatry; and he is therefore represented by some of its votaries as proscribing all amusements, dancing, singing, cards, &c. The fact is, he has never, directly or indirectly, given any opinion on any one of these subjects; and if you happen to hear the thing mentioned, you may most unequivocally contradict it. His usefulness must not be crippled by such absurd reports; if he was in a private station they would be unworthy of notice."

Meanwhile the Bishop himself, *justus et propositi tenax*, was but little moved by the complaints of the few who resented his active rule. When his "Articles of Inquiry" were complained of, though almost entirely identical with those issued by his predecessor, he wrote to a friendly clergyman: "If the clergy are so ready to take offence, they must take it: I shall go on doing my duty." In his Primary Charge he says, "No personal considerations, no apprehension of that unpopularity which is sometimes the portion of those who faithfully and fearlessly put others in mind of their duty, will ever deter me from speaking to you, upon subjects relating to your sacred office, with the utmost plainness and candour; but always, I trust, with the plainness and candour of a friend." He proceeds to show how his sentiments on some questions of clerical duties and habits had been misrepresented.

In the autumn of the first year of his episcopate, and again in 1826, he visited the great manufacturing towns of his diocese, confirming large numbers of young people, preaching to crowded congregations, consecrating churches and burial-grounds, and endeavouring to stimulate the religious life, both of clergy and laity, by all the means in his power.

"MANCHESTER, [*Oct.* 1824].

".... I have been preaching to-day to the two most crowded congregations I ever saw. The Collegiate Church was quite paved with heads, and many hundreds stood on the outside—within, there must have been nearly 6,000 persons. In the afternoon more than 1,000 went away disappointed from St. Anne's, not being able to get standing room. . . . ."

August and September of the next year were occupied by his visitation, in the first six days of which he confirmed 7,991 persons at six different places, delivered his charge and entertained the clergy twice, preached three times, and consecrated one church and four burial-grounds. In the autumn of 1827 he spent some time in the Lake-district, to acquaint himself with the state of Church matters in those remote valleys and mountains. There was much to amend here; and he would often in later life relate anecdotes of the clergy in that district; of his going, for instance, into a poor man's cottage in one of the valleys and asking whether the clergyman ever visited him; the man replied that he did frequently; but, upon further inquiry, it appeared that the reason of the pastor's visits lay in the fact, that there were a good many foxes in the hills behind the house. The time which was not occupied in these visitations he spent either in London or at Chester. In London, besides preaching twice in his own church, and sometimes a third time elsewhere, and superintending the affairs of his parish, he was regular in his attendance at the House of Lords (when ecclesiastical matters were in debate), and was constantly to be found at committees of the Bounty Board, the Church Building Society, the Societies for Promoting Christian Knowledge and for the Propagation of the Gospel, the Negro Conversion Society, and at meetings for establishing King's College, or (in 1826) for administering relief to the distressed weavers of Spitalfields and the operatives of his own diocese.[1] At Chester he did not forget that he had duties to perform, not only as Bishop of the diocese, but as the most important resident of the city. All local matters were actively taken up; the parochial schools especially were raised to a high state of efficiency; the state of hospitals and prisons, the improvements of the town, and its sanitary condition, did not escape his vigilant eye; so that it was the opinion of a Chester citizen, well qualified to speak on the subject, that the affairs of the city had never been so well looked after before or since, as during the short episcopate of Bishop Blomfield. He had an eye for everything, and an ear for everybody. He lived himself in an atmosphere of work; and few of those around him could long escape the contagion of his example.

Among the means employed by the Bishop to stimulate the religious activity of his diocese, it should not be forgotten to mention the diocesan branches of the Society for Promoting Christian Knowledge, and the Church Building and National Societies, which he either established or made much more efficient than they had ever been before.

And, here, before leaving this part of our subject, it may be well to extract from his letters and other documents his opinions on certain points, more or less important, which, at a subsequent period, became matters of controversy.——He censured the unnecessary use of Private Baptisms, and thought that the clergy could not refuse non-communicant or illiterate

[1] This was the season marked by an unprecedented number of commercial failures, when O'Connell said in Ireland, "I cannot help being gratified by the national misfortunes of England."

sponsors; he insisted upon the gown being worn in the pulpit, alleging that the use of the surplice was a departure from the usual practice only found in remote and small parishes; he would not support the Church Missionary Society, disapproving of the principles of its management: he thought that charity was too much diverted to distant objects, to the neglect of those nearer and more immediate; he considered that the revival of an *operative* Convocation would be inexpedient; he refused to sanction any collection of hymns for use in churches; he declared that it was binding upon the clergy to preach the sole merits of Christ, and the corruption of human nature, but discountenanced Calvinistic opinions; he disapproved of Wednesday evening lectures, as leading the people to overvalue preaching and undervalue prayers, and thought that where there were two full services on Sundays, such week-day services were not required; he would rather that the sermon should be omitted on Communion-Sundays, than the elements administered to more than one communicant at a time; he questioned the propriety of holding oratorios in churches, and the profit of converting a dinner-party into a prayer-meeting; and in all his communications, he maintained that the first duty of bishop and clergy is to act strictly and punctiliously according to law. Lastly, in his charge of 1825, he insists upon the same principles with regard to rubrical observances which he had already expressed in 1823, and which he repeated in 1842; "a strict and punctual conformity to the Liturgy and Articles of our Church is a duty, to which we have bound ourselves by a solemn promise, and which, while we continue in its ministry, we must scrupulously fulfil. Conformity to the Liturgy implies, of course, an exact observance of the Rubrics. We are no more at liberty to vary the mode of performing any part of public worship, than we are to preach doctrines at variance with the Articles of Religion. If there be any direction for the public service of the Church, with which a clergyman cannot conscientiously comply, he is at liberty to withdraw from her ministry; but not to violate the solemn compact which he has made with her. .... It is, surely, not too much for me to request, that in performing all the different offices of public worship, and especially in administering the sacraments of Baptism and the Supper of the Lord, your practice may be exactly conformable to the Rubrics, by which it ought to be guided, and to the observance of which you are bound both in law and conscience; with this proviso only, that the thing enjoined be practicable."

Those who are familiar with the Bishop's later acts, will see from these extracts, that while the main bent of his mind, and the principles on which he acted in discharging his episcopal duties, remained the same throughout his life, he was guided in the application of those principles by the complexion of the times, the necessities of particular cases, and the fluctuations of public feeling on ecclesiastical matters. Hence he laid himself open to a charge of vacillation and inconsistency and a temporising policy; the fact being, that it was his rule to give up or modify, if occasion seemed so to require, *everything except a principle;* while in deciding what *were* principles, if he took the usual liberty of individual judgment, he must of necessity differ, on the one side or the other, from very many of his critics.

The following letters will illustrate more at length Bishop Blomfield's opinions and mode of dealing with his clergy while Bishop of Chester:—

To a Clergyman who had attended a Meeting at which a Female preached.

"CHESTER, *Nov.* 12, 1824.

".... I have to acknowledge the receipt of your answer to my inquiry concerning an act of irregularity, which, as you assure me it shall not occur again, I am not disposed to visit with any further censure. At the same time, I cannot but observe that, as the late Bishop had cautioned the clergy of —— against the practice to which I allude, the circumstance of your having attended the meeting in question immediately after his quitting the diocese, does not wear the appearance of inadvertence. I trust that I am well disposed to value and encourage the pious exertions of faithful and laborious ministers; but as I am convinced (and every sincere clergyman must be convinced) that those exertions will be most effectual when they are in close conformity with the doctrine and discipline of the Church, I never will tolerate any intentional departure from that strict canonical regularity which every clergyman is solemnly pledged and sworn to observe. No personal or present benefit which an individual thinks he may derive from a breach of Church discipline, as to his own improvement or that of others, can compensate for the mischief which would ultimately result from the subversion of order and uniformity, nor justify any minister of that Church in breaking his solemn engagements. With respect to your own case, surely it might have occurred to you, without your having been admonished by others, that the attendance of a clergyman at a conventicle is the most effectual of all methods to persuade the laity, that it makes no difference whether they go to the Church or to a conventicle: and even were it true that it does make no difference, yet, since in that case the Church must be in error, the part of a sincere man would be to secede at once from her communion, and not to make her ministry and privileges the abettors and auxiliaries of Dissenters. Believe me, the efficacy of your ministry will in no degree be impaired, nor need your zeal be abated, by a strict adherence to the discipline of that Church which you are sworn to uphold and obey. For my own part, I am convinced that I shall consult the interests of true religion by a strict enforcement of the laws by which that discipline is regulated. In conclusion let me remark, that while you continue to be a clergyman of the Established Church, as you are bound by a sacred pledge to comply with all her prescriptive forms and orders, you can never do wrong by a strict observance of your promise; but that you *may* do harm, and cannot be quite in the right, if you deviate from it. . . . . "

To the Very Rev. Dr. Calvert, on the necessity of showing the Church to advantage in Manchester.

"LONDON, *Feb.* 2, 1825.

" . . . . I shall be much obliged to you if you will express to the Manchester clergy, as opportunity may offer, my particular *wish* that they should wear their *gowns* and clerical hats, or at least the former, on Sundays. I am quite sure that in a place like Manchester, it is very desirable that they should keep up all the *appearance* of ministers of the Established Church.... In the present day, I am persuaded that the more the clergy come forward *as clergymen*, the more they distinguish themselves from the rest of the community, not only by their devotion to the duties of their calling, but by their attention to all outward decencies, the more effectual will be their ministry.

The question whether such a place as Manchester shall continue to be a stronghold of the Church, or shall be converted into a vast treasure-house of Dissent, is so fearful, and lays such an awful weight of responsibility on the clergy, that I cannot suspect any unwillingness on their parts to comply with the wishes which I may express on the subject of their professional duties, at least while I call for no sacrifice of interest or ease."

To a former Pupil, who thought of leaving the Ministry of the Church, from scruples about the Athanasian Creed.

".... If you object to the *doctrine* of the Athanasian Creed, I have not a word to say against your quitting the ministry of the Church, when you shall have carefully and exactly studied the subject, and satisfied yourself that the doctrine is not true. This, however, I have but little apprehension of your doing, because I am sure you are not prepared to give up the doctrines of the Divinity of the Son, and the personality of the Holy Ghost, upon the former of which hangs the whole scheme of the atonement and redemption, and upon the latter the certainty of a Comforter, to abide with and to sanctify the Church of Christ even unto the end. What you object to in the Athanasian Creed is the form in which these doctrines are *asserted;* not the form in which they are *declared* (although that may be considered as an attempt to define what is undefinable by human language, rendered necessary by the subtilties of some early heretics), but the words in which you suppose all persons to be condemned who do not receive that declaration. If men are accountable to God for their faith as well as their practice (and I do not see how this can be denied), it is a necessary consequence that a man must believe rightly in order to salvation. This is the general proposition, which we may lay down broadly. Its limitations are to be made by Him who searcheth the hearts, and can alone judge of every man's opportunities and means both of believing and doing what he ought. The exercise of this prerogative of the Divine omniscience and goodness is taken for granted through all the formularies of a Protestant Church; the denial of it being on the other hand characteristic of a Church which rests its authority upon the traditions of men. And with respect to all its doctrines, the language of a true Protestant Church is that which our own Church distinctly holds in her Articles [quoting from Articles vi. xvii. and xxi.]. Now I consider it to be evident upon the face of it, that a Church which holds such language as this can never intend to pronounce sentence of condemnation (or rather to declare that sentence will be given) against those who do not implicitly admit the minute dogmatical *illustrations* of a doctrine which she herself has laid down, as fully and as particularly as she requires it to be believed, in her first five Articles. In those Articles no such sentence is passed even by implication. Nevertheless it is certain that whatever the true faith be, it is necessary to salvation as far as we can determine; for if this be not admitted, a Christian belief becomes a matter of no importance. And if the Christian faith be rightly set forth in the Athanasian Creed, the Church has a right to say that the belief of the doctrines therein contained is necessary to salvation—provided that this be said with those implied limitations, with which equity and the Scripture teach us that all such declarations must be fenced and qualified. Suppose that after reciting the two great commandments, or rather a collection of Gospel precepts, the Church were to declare, 'This is the true Christian practice, which, except a man faithfully perform and follow, he cannot be saved;' who would be offended at the declaration? Yet even there it would not be intended to exclude, but rather to take for granted, the allowances to be made for natural weakness and inability, and the necessity of repentance and faith.

I think it a supposition so probable, that I have no hesitation in adopting it, that whereas the Eighth Article declares that the three Creeds may be proved by Scripture, it means, strictly and properly, the *doctrine* of those creeds. Now the damnatory clauses are no part of the *Christian doctrine* set forth in that Creed, nor even, strictly speaking, part of the Creed itself; but a particular form of asserting that the doctrine of the Creed is true; as if you were to subjoin to the Apostles' Creed some such clause as this—'This is the true Catholic faith,' no one would look upon it as part of the Creed.... Taking then into account the uniform moderation and wariness of our Church in dogmatizing; the unvarying language which her most eminent divines have held respecting the restricted import of the condemning clauses; the formal (but by accident not official) exposition of the Church itself by its commissioned interpreters in 1689;[1] the admission of the most scrupulous and captious Baxter that such exposition may be received; and the undoubted fact that when you

[1] That the condemning clauses "are to be understood as relating only to those who obstinately deny the substance of the Christian Faith."

subscribe the Eighth Article, you are considered to subscribe it in this sense and no other (and that too a sense perfectly consisting with 'the literal and grammatical sense')—surely it is symptomatic rather of pride or weakness than of a conscientious sincerity, to persist in affixing your own sense to the Article, rather than that in which every authority deserving of respect assures you that you may and ought to take it. And if you object, that although you may yourself use the Athanasian Creed with this qualifying exposition of the condemning clauses, the people will not know that they are to be so qualified, the obvious answer is, 'Then take care to inform them....'"

The next three letters are to Clergymen in his diocese, on various disputed points.

Improper to collect in Churches for the Moravians.

"*June* 1, 1826.

"....Without entering into the question of the merits of the Moravian Brethren, I may say that I respect them, and think that they have been particularly judicious and successful in the conduct of missions. But some limit must be drawn in the preaching of Charity Sermons; for it is obvious that if individual clergymen are to follow no rule in this respect but their sense of propriety, great inconvenience and irregularity may ensue, and a wrong direction may be given to the charity of our congregations. The practice of modern times permits a greater latitude in this respect than was allowed a hundred years ago, when Lord Chief Justice Powys declared all Church collections not made under the authority of a king's letter (except the Eucharistic offerings) to be illegal. I am not disposed to go so far as this, but I certainly think that no collections should be made in churches except for objects of local or diocesan charity, or for institutions in immediate connexion with the Church; and were it in any case allowable, it ought not assuredly to be done without the sanction of the Ordinary. I believe the modern Moravians would find it difficult to prove the succession of bishops amongst themselves, previous to the assumed episcopate of Count Zinzendorf. . . . ."

The Doctrine of the Atonement must be distinctly preached.

"*Sept.* 4, 1826.

". . . . I return Mr. ——'s letter. I hope that the charge which he insinuates against you, of not preaching the peculiar doctrines of the Gospel, is not true. Much as I lament and disapprove of that enthusiasm which has expressed itself so unintelligibly in his letter, I entirely agree with him in thinking that no minister of the Gospel does his duty, who does not frequently and strongly insist upon the necessity of an *exclusive* reliance upon the merits and death of Jesus Christ, a disclaiming of all desert upon our own part, the great corruption of human nature, the indispensableness of Divine grace, and the necessity of good works, not as the efficacious cause or instrument of our salvation, but as a fruit, and part, and token of true evangelical faith. Any discourse in which the arguments are not grounded upon this view of the Gospel scheme, will be without effect upon the hearers. If you have never met with Mr. Sumner's 'Apostolical Preaching,' I earnestly recommend it to you for perusal. . . . ."

A check must be put upon Sermons for Religious Societies.

"PALACE, CHESTER, *July* 20, 1827.

".... A circular letter has been put into my hands, announcing a sermon to be preached in your church, on the 8th of July, on behalf of a society called the Continental Society, by the Rev. ——. This open defiance of my directions, with respect to these itinerant preachers, calls for some expression of my displeasure. I would put the question to your common sense, whether there must not be *some* check upon the preaching of sermons for societies, the object of which may sometimes be completely at variance with the principles of our Established Church; and who is to exercise that check but the Bishop? Your perseverance in the practice of which I complain will reduce me to this necessity: I must employ some person to give me previous notice of such sermons, and I will then issue beforehand a formal prohibition, both to you and the preacher. I am aware of the doctrine which you maintain with respect to canonical obedience, but I believe I shall be able to convince you of my power to enforce it in this instance. I have prohibited Mr. —— from preaching again in my diocese...."

To Mr. Mawman, the Publisher, on the Warnings of Sickness.

"BURY ST. EDMUNDS, *June* 21, 1827.

"MY DEAR SIR,—I am happy to learn from Mr. Fellowes, whom I desired to send me an account of your progress, that you are better than when I saw you. I trust that we may now look with confidence towards your restoration to health. Nevertheless, I am sure you will attribute it to the regard which I feel for you, if I remind you that these visitations of sickness are serious warnings, and ought not to pass away unimproved. Whatsoever makes us aware of the uncertain tenure by which life is held, should make us, at least in an equal degree, anxious about that which is to follow after. The question seems at such times to be *directly* proposed to us by God, whether we have been preparing ourselves agreeably to the plain instructions which He himself has given us. All have too much reason to look back with regret to the past; and they alone can bear the retrospect, who are sensible of the true grounds upon which they may look forward with confidence to the future. In what degree you have made religion the subject of your thoughts, I am not able to judge; but I am sure that it must, in some shape or other, present itself to your mind in the hours of sickness; and I hope, most sincerely, it may be in the shape of comfort and encouragement.

My office, no less than my friendship, suggests these observations. More I will not add at present. I trust that a kind Providence may grant you many years to consider its goodness and its requirements.

I will call upon you as soon as I return to town.

Believe me, my dear Sir,
Yours very sincerely,
C. J. CHESTER."

To the same.

"RYDAL, NEAR KENDAL, *Aug.* 13, 1827.

"MY DEAR SIR,—I have heard from two or three quarters, since I left London, accounts of the state of your health, which have excited in me great uneasiness. I was not satisfied with what I observed when I last saw you, but as I heard afterwards that you were considerably better, I hoped that my fears had been unfounded. What I now hear leads me to apprehend, that you are not in so hopeful a way towards recovery as you have hitherto believed; if it be not so, you will easily satisfy yourself of the fact by a distinct and categorical appeal to your medical friends; but if it be so, as, indeed, I cannot help fearing, surely it is of the highest importance that it should not be concealed from you, either by others or by yourself. In expressing, with great earnestness, a wish of such a nature, I use the freedom and candour, to which, I hope, I am entitled, not only by the nature of my office, but by a very sincere esteem and regard for you, now of seventeen years' standing, of which I trust you have had many proofs, but none more sure, because none has been more reluctantly given, than this.

Let me entreat you, my dear Sir, to ascertain by a bold inquiry, your real state and prospects. Nothing but good can result from it. Should the issue be such as to excite apprehension, you will only be sorry that you did not know it before. Should no cause for such apprehension exist, it will still be good for you that it should have been excited, and that you should have been led, by whatever motive, to think seriously of your eternal state. Convinced as I am myself, that there is no hope of acceptance with God, but that which rests upon the Gospel of Jesus Christ, producing repentance and faith, I cannot but be deeply solicitous that all whom I value should be possessed of that hope, and fulfil those conditions. If the cares of business, or too great a reliance on your own reason or goodness, should have led you to undervalue that possession, consider what there is which will stand you in stead of it at the last; and whether hours and weeks of sickness and pain may not be intended to humble pride, and discipline the soul to penitence, and elevate it to faith.

You know me too well to accuse me either of insincerity or enthusiasm. I am actuated by neither when I beg you to consider, that it is God himself who reasons with you by His afflictive dispensations, and in mercy gives you time and space for reflection. Should the fears which I express turn out to be unfounded, still I shall not regret having written this letter to you. May God prosper it to your good, to whose gracious Providence I most earnestly commend you."

CHAPTER V.

BISHOP BLOMFIELD AS A PUBLIC SPEAKER—HIS DEFENCE OF THE CHURCH IN PARLIAMENT—HIS REPLY TO CHARLES BUTLER—OPPOSES ROMAN CATHOLIC EMANCIPATION—ATTACKED IN CONSEQUENCE BY THE PRESS—HIS COLLISION WITH BISHOP BATHURST—THE "TIMES" NEWSPAPER—ADVOCATES THE ABOLITION OF THE TEST AND CORPORATION ACTS—IS TRANSLATED TO LONDON—FEELING OF CHURCHMEN ON THE OCCASION—CONGRATULATORY LETTERS.

THE elevation of Dr. Blomfield to the Episcopal Bench introduced him to the public in the new character of a legislator and speaker on public affairs, by virtue of his position as a Peer of Parliament. In this character he perhaps appeared to greater advantage than in any other by which he was known to the world. Impressive as a preacher, thoroughly efficient as a man of business, he was still more admirable as a public speaker. Gifted with a clear and musical voice, and a pleasing delivery, a ready facility of expression, and a mind quick to seize and to appreciate the points on which it had to deliver itself; accustomed by long habit to spare no pains in accumulating and digesting the facts upon which decision must be built [1] (so that his speeches were those of one who had something to say, not of one who had to say something); and possessing an almost complete mastery over a temper naturally liable

[1] The pains which he took in preparing his more important speeches are attested by the copious MS. notes which he has left behind him.

to be soon roused by the angry recriminations of debate; he was just the man to carry weight and produce a favourable impression, whether in such an assembly as the House of Lords or in a more mixed audience. "As a public speaker" (wrote Bishop Copleston) "he is the best I ever heard. For he is ready, fluent, correct, always addressing himself to the point, never seeking admiration by sarcasm, and ornament, and rhetorical flourishes. He is above all that."[1] "He always brings out original thoughts, bearing well upon the subject. His diction the readiest, the purest, and most correct of any speaker."[2] "No report can do him justice. It is always below the truth."[3] Archdeacon Sinclair, on a visit to the United States, met with the eminent American lawyer and politician Daniel Webster, who, speaking of Bishop Blomfield, declared that, having heard speeches delivered by the most noted orators of this country, "in dignity of manner and weight of matter, no speaker in Great Britain was, in his opinion, equal to the Bishop of London." He added that such was also the opinion of M. Guizot. The Archdeacon also remembers that the Bishop once told him in conversation that he had never felt nervous when rising to address a public meeting, not even when he spoke for the first time in the House of Lords. There was something in his tone and manner which arrested the attention of the hearer, even when his remarks were brief, and their subject unimportant. His after-dinner speeches were always apt and happy, neither too ponderous nor too jocose. It may be added, that in the

[1] From an unpublished letter.

[2] Memoir of Bp. Copleston, p. 170. [3] Id. p. 178.

House of Lords he never spoke except in his character of a *spiritual* Peer, and upon subjects affecting, directly or indirectly, the interests of religion, or the welfare of the Established Church.

The principal question which agitated the House of Lords at the time at which Bishop Blomfield took his seat (Feb. 3, 1825), was that of the claims of the Roman Catholics to be admitted into Parliament. In a letter written to Mr. Lyttelton about this time he defends the active part taken by the clergy in the discussion of this question:—

"*June* 22, 1825.

"…. I am sure you will excuse me if I take the liberty of offering a remark upon one part of your letter, which relates to the interference of the clergy in 'the angry controversies of the political world.' I conclude that you refer to the discussion of the Roman Catholic question, for I am not aware that for the last twenty years the clergy have meddled with any other political matters. I never could understand with what justice *that* question could be considered purely political. The assuming it to be so is a complete *petitio principii;* for we argue, and I think justly, that it directly concerns the safety of that Church of which we are the ministers, and which we value as the most effectual instrument of diffusing and upholding true religion. Whatsoever measure threatens the Established Church with a diminution of its property, its privileges, and its security, is justly regarded *by us* as hostile to the interests of religion itself; and nothing, I think, can be more unjust or more unreasonable than to require of us that we should sit quietly, and contemplate the progress of such a measure without even a remonstrance, or an expression of our opinion. Every other profession is allowed and expected to petition and remonstrate when any measure is in contemplation which seems to threaten its interests; but as for the clergy, when not only their personal interests, but, as they believe (mistakenly perhaps), the interests of religion itself, certainly those of the established religion, are at stake, their mouths are to be stopped, and they are rebuked and reviled as agitators if they express an opinion upon what is to them the most important of all subjects. But we are told that we ought to leave these matters to the wisdom of others, and to acquiesce in their determination. If the clergy were persuaded, if they had any reason to be persuaded, that all those *other* persons, or even a very great majority of them, were really and firmly attached to the Church, that they understood its interests, and would suffer nothing to interfere with them, *then* they might be content to remain silent, and leave the question wholly to *them*. But when this is notoriously not the case, when a very large number of persons in the House of Commons declare their hostility to the Church, and a still larger number display an incredible ignorance of its doctrines, its constitution, and its securities, it would be the height of folly in the clergy not to raise their voices in its behalf, and to deprecate the enactment of laws which they believe to be greatly injurious to it. Only let them do it in such a manner as to show that their real motive is a concern for the Church, as the depositary of sound Christianity."

Many clergymen, amongst others, having petitioned the House against these claims, the Liberal peers enlivened the debates with a good deal of indiscriminate abuse of the Established Church in England and Ireland. Conspicuous in the attack were Lord Holland and a now forgotten nobleman, Lord King; and it was in answer to the former that Bishop Blomfield made his first speech. No Bishop was prepared to answer the attacks of Lord Holland, so the Bishop of Chester rose on the spur of the moment, and, as he said himself afterwards, had finished his speech before he had time to reflect that he was addressing for the first time the most dignified assembly in the world. Several peers congratulated him on his speech; and Lord Holland himself generously crossed the House, and offering him his hand, predicted his future success as a debater. Of this speech he writes to Dean Monk:—

"U. U. Club, *March* 3 [1825].

"…. I made my first speech in the House of Lords on Monday, very unexpectedly, but I have since learned with good effect. The newspaper report of what I said is, as usual with the reports of Bishops' speeches, very incorrect. I have learned from Lady Spencer what the Opposition Lords thought of it; and she tells me that their artillery will be pointed at me for the rest of the session—a compliment I could very well dispense with.

I am sorry for the decision of the House of Commons on the Catholic claims"—alluding to a partial Relief Bill which had just passed the Commons, but was afterwards rejected by the Lords.

With Lord King he had many a struggle in this and subsequent sessions, very much to the disadvantage of the lay peer. "It can hardly fail to go well with us on both sides of the Channel (wrote Bishop Jebb, in 1827) so long as we have Lord King for an opponent, and the Bishop of Chester for a defender." That the

Bishop himself was conscious of his powers as a debater, and anxious that he might never be tempted to abuse them, may be seen by the following extract from his diary :—

"1825, *April* 21.—Presented petition from a congregation of Dissenters; spoke on it, and was well heard. I humbly pray that Almighty God may subdue in me all love of the applause of men, all conceit of my own strength or wisdom, all trust in my own goodness; and enable me by His grace to bring every thought into subjection to the law of Christ, and be in spirit and temper 'as a weaned child.' O Lord, to thee be ascribed all the praise, and honour, and glory, by us, thy sinful, weak, unworthy creatures."

About the time of his first speech in the House of Lords, Bishop Blomfield published a pamphlet bearing on the subject of the day, in the shape of a letter to Mr. Charles Butler, who, in his 'Book of the Roman Catholic Church,' (intended as an answer to Southey's 'Book of the Church,') had accused the English clergy and laity of not believing, as a body, in the cardinal doctrines of the Trinity, the Incarnation, the Divinity of Christ, and the Atonement; and the clergy of signing the Thirty-nine Articles, in Gibbon's language, *with a sigh or a smile.* These charges the Bishop indignantly repudiates, and defies their assertor to substantiate them ; and he "availed[1] himself of this opportunity to fix upon the Romanists of the present day the charge of still believing in the obnoxious and anti-social doctrines which had long been a standing

[1] Biber, 'Bishop Blomfield and his Times,' p. 45

reproach to their Church, and the cause of the civil disqualifications of which they at this time so loudly complained," appealing in proof of his accusations to the Creed of Pius IV., 1564, to which Butler had himself referred for an exact account of the faith of Roman Catholics. This letter was well received by the public, and speedily ran through several editions.

Upon the proposal to the House of a distinctive measure of Relief to Roman Catholics, in May of the same year, the Bishop of Chester took the opportunity of stating his views more at length. The arguments which he employed against the proposed measure were the usual ones—that the concessions in question were required neither by justice nor expediency, that the measure would not be one of final pacification, and that an unquestioning and unbounded submission to the authority of the Pope was so essential a part of the creed of Romanists, as to make them unfit to exercise the office of legislators in a Protestant country. What made the speech open to unfavourable comment was the confession which the Bishop had to make, that his objections to the Relief Bill were in opposition to the sentiments of some of his most valued friends, and to his own early convictions. "The change, indeed, is not of recent date, but I do remember the time when my mind, imbued with those principles of civil and religious liberty which are interwoven with the very rudiments of education in this country, and disgusted with the severity of the penal code in some of its more hideous features, was inclined to regard the claims of the Roman Catholics with favour. But when I became more thoroughly acquainted with the doctrines and constitution of the Romish Church .... then, my lords, my opinion was changed."

The Liberal press and the Edinburgh Review were not slow in seizing upon such a confession as this; it was pointed out that his early patrons, Lord Spencer and Lord Bristol, were both in favour of Emancipation, while the Government now in power were opposed to it; and he who had till lately been the model parish priest, and the distinguished scholar, now became the servile courtier, the interested hunter after preferment, and the intolerant bigot. A writer in the Edinburgh Review,[1] with equal accuracy of statement and felicity of style, described him as having been "raised from a humble station to be a Lord Bishop, with 8,000*l.* a year, and the privilege of venting his matter by the hour in the first assembly of the empire," and as "doing his uttermost to serve both the court, the minister, and the heir presumptive, with a forwardness of obsequiousness that distinguishes him even on the bench of Bishops." Lord Hervey, the present Marquis of Bristol, on hearing of these charges against the Bishop, wrote the following letter to his father, the late Marquis:—

"PARIS, *June* 4, 1825.

".... In Saturday's Morning Chronicle I found a letter signed *Vindex*, commenting upon one which had been addressed a few days before to the editor of the Courier, with the view of rescuing our friend the Bishop of Chester from the charge of having abandoned his former opinions on the Catholic question, in the hope of promoting his own private and temporal interests.... It is more than insinuated, that in his early life, and so

[1] Vol. xlii. April, 1825.

long as your protection or Lord Spencer's could be of use to him, he took care to express sentiments favourable to Catholic Emancipation, with a view of ingratiating himself with those who he thought were at that time able to contribute to his promotion in the Church; but that as soon as you had, by bringing him under Lord Liverpool's notice, opened a new prospect to his ambition, he turned his back upon his former friends and protectors, and recanted those political sentiments which he conceived likely to stand in the way of his advancement. The conduct of the Bishop of Chester is said by the writer of the letter (who professes to speak from authority), to have caused much pain and disappointment to his early friends, and to be considered by them as exhibiting not only a want of public principle, but a want of gratitude..... The assertion that his friends had been induced by any reference to his political sentiments to forward his worldly interests, is one which it is easy to deal with, being a simple question of *fact*. As far as I am concerned, I am sure that any wish which I may at any time have either felt or expressed for his promotion in his profession, has arisen entirely from my admiration of his great talents and superior acquirements, and from the sincere and well-grounded regard which I entertain for his excellent moral qualities, and eminently virtuous character. When Lord Liverpool was so kind as to make me the channel of communicating to Mr. Blomfield (as he then was) the intelligence of his being presented to the living he still has in Bishopsgate, I certainly informed him of his good fortune with very great pleasure and satisfaction; not, however, from any regard to his political tenets, but because I was sincerely glad to see a clergyman, whose assiduous and exemplary discharge of his parochial duties I had myself witnessed during the few months I was under his roof, and of whose qualifications on the score of learning and ability no one can speak disparagingly, placed in a situation where he might make himself more extensively useful. The effect of his residence in his parish has been such as was anticipated by those who knew his character. The value of his labours has been felt, and I believe has been publicly and repeatedly acknowledged, by his parishioners; and I am told that he has contrived, in that very populous district, to conciliate the good opinion of the inhabitants, of all sects and denominations...... How far the Bishop of Chester's opinions on the Catholic question may have been gradually altered by mixing in the society of men connected with the High Church party, who are too apt to look upon any one who differs from them on certain points, as an enemy to the religious establishments of the country—how far that sort of *esprit de corps*, which has always existed among Churchmen, may have been prejudicial to his understanding and judgment, or whether this has been so at all, I do not presume to determine; but I cannot help feeling very much hurt at seeing such accusations published to the world; not only because of the true and sincere friendship which, in common with you, I bear towards the Bishop of Chester personally, but because it is so much to be lamented that the influence and usefulness of such a man should by possibility be lessened by any suspicions being thrown out against the honesty and integrity of his character....."

The Earl of Bristol to the Bishop of Chester.

"ST. JAMES'S SQUARE, *June* 9.

".... The sentiments he [Lord Hervey] expresses are so entirely my own, that I derive a double satisfaction from them. My son, as a young man, feels too strongly the attacks upon you to which he alludes. I have lived long enough to know how contemptible they are, and that a character like yours will rather profit than suffer by them. I know, perhaps, better than any man in England the pure gold of which that character is composed, and I can say with truth that the affectionate attachment I have long borne you had not at any time the remotest connexion with politics of any description."

Bishop Blomfield's character was, indeed, too high to suffer much from such charges as those here alluded to, and before the Roman Catholic question was finally settled, they had ceased to be heard. Among the testimonials which he received for his speech on this question was an enormous cheese, presented to him by a zealous Cheshire Protestant, who at the same time forwarded another of the same dimensions to the Duke of York, who had lately expressed himself strongly against the Roman Catholic claims.

A circumstance occurred in the summer of 1827, involving Bishop Blomfield in a misunderstanding with a brother prelate, which would probably have attracted no notice, had it not been that the former was still a mark for the political hostility of the Whig press. Bishop Bathurst, whose laxity in the matter of ordinations was notorious, had ordained, without a title, a young man who had before been refused as a candidate by the Bishop of Chester, and who immediately returned to the diocese of the latter, and proceeded to officiate without licence or permission. Having had to complain before of a similar irregularity on the part of the

Bishop of Norwich, and having received no answer to his remonstrance, Bishop Blomfield on this occasion addressed himself to the Archbishop of Canterbury, and represented to him the conduct of his suffragan. The Primate thereupon wrote to Bishop Bathurst, and admonished him in rather strong terms for his violation of the canons. The Bishop replied in defence, that he was not aware that the young man had been rejected by his brother prelate. And here the matter might have ended; but towards the end of the year, the *Old* Times newspaper, as it was then called, got hold of some fragments of these transactions, which, by some process known only to itself, it transmuted into the extraordinary story, that the Bishop of Chester had complained to the Archbishop of Bishop Bathurst's habit of whiling away his evenings by *playing a rubber of whist;* which the Times pathetically represented him as doing "more for the benefit of his poorer fellow-Christians than his own:" meaning, apparently, that the Bishop, like Parson Dale in Sir E. Bulwer's 'My Novel,' always gave his winnings away in charity. The sting of the Times article was in its tail: "If his Lordship, *now that he has lost his hold over the King's Government*, seeks to establish a fresh and strong position in the country, by founding a new and inexorable sect, of which he is himself to be the chief, we are only sorry that he cannot effect his aim without disturbing the peace and innocence of the best of Christian Bishops." "What a hateful thing," it was added the next day, "is an intolerant and meddling priest." The matter was taken up by Archdeacon Bathurst, the Bishop's son, who gave the real facts out of which this extraordinary *canard* had grown, and drew a graphic picture of the aged prelate spending his evenings, not at the whist-table, but in "straining his eyes, and exercising his still vigorous understanding and incredible memory and attention, over the pages of Hoadley, or Jortin, or Jeremy Taylor, his favourite authors:" and the Times was compelled to eat its own words with a completeness of retractation to which, in its present days of power, it probably would not condescend for any Bishop on the bench. The first article on the subject had appeared on December 1st; on the 7th, the editorial 'we' "contradicted, in the most positive terms, the statement presented to the public, that his Lordship had appealed, or applied, to the Archbishop of Canterbury, on the subject of the venerable Bishop of Norwich's occasional rubber of whist;" but this not being considered by the Bishop's friends a sufficiently explicit retractation, another paragraph appeared on the 8th, which declared that there "was *not a shadow of foundation*" for the original statements, and concluded with these words: "We can offer no more than our absolute negation of what we had before stated; and must again express our regret at the insertion of the unfounded paragraphs. We are sure that after this the Bishop of Chester's character will stand as high with his countrymen as it did before this affair."

It is only due to Bishop Bathurst to add, that he was far too good-tempered a man to feel more than a momentary annoyance at the rebuke indirectly administered to him by his brother Bishop; as the following extract from his Life, by his daughter, Mrs. Thistlethwayte, will show:—

"Mr. Tavel and Lady Augusta spent a day or two with my father at Norwich during the autumn of this year (1828), soon after the period of Dr. Blomfield's translation from the diocese of Chester to that of London. Mr. Tavel was formerly tutor to his lordship. My father, in the course of conversation, expressed his pleasure at the fact of Bishop Blomfield's translation to London, as he thought him so active and clever a man, and so proper a person for that diocese. Mr. Tavel, in a letter to Bishop Blomfield, mentioned what my father had said; and when the latter afterwards moved to London for the winter, early in November, Bishop Blomfield, having heard of his arrival, sent him a note to say he was anxious to call upon him, and begged he would let him know when he might find him at home. My father wrote to Dr. Blomfield in return, and fixed a time for receiving his lordship, who accordingly paid him a visit, and sat with him for some time, conversing on various subjects. In the course of conversation, he took an opportunity of complimenting my father on the calmness and benignity of his temper. Dr. Blomfield has also evinced the kindness of his heart by the constant and useful attention which he paid to my father ever afterwards."

The last words allude to Bishop Blomfield's having taken confirmations, on two or three occasions, for Bishop Bathurst.

The only other measures of importance on which Bishop Blomfield spoke in Parliament, before his translation, were a Bill to relieve Dissenters from the compulsory use of the Church service in their marriages, to which he expressed himself favourable; and the repeal of the Test and Corporation Acts, of which he was also a supporter, and which was carried in the spring of 1828. It is well known that Lord Eldon and the High Tory peers looked upon these Acts as the great securities of the Church, and branded as inconsistent and unprincipled those Churchmen who were ready to see them abolished; [1] but the Bishop was supported in his views on this subject by the whole of his brethren on the bench.

In conjunction with some of them, he had been in communication with Mr. Peel on the Declaration to be substituted for the Sacramental Test, and other details of the proposed measure. Mr. Peel writes to Bishop Lloyd, March 4:—

"I have had opportunities of ascertaining the opinions of the Archbishop, Bishops of Durham, London, and Chester, on the present state of the question regarding the Corporation and Test Acts. . . . The Declaration proposed by the Bishop of Chester is, I apprehend, too strong."

And March 15—

"I have been all morning at Lambeth with the two Archbishops, Llandaff, Durham, London, and Chester. We settled a Declaration which, I think, will go down in the House of Commons, which we can carry against the Dissenting interest there; and will, in my opinion, or, at least, ought, under all circumstances, to be satisfactory to the Church."[2]

While holding these exclusive measures to have been defensible at the time of their enactment, Bishop Blom-

1 "In Committee he [Lord Eldon] moved amendments, upon which there arose some altercation between him and the then Bishop of Chester, Dr. Blomfield, respecting the consistency of each."—*Twiss's Life of Lord Eldon*, vol. iii. p. 41.

2 Memoirs of Sir R. Peel, vol. i. p. 73.

field maintained that they had failed of the object for which they were intended, had become unnecessary in an altered state of things, and tended to bring religion and the Church into discredit, by the profanation involved in the use of the Sacramental Test. He ridiculed the idea that the safety of the Church could be endangered by the loss of such bulwarks—"bulwarks which it has been necessary to prop up year after year with the shoring of an Indemnity Act, lest they should fall on the heads of those whom they were intended to protect"—and declared that, in his opinion, much more danger was to be apprehended to religion from the existence and success of schemes of education for the young from which Christianity was by name excluded; alluding to the recent establishment, by Mr. Brougham and others, of the London University, and the Useful Knowledge Society.

To the Dean of Peterborough.

"LONDON, *April* 22, 1828.

". . . . Upon the most mature consideration which I have been able to give to the question of the Sacramental Test, I am of opinion that the Church is clearly a gainer by the repeal. It was under this conviction that I strenuously urged the concession, at a moment when there was a strong inclination in certain quarters to throw out the Bill in the House of Lords, and to stave off the question for another session. The present measure is strictly and literally a measure of the Bishops. The Dissenters acknowledge the concession, but consider it any thing rather than a triumph on their part. The more violent regard the proposed Declaration as a fetter, where there was none (in practice) before. Cobbett abuses Lord John Russell for acceding to such a security, and laughs at the Dissenters for having been made fools of by 'sly old Mother Church.'

I will take care that you shall have a report of the whole debate on this question, which is about to be printed, with a *correct* account of all our speeches. The Bishop of Lincoln spoke well on Thursday night, as did the Bishop of Llandaff on Monday. Of what *I* said, you will be able to judge. The Bishops took the lead, and were heard with great attention."

The illness and retirement of Lord Liverpool, early in 1827, had been rapidly followed by the short-lived administrations of Mr. Canning and Lord Goderich; and in February, 1828, the Duke of Wellington became Premier, with Mr. Peel and Lord Lyndhurst in his cabinet. Bishop Blomfield had written to Dean Monk, in March, 1827, "We must look *ultimately* to Peel as the only person on whom we can thoroughly rely;" and his expectations were thus partially realized. The new ministers had not yet determined, when taking office, that Roman Catholic Emancipation must be passed; so that the expressed opinions of the Bishop of Chester on this subject did not prevent the Duke from designing for him that promotion to which his character and work entitled him. The death of Archbishop Manners Sutton in July, 1828, gave the desired opportunity; Bishop Howley was promoted to the metropolitan see, and that of London was offered to the Bishop of Chester, in a letter from the Duke, dated

July 24. The letter was received late on a Friday evening; and on the following Monday he was to have started on his Visitation. His plans, however, had now to be altered at once: Saturday was spent in writing letters to announce that the Visitation would not take place, and in making the necessary arrangements; and on Monday, the horses which had been ordered to take him northward, carried him in the opposite direction towards London; the Duke having characteristically expressed a desire that he should enter upon his new duties as soon as possible.

The relations of Bishop Blomfield and Bishop Howley had always been, as they always continued to be, of the most friendly and confidential character, and the new Archbishop seemed as much pleased with the appointment of his successor as with his own. "I believe" (wrote a friend of the younger prelate) "my Lord of London almost demanded to have him to be his coadjutor." Nor was the news of the translation received with less joy by the numerous friends of the Bishop, and by the friends of the Church in general. "Glorious times for the Church!" exclaimed one of these as he met another in the street; "meeting-houses will go down fifty per cent." In the diocese of Chester his elevation was, of course, viewed with mixed feelings; and his clergy, in memorializing him on his departure, expressed something more than complimentary congratulation, since they could point to definite works done, and definite qualities displayed. The clergy of Warrington said, in addressing him on this occasion, "You have raised the scale of ministerial qualifications, and quickened the zeal of ministerial services. That which you have required from us, you have yourself performed; you have gone before us in the path of every duty;" and those of Macclesfield enumerate among his titles to their esteem, "the intimate acquaintance with the rights and privileges and duties of our order—the truly disinterested and impartial exercise of power and patronage." "I feel myself happy," wrote his successor at Chester, the late Archbishop of Canterbury, "in succeeding to a road so admirably smoothed and prepared." The feelings of Bishop Copleston upon this translation are worth recording:—

".... This morning I was made quite happy by seeing authentic intelligence that the Bishop of Chester is nominated to the see of London. We two become Bishop and Dean again of the same cathedral.[1] He is by far the ablest man on the bench—the only very good speaker; quite a man of business, and as candid, upright, fearless and conscientious a person as I ever knew. He has also a noble spirit as to money. The diocese of Chester will long enjoy the benefit of his short occupancy. He had saved nothing, but had improved everything, setting a most liberal example himself whenever money was wanted." .... "He is distinguished by ability, learning, firmness, disinterestedness, independence of mind, and an habitual sense of duty beyond any man I ever met with; and such a person cannot be better placed than in the see of London, where he will find continual exercise for all those qualities. He is, besides, thoroughly acquainted with the diocese, and has long taken a leading part in all the institutions connected with the Church."[2]

1 Dr. Copleston was appointed Dean of Chester 1826; Bishop of Llandaff and Dean of St. Paul's about the end of 1827.

2 From unpublished letters.

From the numerous letters occasioned by the Bishop's translation, the following have been selected:—

The Bishop of Chester to the Rev. Augustus Campbell.

"DAVENTRY, *July* 29, 1828.

"…. On Friday evening I received from the Duke of Wellington notice of His Majesty's intention to translate me to the see of London, and he desires my immediate attendance. Under these circumstances I was compelled, very reluctantly, to put off my Visitation; and I believe that it must be altogether foregone; for the Duke wishes the arrangement to be completed as soon as possible, and when once I am elect of London I shall not be at liberty to perform any episcopal function in the diocese of Chester.

It would be foolish affectation to say that I am not pleased with this mark of His Majesty's confidence; but I feel, almost overpoweringly, the weight of the charge which I am about to take upon me, and the necessity for relying for support and guidance upon One who has promised to be with His faithful servants; and I hope that the chief ingredient in my satisfaction is a belief that I may be enabled, in this new sphere of exertion, to do greater good to the cause of religion and the Church."

The Rev. G. F. Tavel to the Bishop of Chester.

"CAMPSEY ASH, *July* 30, 1828.

"Your letter, dated 26th, reached me only this morning (having, by as vile a wrong reading as ever befel calligraphy such as yours, been mis-sent to Northampton). I cannot tell you all the delight which it has given me. Of your being by far the fittest person for the see of

London I was well assured in my own mind, and did indulge secret hopes that your qualifications were so manifest that others, more to the purpose, could not but be assured of it too; though I was somewhat fearful of the Eldon influence. But I rejoice to see the willingness of Government to avail themselves of the talent, activity, and pious zeal which Providence offered to them in your person.

It is a noble triumph, and to which I conceive you are indebted, through the blessing of God, to your own ascensive force of merit solely.

May Heaven pour all its benedictions upon you, and grant you health, vigour, and every requisite for that elevated and deeply responsible situation. But such has ever been the happy elasticity of your mind, and such the blessing shed upon it, that its nerves have always found a tone which gave you easy command over the weight imposed.

I remain, in very truth,
My dear Bishop,
Your most affectionate friend,
G. F. Tavel."

J. D. Powles, Esq. to the Bishop of Chester.

"Stamford Hill, *July* 31, 1828.

".... But I have most reason to be thankful to the Divine Mercy for the all-consoling assurance which I am permitted to feel that, as far as human observation can penetrate, my faithful and excellent partner will not be found, whenever the call does come, unprepared to meet her Lord.

For how much of this unspeakable comfort I may be indebted to your lordship it is not in my power to estimate. Certain it is that she who is now to all appearance about to be called to her reckoning, has often told me how deeply she had found all her religious impressions strengthened, all her motives to duty enlarged and invigorated, while she had the blessing of being under your pastoral care. The consciousness of having thus helped thousands on their way rejoicing will sustain your lordship in the midst of the arduous duties to which Providence has called you, and the anxieties inseparable from so extended a sphere of action.

I congratulate your lordship with all my heart on your well-earned elevation. I have only been able to feel, from the moment that I learnt the intelligence, as if some great good had befallen myself and my family. I rejoice for the sake of the Church—for the credit of the King's Government—and in particular I delight to see that the miserable twaddle which it has been the fashion to talk for the last two years, of 'the Bishop of Chester not being a man of sufficient discretion to receive further advancement—of his having lost ground with the Government,' &c. &c. is at once and for ever silenced. The attacks of open enemies, and the timid apprehensions of lukewarm friends, may now be viewed with equal indifference."

Archdeacon Wrangham to the Bishop of Chester.

"HUNMANBY, *Aug.* 10, 1828.

"MY DEAR LORD,—Amidst the increased cares and duties of the new and very exalted station to which your lordship has been recently—may I without presumption add, deservedly?—advanced, I am sure you will forgive one, who has long looked up to you as an example of all that is active, enlightened, and benevolent, for intruding upon you his warmest congratulations.

There is a story of the neighbours of the old saint Romuald—that from the intense desire of keeping all they could of him amongst them, on hearing of his projected departure from their vicinity, they meditated killing him in order to secure his relics. We of Chester are, I trust, more disinterested; though, if it could have been achieved without your detriment, I believe the whole diocese would have made every justifiable effort to detain your lordship amongst them, and none more earnestly, or more honestly, than

My dear Lord,

&c. &c."

The Bishop of Chester to Joshua Watson, Esq.

"PALACE, FULHAM, *Aug.* 14, 1828.

"MY DEAR SIR,—Amongst the numerous congratulations which I have received from kind friends upon the occasion of my nomination to the see of London, there are few which I value so much as yours; for I am accustomed to appreciate the applause and good wishes of others, according to the worth of those that offer them. My removal to London is, indeed, an important event in my life—gratifying it must naturally be on many accounts; but the pleasure which it inspires is mingled with a deep and awful sense of the responsibility which I am about to take upon myself; yet not a *fearful* sense, because I have always been accustomed to put my trust in One who has never failed me, and who will not be wanting to me in the arduous office to which He has been pleased to call me, if I be not wanting to *Him*. Whatever zeal and energy I may have felt or exhibited in less important stations, I shall carry with me in that which I am about to fill; with somewhat more, perhaps, of prudence and discretion; for I should esteem it no mark of real wisdom, if I did not profit by the experience of every succeeding year. I reckon with confidence upon the countenance and support of the wise and good; and if I were called upon to mention individuals, I should say that I have an especial reference to *your* counsel and assistance, which I am sure you will give me with the same candour and cordiality which I have always experienced in my communications with you."

It is said that when Lord Liverpool, then weak from paralysis and near his end, was told of the death of Archbishop Manners Sutton, he asked, "Who goes to Lambeth?" "The Bishop of London," was the reply. "And who to London?" "The Bishop of Chester." "Good," said the ex-minister, "that is all right."

The new Bishop of London kissed hands, and was sworn a Privy Councillor, July 31st, 1828; was elected August 20th, and his election confirmed at Bow Church, August 23d; was admitted Dean of the Chapels Royal, December 12th (an office usually, though not invariably, annexed to the bishopric of London); and was enthroned in his cathedral, January 16th, 1829.

The circumstances which make London the most important and onerous of English bishoprics, are too well known to need enumeration. Suffice it to say, that the most obvious of them—the enormous overgrowth of the population of London—was a difficulty which had only lately assumed a very formidable magnitude, but which, when Bishop Blomfield entered upon his new duties, was every year becoming greater and greater. The population of the county of Middlesex increased from 818,129 in 1801, to 1,358,200 in 1831; while no corresponding increase had taken place in the number of churches and clergymen. "The successor of Sherlock and Lowth (wrote Mr. Lyttelton in congratulating him) had need to be no common divine; the successor of Porteus and Howley, a Christian of no common meekness and humility;" but evils unknown to Sherlock or Porteus had arisen in the meantime, rendering necessary other qualifications for one who should worthily fill their place. Add to this, that the unpopularity of the Church, occasioned by the Roman Catholic question, and heightened subsequently by that of Parliamentary Reform, made it of the highest importance that the Episcopate should be represented in London by one who could at once by his own example prove the usefulness and efficiency of the Establishment, and vigorously defend it in his place in Parliament; and it will be seen that no light task was before Bishop Blomfield when he exchanged Chester for London.

CHAPTER VI.

ROMAN CATHOLIC EMANCIPATION—SENTIMENTS OF GEORGE IV.—EDUCATION—KING'S COLLEGE—LETTER ON THE LORD'S DAY—ITS RECEPTION—ACCESSION OF WILLIAM IV.—CHARGE OF 1830—THE REFORM BILL—THE BISHOP'S CONDUCT WITH REGARD TO IT—DEATH OF HIS FATHER—THE REFORM BILL PASSED—LETTERS TO CLERGY.

THE first question of general interest with which the new Bishop of London had to deal, was the still unsettled one of Roman Catholic emancipation. Upon this subject he repeated the opinions to which he had given utterance as Bishop of Chester, though expressing his regret that he had now to oppose, not only many of his most valued friends, but also the Government which had just honoured him with so high a mark of confidence; and he again recorded his vote against the measure when it was eventually carried in April, 1829. With reference to the sentiments of George IV. on this point, Bishop Blomfield records in his diary, that in April, 1827, the then Archbishop of Canterbury related to him the circumstances of an interview which he and the Bishop of London (Howley) had had with the King on the subject: "The King spoke for five hours, and gave a history of his own conduct on the Roman Catholic question from the beginning of his political life; said that he had stipulated with Mr. Fox that he should do all in his power to prevent its being agitated during the Regency; while, in administration, that Mr. Fox questioned him as to his sentiments, which he acknowledged to be as strong against further concessions as those of his father—that he had insuperable scruples about the Coronation oath; that he was now desirous of having a Lord Lieutenant, a Chancellor, and a Secretary in Ireland, decidedly Protestant; that his own opinions on the subject were as strong as ever, and that he wished this to be generally known."[1] On another occasion, at the end of 1828, Bishop Blomfield met the Duke of Wellington and the Bishop of Durham (Van Mildert) at Lambeth, to discuss the question. The Bishop of Durham was the principal speaker, and urged all the best arguments against concession. The Archbishop said but little: the Bishop of London pointed out that the measure was not likely to satisfy the Irish. The Duke brought no argument in reply, except the alternative of civil war.

This interview is thus described by Sir R. Peel (Memoirs, vol. i. p. 276):—

"In the early part of the month of January, 1829 [December 26th, 1828], the Duke of Wellington had an interview with the Archbishop of Canterbury, the Bishop of London, and the Bishop of Durham. He sought that interview for the purpose of laying before them the state of affairs in Ireland, and in the hope of

[1] This statement is confirmed by Sir Robert Peel :—

"There was a general belief that when the King appointed Mr. Canning to be his chief minister, His Majesty had personally given assurances to the Archbishop of Canterbury and other of the bishops, that his own opinions on the Catholic question were the same with those of his father, and that it was his determination to resist to the uttermost the repeal of the disabling laws."—*Memoirs of Sir Robert Peel*, vol. i. p. 275.

convincing them that the public interests, and those interests especially which they must naturally regard with the greatest solicitude, demanded the adjustment of the Catholic question, and the adoption of other legislative measures which, without such adjustment, it was hopeless to attempt. A disposition on the part of such high ecclesiastical authorities favourably to consider this proposal, or even to admit the necessity for grave deliberation by an united government on the whole condition of Ireland, would, no doubt, have had great influence on the mind of the King, and would probably have removed one of the main obstacles to concession on the part of his Majesty.

At the interview, however, to which I have referred, or at a second interview immediately following the first, the Archbishop of Canterbury and the Bishops of London and Durham informed the Duke of Wellington that they could not lend their sanction to the proposed course of proceeding, but must offer a decided opposition to the removal of Roman Catholic disabilities."

The party who had been pressing forward the cause of Roman Catholic emancipation, had also been active in promoting secular, or, as it is called, non-sectarian education. With this object the London University had been founded, in 1827, by Mr. Brougham, Lord Lansdowne, and others of the same party. The exclusion of religion from this institution incited the friends of the Church to make some corresponding effort on their own side. Their feelings may be expressed in the following words of Bishop Blomfield:—

"A very general opinion has long existed, that the metropolis of this great country is deficient in institutions for the education of the middling and upper classes of society, especially with reference to those young persons who are destined to a professional or mercantile line of life. Of this opinion the founders of the institution called the London University have taken advantage; but in their plan for supplying the defect complained of, they have omitted, what the friends of religion and good order must ever deem an indispensable and essential branch of education, religious instruction. The remedy which they propose to apply to the existing evil is not only defective, but, in its tendencies, injurious. A sense of the want which really exists of some establishment for the purposes of a *complete* education, together with a conviction of the indispensableness of religious instruction, ought surely to induce those who are attached to the cause of knowledge and of virtue, to come forward and lay the foundation of an institution which shall combine the two objects. We have heard, with great satisfaction, that this subject has not escaped the notice of those who may be supposed to be most interested in the question; and we sincerely hope that there will be such a demonstration of public feeling amongst the supporters of sound principles in Church and State, as will justify the parties alluded to in coming forward with some distinct and substantive plan for effecting this great national object."

A large meeting to further the object thus described was held in London, in June, 1828, with the Duke of Wellington in the chair; smaller meetings, of merchants and others, were held at the Bishop's own house; and with Joshua Watson, Bishop Lloyd, Dr. D'Oyley (who had written an able pamphlet on the subject, under the name of 'Catholicus'), and other zealous Churchmen, he took a leading part in giving shape and consistency to the plan. The result was the foundation of King's

College, which, however, was not opened till 1831. To this institution Bishop Blomfield continued to give his cordial support and the benefit of his counsels, throughout his Episcopate; and its success, during a probation of thirty years, has been, in no inconsiderable degree, owing to his care. It is needless to add that the Bishop contributed largely in money, as well as in time and thought, to the new institution.

His general sentiments on the education of the middle and upper classes, were thus expressed, about this time, in writing to a zealous and munificent layman, on a proposition to found schools in which Dissenters and Churchmen were to be educated together.

"FULHAM, *Nov.* 25, 1829.

"MY DEAR SIR,—I am well assured that you will not lend yourself to any measures which can be shown to your satisfaction to be injurious to the interests of the Established Church, as the best instrument of conveying religious instruction to the people of this country. But the same measures may be viewed in different lights by different persons, equally attached to the right cause; and I have no scruple in saying that I consider an institution founded on such principles as those which I understand are the basis of the school at ———, to be fraught with considerable danger, and to be at all events at variance with sound Church principles. It is agreed that religious instruction is to form a part of the course of education which it is proposed to afford. Religious instruction is *necessarily* instruction in the doctrines as well as the duties of Christianity. It must, therefore, be in accordance with the doctrines of the Church of England, or at variance with them. If in accordance, what objection is there to making that a fundamental rule of the school? If at variance, how can a Churchman sanction it? Again, the head-master is, *in the first instance*, I am told, to be a clergyman. He, of course, will teach the doctrines of his Church. His successor *may be* a Dissenting minister; he, in *all probability*, will *not* teach the doctrines of the Church. Is not such a system a distinct avowal, on the part of its supporters, of *indifference* on these points? and must not the pupils necessarily grow up in a belief that it is perfectly indifferent whether they are Churchmen or not? In short, although there are many schemes of charity in which Churchmen and Dissenters may cordially unite, yet, in a scheme of religious education, it is not possible they should unite without a compromise of principle on one side or the other, if, as I think, it is the duty of a Churchman to bring up children in the principles which he himself entertains, and if, as I suppose is the case, a conscientious Dissenter considers it to be his duty to deny those principles in their full extent. The founders of the London University were quite aware of this difficulty, and as it was not consistent with their views to confine the benefits of that institution to members of the Church of England, they got over the difficulty by omitting religious instruction altogether. I hold it to be morally impossible to give *religious instruction* which shall not *have a tendency* either to promote or to weaken the interests of the Church. This is only my own opinion, which I can entertain without imputing to those who think otherwise any want of affection to the Church, and without intending peremptorily to assert that my opinion is right and theirs wrong, especially where, as in your case, I see so many clear evidences of a true spirit of piety and charity....."

In May, 1830, he was gratified by the elevation to the bench of Dr. Monk, a tried friend of more than twenty years' standing; "an event (he says) which I have always most earnestly desired, and which, I pray God, may be blessed to your own comfort and to the good of His Church. In times such as these, we want a reinforcement of such learning and zeal and discretion as you will bring amongst us."

About the same time his thoughts were much taken up with a subject respecting which he had not been unobservant during the ten years of his residence in London, and on which he now felt able to speak with some authority—the non-observance of Sunday in the metropolis. On this point he entertained rather strict, or what would now be called "Sabbatarian" notions. He wrote to Lord Lowther, then Lord Chamberlain, requesting that the new pleasure-grounds in St. James's Park might be closed during the hours of morning service on Sunday. When invited to dinner on a Sunday by William IV., soon after his accession, he explained, through Sir Herbert Taylor, that he never dined out on that day, and the good-natured King excused him, saying, "Ask him to dinner on Wednesday;" and in later life he always opposed the opening of the Crystal Palace, or any places of amusement on Sunday. In October, 1829, he had received a deputation of Dissenting ministers, who wished him to publish an address on the profanation of the Lord's Day; and being encouraged by this circumstance to take some public notice of the evil, he published in May, 1830, a "Letter on the present neglect of the Lord's Day, addressed to the inhabitants of London and Westminster." In doing this he was following the example of Bishop Porteus, who had published a letter or declaration on the subject, addressed, however, only to the clergy. After touching upon the Sunday traffic, the dram-drinking, the "short stages" to the suburbs, the steam-packets on the Thames, "crowded with gaily-dressed Sabbath-breakers," and the Sunday news-rooms and newspapers, as specimens of the way in which the day was profaned by the poor; the Bishop proceeded in the latter part of his pamphlet to speak more particularly of the sins of the upper classes in this respect—Sunday travelling (instancing his own experience at Chesterford), Sunday dinner-parties, *conversazioni*, and card-parties, and the additional labour imposed upon domestic servants by these festivities. He called upon the rich and the educated to return to a better practice by way of example, as well as for their own sake. "In spite of the increased numbers of our churches, in spite of the increased exertions of a zealous and laborious clergy, religion is, we fear, on the wane amongst the poorer classes; and the surest and the most alarming symptom of this is the profanation of the Sabbath. Surely, then, I am justified in calling, with great earnestness of intreaty, upon those who have it in their power (I do it in the name of the clergy, and of all well-wishers to the cause of true religion), to assist us in stemming the torrent of ungodliness; and to make, by their conduct, a practical declaration of their pious resolution, *as for me and my house we will serve the Lord.*"

The plain language of this latter half of the Letter (which ran speedily through no less than seven editions), excited a considerable sensation, and gave no little offence among those whose habits it held up to reprobation; and an expression of which the Bishop made use, "the Athenian curiosity of the present age, to which the public press is pander," drew down upon him the wrath of the newspapers; not only of the Times and Morning Chronicle, but even of the John Bull, the organ of the old-fashioned Tories, and the supporter of the Established Church, the humorous articles in which were at this time frequently written by Theodore Hook. The Times accuses the Bishop of cowardice in not venturing to stigmatize the Cabinet Ministers among Sunday dinner-givers (illustrating this accusation by comparing him to Gehazi, and the Duke of Wellington, from whom he had received his preferment, to Naaman), and speaks of consulting with its brethren whether legal steps should not be taken against him for his remarks upon the public press; the John Bull considers that "the expression of his lordship's views on this point savours considerably of that disposition to gloom and Puritanism which first disgust, and then drive from the pale of the Church of England, those who have always held the belief that the Protestant religion has nothing of austerity in its composition."

But the most remarkable utterances of the press on this subject were those of the Morning Post, which, as the representative of the "fashionable world," was particularly hurt by the Bishop's strictures upon Sunday parties. Its transformation will best be seen in parallel columns:—

Morning Post, May 11.

"The Bishop of London is said to be the author of a pamphlet, just published, complaining of the Sabbath not being duly observed: but from the opinion we have hitherto on all occasions been induced to form of this excellent prelate, we are led to doubt the authenticity of the work. . . . The observations respecting dinner-parties could never have proceeded from such a man as the Bishop of London, while the accompanying misrepresentations can only be intended for purposes to which so great and good a man could never deign to stoop. Our conclusion on the whole therefore is, that a production so utterly unworthy of such a character must be an audacious forgery, and a wanton libel upon one of the brightest ornaments of our pure and heavenly Church."

Morning Post, May 13.

"The letter of the Bishop of London to the inhabitants of the metropolis, is a production which denotes great earnestness and a very considerable zeal on the part of the Right Reverend Prelate in the cause of religion, although it may be thought that some particular passages in it (and we have ourselves expressed this opinion,) breathe a spirit somewhat too unaccommodating to the actual condition and exigencies of society, and that this circumstance is likely to impair, in some degree, its usefulness and efficacy as a pastoral admonition. . . . We do not hesitate to say, after an attentive perusal of this letter, that it is highly honourable as a whole to the zeal and talents of its eminent author, and well calculated to promote the object which evidently lies nearest to his heart, 'the maintenance of true religion and virtue.'"

While the London world was still talking of the Bishop's Pastoral Letter, its attention was diverted to more exciting topics by the death of George IV., which occurred June 26th. Bishop Blomfield's acquaintance with the Sovereign who now succeeded to the throne had a singular commencement. He addressed a letter to the Countess of Dysart, at Ham House, requesting permission to see that ancient mansion. The Countess, hospitable as she generally was, at first declined, saying, "I never saw any Bishop here in my brother's time." Afterwards, however, she relented, and, as the most agreeable arrangement to all parties, desired Sir George Sinclair, who had married her granddaughter, to fix a day for the Bishop to dine there, adding that he might invite William IV., then Duke of Clarence, and a large party to meet him. Sir George was not aware that the Duke had taken great offence at the Bishop for his recent speech and vote on Catholic emancipation. Observing that they took no notice of each other, he presented the Bishop to the Duke, who immediately addressed him in a voice loud enough to be heard by all the company, "I had lately the pleasure of seeing the Bishop of —— along with me in the lobby of the House of Lords, but I had not the pleasure of seeing the Bishop of London." The Bishop courteously replied, "It is with regret that I ever vote on a different side from your Royal Highness." The Duke resumed, "I was the more surprised, and I consider you the more in the wrong, because I thought I had reason to expect the reverse." "Whether I was actually in the wrong or not," replied the Bishop, "my conscience told me that I was in the right." The Duke was about to continue, when dinner was fortunately announced. At table, the Bishop drew him into conversation, and so completely conciliated his good opinion that some days afterwards he said to Sir George Sinclair, "I like the Bishop far better than I expected, and I do not care how soon you invite him to meet me again." He felt that he had gone too far, and asked, "How did the Bishop look when I told him my mind?" "I did not see," replied Sir George, "for my eyes were fixed upon the ground." "Did any one else observe how he looked?" "No; I believe their eyes were turned in the same direction." This anecdote is given on the authority of Sir George Sinclair.

The new king was generally supposed to be more favourable to the agitators for radical changes in Church and State than his predecessor had been; and his accession was hailed by them as a good omen for their cause. Being aware of this general impression, and wishing apparently to allay any apprehensions which might be entertained by the heads of the Church as to those among the questions of the day which most nearly affected themselves, William IV. took an early opportunity of declaring his sentiments to them, as will be seen by the following extracts from Bishop Blomfield's diary:—

"*July* 1.—Had an audience of the king at Bushy, concerning the service for Sunday. His Majesty expressed himself strongly in favour of the Established Church; wishes to annex commendams to bishoprics, so as to make them £6,000 per annum, but not interfering with those which are richer.

July 4.—Preached at the Chapel Royal[1] before the new King, who received the sacrament..... Afterwards the King received the Bishops (Canterbury, York, Armagh, London, Sarum, Carlisle, Rochester, St. Asaph, Exeter, Llandaff, Chester, Chichester, Lincoln) in his closet, and made a strong declaration of his attachment to the Established Church, and his determination to maintain and defend it; as also of his conviction that its revenues were not only not too great, but not great enough—that toleration had its limits, and had been carried as far as was just or safe, and that no description of persons had now any ground of complaint on that head. His Majesty then thanked me particularly for my sermon,[2] which he said had made a deep impression on him, and especially for not having

[1] As Dean.

[2] On the nature of the Holy Communion, and its importance to all classes of persons.

approached him with flattery, but for having stated plainly, yet with delicacy, the great principles of duty by which his conduct should be regulated; and he desired me to let him have a copy of the sermon, that he might refer to it at his leisure. His Majesty also desired me to make a minute of the proceedings of the day in the Register Book of the Chapel Royal.[1]

July 21.—Had an audience of the King, and presented my sermon, preached at the Chapel Royal on the 4th, and published by his command. The King again assured me of his firm attachment to the Church."

It soon became evident that the changes in the constitution of the country, which had for some time been anticipated, could not now be much longer delayed. The popular impulse in a democratic direction was heightened by the news of the revolution in France, and the abdication of Charles X.; and the Whig ministry under Lord Grey, which displaced that of the Duke of Wellington soon after the assembling of the new Parliament, was virtually pledged to some measure of Parliamentary Reform.

Meanwhile the Bishop of London met his clergy at his primary Visitation, and delivered his Charge. After touching upon the critical nature of the times, and the danger to be apprehended from the prevalence of an infidel spirit, which it was the duty of the clergy to watch and meet, he proceeded to urge the duty of residence, and a regular performance of the offices of the Church; suggesting, by the way, that the experiment might be tried of substituting "early prayers or

[1] In 1834, William IV. gave a similar assurance to the Irish bishops.

matins" on all week-days, for morning services on Wednesdays and Fridays. He next called their attention to the importance of superintending the education of the poor by means of national and infant schools, and the duty of public catechising; and concluded by touching on the subject of ministerial qualifications; the standard of which, with respect to learning, he announced his intention of raising considerably, while he expressed a hope that he might be aided in this reformation by the establishment of one or more theological seminaries. In speaking of residence, the Bishop had his eye more particularly on the Essex incumbents, many of whom had licences of non-residence on account of the alleged unhealthiness of the district, and left their duties to be performed by curates. On some less formal occasion, he reminded the clergy that curates were, after all, of the same flesh and blood as rectors, and that the residence which was possible for the one, could not be quite impossible for the other. "Besides," added he, "there are two well-known preservatives against ague; the one is, a good deal of care and a little port-wine; the other, a little care and a good deal of port wine. *I* prefer the former; but if any of the clergy prefer the latter, it is at all events a remedy which incumbents can afford better than curates."

In this Charge the Bishop alludes to his long connexion with the diocese over which he was now called upon to preside: "In addressing for the first time, from this chair, the clergy of the diocese of London, I may be allowed to testify the satisfaction which I feel, in reflecting, that during the whole of my ministerial life, with the exception of a few years, I have been numbered amongst them, first as a curate; then as the incumbent of a country living; next as rector of an important parish in the metropolis; and, lastly, as an archdeacon of the diocese." The practical turn of his mind, and his unwillingness to waste a moment in idle regrets for that which was irrecoverably past and gone, are evinced by his dismissing the whole subject of Roman Catholic emancipation, and the repeal of the Test and Corporation Acts, in the following sentence:—

"With respect to ourselves, the repeal of those laws, which were long considered to be indispensable to the safety of the Established Church, if it be no just cause of alarm, at least places us in a new position, compels us, for the future, to depend more entirely upon our internal resources, and will be a test of their sufficiency."

It is, perhaps, also worthy of note, that in this Charge he makes no allusion to the necessity or desirableness of Church Reform. This, however, arose rather from a dislike of taking too many people into his counsels, and a fear of exciting groundless alarm, than from any doubt as to the inevitable tendency of public feeling in that direction. As early, at least, as November, 1830, he expressed, in his correspondence, his disapprobation of a kind of defence association which some zealous conservative clergymen proposed to establish, as a means of resisting all change in the organization of the Church. In January, 1831, he wrote to Bishop Monk:—

"Mr. Hume intends to move for a committee, or a commission (probably the latter) to inquire into the whole subject of Church property.[1] And inquired into it must be, and most safely by a commission properly appointed. But surely the application for a commission ought to proceed from ourselves. We shall die of dignity, and of a St. John Long excoriation, for want of calling in a regular practitioner in time."

And in February:—

"The Archbishop has proposed to us the outlines of a plan for the restraining pluralities and non-residence. As soon as it is put into any shape, you shall have a copy of it. We shall probably have settled the whole matter of pluralities and commendams before Easter. It has been thought right that the recommendations for reform should come to the King from the Bishops who are Privy Councillors, after consultation with their brethren, rather than from a commission."

Again, in March, in the prospect of Reform in State as well as Church:—

"....It has been thought prudent to abstain from all episcopal conference on the Reform Bill till we see whether the measure will come before us. If it should, much, I think, will depend upon its shape, and upon the weight of majority which sends it to us.

I do not intend to subscribe to the Irish, till the Irish proprietors have done their duty: the last subscription was grossly misapplied. I have not added my name to the anti-repeal declaration, because I have always kept as clear as possible from all questions purely political; but if I were pressed to do so, I should have no great objection. The measure of reform now proposed, I view precisely in the same light with you—'Caput

[1] As Mr. Hume, in 1825, had spoken of the "enormous sinecures called rural deaneries," his object was perhaps to obtain more accurate information on ecclesiastical matters.

inter nubila condit'—we can do nothing but trust in Providence. Our deliberations on pluralities, residence, &c. are going on, and I wish you could have been amongst us. What is your own notion as to the proper limitation of pluralities?"

A commission "to inquire into the revenues and patronage of the Established Church," was, in fact, appointed by letters patent bearing date June 23, 1831, and Bishop Blomfield was one of its members. Its existence was again renewed in 1833 and 1834, and in 1835 it presented its report to Parliament. Further mention of it may therefore be reserved for a later place.[1] About the same time he had more than one encounter in Parliament with his old opponent, Lord King; whom he reminded that the non-residence of the clergy was in great measure owing to the existence of lay impropriations; and informed him that the total revenues of the English Church, if divided equally among the clergy, would hardly give them £200 a year a piece.

The second dissolution of Parliament in April, 1831, and the decidedly radical tendencies of that which assembled in June, brought to an issue the question of Parliamentary Reform; it being obvious, that whatever might be the course pursued by the Lords, some measure of reform would pass the Commons during

[1] This Commission, though often called at the time and since, "The Ecclesiastical Commission," being only a commission of *inquiry*, must not be confounded with the present "Ecclesiastical Commission," which was constituted a corporate body by an act passed in 1836.

that session. On this question, as being a political one, not necessarily affecting the welfare of the Church, Bishop Blomfield would have been glad to remain neutral. But if compelled to vote, his feeling was that the dangers which must ensue if reform were refused by the Lords, were so great as to outweigh any objections which could be urged against granting it. Circumstances, however, were to arise, which rendered the course of the Bishop less simple and easy than it would otherwise have been.

In the meantime, public attention was for a moment diverted from the absorbing topic by the ceremonial of the coronation of the new king and his queen, which took place on the 8th of September. On this occasion Bishop Blomfield preached the sermon; which is marked by a tone of manly simplicity, and an absence of all flattery, either towards the new king or his predecessor. It is essential to a consecration sermon, occurring in the midst of so lengthened a ceremonial, and being heard by so small a proportion of those present, that it should be *short;* and this condition the Bishop's sermon fulfilled. Some years after, he said that he could not in the least recall what had been his text or what he had said on this occasion. It was either this sermon, or that which he preached at the coronation of Queen Victoria, which, when read by the late King of Prussia, drew from him the remark, that he wished his court chaplains could preach so. On both occasions, the duty of preaching properly belonged to the Archbishop of York, who deputed it to the Bishop of London.

At this time the following entries occur in his diary:—

"*Sept.* 21.—Had an audience of the King, who stated very emphatically his attachment to the Church, and his wish to make proper appointments. Presented to him my Coronation Sermon.

Sept. 24.—Had an audience of the Queen, and presented my Sermon. Her Majesty expressed her sense of the dangerous state of affairs, and her trust in Providence, as well as her desire to promote the cause of religion. I told her that great good was likely to result to that cause from her attention to the public duties of religion; that I believed there was more religious feeling in England than in almost any country, though far less than there ought to be; that we must all do what we conscientiously believed to be the best, and trust to God to direct things to a prosperous issue."

Three days after this interview, he received intelligence that his father, who had been for some months suffering from a painful illness, was in a dangerous state, and setting out immediately from Fulham, he reached Bury not many hours before the end.

"*Sept.* 28.—This day, at half-past four, my dear father breathed his last, after a long and painful decline, which gradually weaned him from the world, and prepared him for his change, which he met in patience and hope.[1] May God forgive me for all my faults towards so kind and excellent a father, whom I have endeavoured to please and comfort since I knew the value of his care, and who lived to see me attain this honour which I so little deserve. May I be prepared to meet my God.

[1] The remainder of this paragraph is written in cypher, in the original.

Oct. 5.—Exuvias patris desideratissimi terra condimus, mœrentes, sed non 'sicut cæteri, qui spem non habent;' nam qui in Christo dormiunt, in Christo resurgent. Faxit Deus O. M. ut illo die patrem carissimum lætabundus revisam!"

The great question was now approaching its issue in the House of Lords. The Reform Bill, as passed by the Commons, was introduced for a second reading by Lord Grey on the 3d of October, and the debate continued for five successive nights. But the position of Bishop Blomfield towards the Bill was not the same now as it had been some weeks before. For whereas it was then probable that, at least, a majority of the Bishops would vote in favour of the measure, on the understanding that its provisions might be modified in Committee; it now appeared that the entire bench, except the two professed Whigs, Maltby and Bathurst, and one or two more intentionally or unavoidably absent,[1] had determined to range themselves on the side of its opponents. To class himself with a party with which he had no sympathies, and to act in opposition to so many of his brethren, including one whom he so unfeignedly loved and revered as the Archbishop of Canterbury, was a course which the Bishop would not take if he could possibly avoid it.[2] He determined, therefore, to avail himself of the reason which his recent loss afforded, for

[1] Bishop Carr, of Worcester, who had just received his promotion to that see, was one of these, and was called by the newspapers "The runaway Bishop."

[2] This was the reason for his conduct given by the Bishop in Parliament, April 11, 1832.

absenting himself altogether from the House on the memorable occasion, when, at half-past six o'clock on the morning of the 8th of October, the Bill was thrown out by a majority of 41, of whom 21 were Bishops: though fulfilling at the same time his engagement to preach the sermon at the opening of King's College on the same day. Three days afterwards (11th) he was in his place in the House, and took occasion to defend the Bishops from the charge which had been brought against them of intending, by their vote on the 8th, to trip up the Government; adding, that in his opinion, so far from the Bishops having any ground of complaint against the existing administration, it could not be for the interests of the Church that that administration should be dissolved.

In the storm of popular indignation which followed the rejection of the Bill—when the Whig press declared, with one voice, that the doom of the episcopal bench was sealed, and that its members must pay the penalty of their vote by walking out of the House of Lords[1]—when bishops were burnt in effigy in their own cathedral cities—when the Bristol mob burnt down the episcopal palace, the prisons, and the Mansion House, while Sir Charles Wetherell, the Recorder, was escaping in disguise over the roofs of the houses—Bishop Blomfield did not escape entirely unnoticed. "The Bishop of London," said the *Times*, "did not vote against the Bill; but, then, he did not vote for it; and the nation will not be served

[1] "The Bishops should not have challenged public attention to their base history, unredeemed by a single virtuous act."—*Morning Chronicle*. On the day after the rejection of the Bill, this paper had its columns *in mourning*.

by halves." The parishioners of St. Anne's, Soho, seeing it announced that he was to preach in their church on October 23d, signified to the rector their intention of walking out in a body when the Bishop should appear in the pulpit. "Such a proof ...." said the *Times*, "of public antipathy towards the entire order, is without example in modern history, and is worth a whole library of comments." The Bishop accordingly thought it prudent not to fulfil his engagement.

Meantime he was looked upon by the Government as a person through whose mediation some terms of capitulation might be arranged with the Bishops, and the question eventually settled. He records, in his diary, interviews with Lord Wharncliffe and the Archbishop of Canterbury, who were discussing the possibility of a "moderate" measure which might reconcile all parties. About the same time he received the following letter from Lord Grey:—

"EAST SHEEN, *Nov.* 20, 1831.

"MY LORD BISHOP,—It has, for some time, been my wish to have the advantage of a personal communication with your lordship, on the question of Parliamentary Reform; which is daily becoming more important to the peace and good government of the country, and must be again brought before Parliament immediately after the opening of the approaching session. My object in requesting this communication is to consider, with your lordship, whether it may be possible to find any means for putting a stop to the evils which have arisen from the rejection of the late Bill, on the second reading, in the House of Lords.

For this purpose it is my earnest desire to do anything in my power, consistently with the pledges I have given, to conciliate the opinions of those who have doubted the expediency of this measure, and to remove the objections of those who have been more directly opposed to it. But your lordship must be aware that I am bound by repeated declarations to adhere to the principles, and to consent to no diminution of the efficiency of the late Bill; being most firmly and conscientiously persuaded that nothing less would satisfy the public, or produce the salutary effects which, I trust, may be expected from a speedy settlement of this question."

The interview accordingly took place three days afterwards; but with what result the Bishop does not record.

A letter addressed, at this time, by Lord Brougham to Bishop Maltby, was, by the latter, sent to the Bishop of London. In it the Chancellor expresses in strong terms, his alarms for the safety of the Established Church, which, he declares, he regards as *the best thing of the kind going;* and concludes with these words:—

"I wish you would consult with the Bishop of London on the subject. If any one can see daylight through all these clouds it is he; for he has a good understanding and sound principles combined. I want to hear what you think, and whether you have a less gloomy view than I have, and in which, I must say, many, many join me..."

The Bishop himself writes to Bishop Monk:—

"*Nov.* 24, 1831.

"For my own part I am still of opinion that it would have been wiser to go into Committee on the former

Bill. Amendments would have been looked on with less suspicion than they will now. But I am so convinced that a great political convulsion will follow upon the rejection of a new Bill without a second reading; and, on the other hand, that if the second reading be carried by a batch of new peers, it will be all over with the House of Lords and the Church, that I have no hesitation as to the part which I shall take. With respect to the Bishops in general, I think it will not *now* be sufficient that they should stay away and take no part in the debate or decision: and I cannot help wishing that most of them may be induced to vote for the second reading, reserving to themselves the liberty of supporting any amendments in Committee."

And again, in February, 1832:—

"MY DEAR LORD,—I have had several conversations with Lords Harrowby and Wharncliffe on the present position of the House of Lords with respect to the Reform Bill. They are most strongly impressed with the belief, that if Ministers are driven to a creation of peers for the purpose of carrying the second reading, the country is ruined. The Bill will then be carried without any modification, and Ministers will, thenceforward, be in the hands of the Radicals. That they have an *unlimited* authority for the creation of peers, and that they have resolved to act upon it, if necessary, you may consider to be a *certain fact.* That they wish to avoid such a measure if the Bill can be read a second time, and that they will not have recourse to it for the sake of avoiding any reasonable modifications, is not less certain. That the House of Commons will accept the Bill, however modified, seems to be quite clear. Lord Harrowby says that he feels himself perfectly free, on the score of consistency, to vote for the second reading, as the most probable method of avoiding the evils of the unmitigated Bill; and as the only method of showing the country, even if the intended modifications should not all be carried, what the House of Lords really *will* do in the way of Reform. It is generally understood (and Lords Harrowby and Wharncliffe treat the question in that light) that the creation or non-creation of peers depends upon the course which the bishops will pursue. It is already known that the second reading will be supported by the following bishops:—

YORK,	CHESTER,	KILLALOE, and
LONDON,	BATH AND WELLS,	LICHFIELD.
LINCOLN,	CHICHESTER,	
LLANDAFF,	NORWICH,	

I cannot help hoping that the Archbishop will see the matter in the same point of view. There was certainly nothing in his speech which need preclude him from voting for the second reading of the new Bill, with a reservation as to the alterations to be made in Committee. But, if he does not determine quickly, it will be too late, and peers will be created—in which case it is all over with us. Pray think this over, and if you can make up your mind to vote for the second reading, it would be of great importance that Lord Harrowby should know it, as I believe, that upon the result of his communication to the Ministers on the subject, depends the question of creating peers. When will you be in town?"

In the next session the Bill was again introduced, April, 1832. In the course of the debate, Bishop Blomfield spoke as follows:—

"He could not now but express his conviction, that it would be as vain to expect that the sun would trace back his degrees on the dial, as that the people of England would ever return to the same channel of thought and opinion as before the introduction of this measure. It was true the inundation had subsided, but the current had been turned into a new channel, from whence it never could be diverted: and, therefore, it would appear to him to be the true wisdom to watch and regulate the course of the stream, to embank and secure that course, so that it might fertilize but never overflow and desolate the land." The time for neutrality, he said, had gone by; and he himself was of opinion that there must be an extensive Reform.

The Bill passed its second reading by a majority of 9: but an amendment of Lord Lyndhurst, destructive of its principle, having been carried in Committee, the Ministers applied to the King to adopt the expedient of carrying it as it stood by the creation of a batch of new peers. The King seeming unwilling to press matter to this extremity, the Ministers resigned; but an attempt by the Duke of Wellington to form an administration having failed, they returned to office, and the Bill was eventually passed in its original shape, by 106 to 22, through the personal solicitations of the King to the opposition peers. On all these occasions Bishop Blomfield voted with the Government.

Two letters may be added here. The first is to a clergyman who wished to present a petition to the House of Lords, praying to be released from his subscription to the Thirty-nine Articles, &c.

"*March* 1, 1830.

"....With respect to your having a petition presented to the House of Lords, I have no opinion to give, different from what I stated to you last year. I would only remark, that if you determine upon that course, it will hardly be proper that you should request one of the bishops to present it. With respect to subscription, if you cannot subscribe unreservedly and according to the literal sense of the words, I do not see what difference your *protesting* can make, as to easing your conscience. It will, in fact, be declaring in writing, that you believe certain things, which you take care to assure your friends and the public you do *not* believe. More than this, if you cannot conscientiously subscribe *anew* I do not understand how you can conscientiously continue to hold preferment by virtue of your *former* subscription. But that is a matter which I must leave to your own determination. As this is a question in which it is necessary to deal plainly, I hope you will excuse the freedom of these suggestions. I entreat you to consider well the nature of the step which you are now meditating; and commending you to the guidance and instruction of Him, whose cause I have no doubt you desire in all godly sincerity to promote,

I am, &c.

On this subject the following entry occurs in the Bishop's diary, May, 1829 :—

"Saw Mr. —— about his petition—told him that I thought the Athanasian Creed ought to be retained, but that I wished a rubric could be prefixed explanatory of the sense in which the Church of England uses the damnatory clauses; that I could not undertake to say whether this was likely to be done; that if any change were to be made, it should be made in times of quiet and peace."

The second is to one who thought of quitting the Church, in which he was a minister:—

"SOUTHEND, *Sept.* 1832.

"DEAR SIR,—Your father has sent me your letter to him of the 18th inst., which, after our recent correspondence, has occasioned me less surprise than concern. As you have not stated in detail your reasons for leaving the Church, I cannot, of course, enter upon them; but I would press upon you the *duty* of not taking so important a step without having used every endeavour to enlighten your mind on the subject, by the use of all those means of inquiry which are within your reach, as well as by prayer for a blessing upon the use of them. You appear to have read some books *against* the Church; but if you have not read what has been said *for* the Church, in answer to them, you have not done that which you are bound to do; and I do not suppose that you rate your understanding so highly, as to think it beneath you to notice the arguments of learned and pious men on either side of the question. With respect to Mr. James's[1] book, the *tone* in which some parts of it are written, and still more the language which its author has held at some public meetings respecting the Church, may well lead you to doubt, as to the spirit by which he is actuated. You will not be offended, if I caution you to beware lest your motive in taking the step which you meditate, should be tainted with some degree of vanity and love of distinction; and to consider seriously whether you have any prospect of doing the same good to the cause of your Heavenly Master in any other line, which you certainly may do as a minister of the Established Church.

I have written this with a view to your own comfort and character. As far as the Church itself is concerned,

[1] The late Angell James, of Birmingham.

I do not know that there is any reason to desire the continuance in its communion, still less in its ministry, of persons who entertain such crude and erroneous notions of the end and duties of the Christian ministry, as are held by some persons of the present day. That it is your *duty* to inquire and examine before you take a step which can in any way affect the interests of religion, I am sure you will readily admit; and with an earnest entreaty that you will do so, and a prayer that you may be guided by the Spirit of Truth to do that which is best,

I remain, &c."

CHAPTER VII.

CHOLERA IN 1831-2—REFORM OF THE POOR-LAWS—BISHOP BLOMFIELD'S SHARE IN IT—THE IRISH CHURCH—MEASURES OF LORD MELBOURNE—OPPOSED BY BISHOP BLOMFIELD—HIS SPEECH IN 1835—CHARGE OF 1834—REVISION OF THE LITURGY—SYDNEY SMITH AND THE LIVING OF EDMONTON—CORRESPONDENCE—CHURCH REFORM—CONVOCATION—THE CHURCH AND THE DISSENTERS.

THE close of the year 1831 had been marked by the first appearance of the Asiatic cholera in England. This singular disease, which had gradually made its way from Bengal to the Baltic, was first heard of in the north of England, whence it spread southwards, and was by many regarded as an unmistakeable sign of Divine wrath upon the country. The anticipations of suffering, however, were not fully realized; the cholera disappeared from Great Britain within twelve months after its arrival, having been on the whole much less violent than was expected, and than it had actually been upon the Continent.[1] On the occasion of preventive measures against the disease passing through the House of Lords, the Bishop of London moved and carried the insertion into the preamble of the bill, of the words—"It having pleased Divine

[1] There were fewer deaths in the year from cholera in the United Kingdom than in Paris alone.

Providence to visit this kingdom with this disease:"—words which had been omitted by the Commons in the English bill, though retained in the Scotch, and which Mr. Hume had gone so far as to characterise as "cant, humbug, and hypocrisy." Though not considering it expedient perpetually to refer to the providence of God, the Bishop thought that this was a case in which it was decorous and proper to do so, in conformity with the precedents set on the occasion of the Great Fire in 1666, and the illness of George III. in 1810.

The passing of this measure was soon followed by the appointment of a General Fast on the same account, which was fixed for the 21st of March. Bishop Blomfield issued a circular to the clergy, calling upon them to observe the day with due solemnity, and to stimulate the charity of their congregations towards the suffering poor. He enters in his diary:—

"March 21st.—General Fast. Preached at the Chapel Royal St. James's in the afternoon: Mr. Coxe preached. The day observed with great solemnity: very full churches, and large collections for the poor."

Among the subjects affecting the internal welfare of the nation with which the Reformed Parliament had to deal, none was of more pressing importance than a revision of the existing Poor Laws. The system which might have worked well in the days of Elizabeth, combined, in an altered state of things, the smallest possible amount of beneficial relief, with the greatest encouragement to laziness and deception;

checked the healthy action of the labour-market; heavily burdened farmers and landowners; promoted local jobbery and corruption; and, by the nature of its provisions with regard to bastard children, put a premium upon perjury and incontinency among women.[1] The few cases in which the existing Poor Laws did not produce such consequences, owed their exceptional character to the energy of individual clergymen or magistrates, not to the system. Of these evils Bishop Blomfield had had no little experience, and had been no unobservant spectator, as the incumbent first of a small, and then of a large country parish, and afterwards as Rector of Bishopsgate; and from the attention which he was known to have paid to the subject, as well as from his abilities, he was naturally thought of as one whose services might be desired, when a commission was appointed to inquire into the operation of the existing Poor Laws, and to suggest improvements in them, in 1832. Accordingly, Lord Althorpe, who was then Chancellor of the Exchequer, requested him to be one of the Chief Commissioners; his associates being the late Archbishop of Canterbury, Mr. Sturges Bourne, Mr. Nassau Senior, and others. This request he complied with, but with some reluctance, for reasons which, on a subsequent occasion, he thus stated in Parliament:[2]—

"When I was first applied to by the noble Lord,

[1] One of the Assistant Commissioners says in his Report: "It may safely be affirmed that the virtue of female chastity does not exist among the lower orders of England, except to a certain extent among domestic female servants."

[2] August 8, 1834.

the Chancellor of the Exchequer, to become one of the Commissioners for inquiring into the Poor Laws, I felt a very strong reluctance to embark in that inquiry. I had a pretty clear perception of the obloquy to which I should probably expose myself, by doing my duty in the examination of such a subject—a subject to which I had paid rather close attention for several years past. I knew that many of the recommendations which would probably be made by that commission, and to the making of which I should be a party, would be of such a nature as would be likely to expose me to the imputations which have been since so liberally lavished upon the Commissioners. I yielded, however, to the solicitation of that noble Lord, and consented to take upon me the office. Having done so, I should have been wanting in the duty I owed to the country at large, had I not faithfully and fearlessly applied myself to the duties of that office. If in the execution of those duties I felt myself compelled to adopt opinions at variance with the sentiments of many with whom I am accustomed to concur, I trust I shall not, on that account, be accused of acting under the influence of unworthy motives."

To make the allusions in the foregoing speech clear, it may be well to remind the reader that many of the recommendations of the Commission, as embodied in the bill which eventally became law, were strongly objected to when proposed to Parliament; especially those which related to the position of the mothers of illegitimate children. The *Times* for months contained a series of leading articles in which the proposed Poor Laws were denounced with great severity, and in which the Bishop of London did not escape criticism. In the

House of Lords, among the most vehement impugners of these propositions, as cruel and immoral, was the Bishop of Exeter; and it was partly against his charges that the Bishop of London was defending himself in the words quoted above. He was firmly convinced, and he more than once expressed the conviction, that the new laws, in all their principal features, would tend to discourage immorality, to relieve the burdens of the country, and to raise the social position of the labouring classes by promoting a feeling of independence among them. These expectations have not been entirely fulfilled, and the administration of parochial relief is still one of the least pleasing features of our social system; but no one who recollects the old state of things will be disposed to deny the solid advantages which have resulted from the establishment of the new; nor will it be regarded as the least title to esteem in the life of a Christian bishop, that he laboured to set the public charity of the nation upon a sounder foundation.

Bishop Blomfield was now called upon to take a part in legislation affecting the Irish branch of the Established Church. The disturbed condition of Ireland had long been a source of uneasiness to the Government; and no small part of those disturbances was owing to the Church. The opposition to tithes had become so violent, that more money was spent in enforcing their collection than was gained by collecting them; and so great was the consequent distress of the clergy, that besides the sums raised by subscription in England on their behalf, a million sterling was voted by Parliament to make up the arrears of tithes. There were some members of Lord Grey's Government who were prepared to remove the popular discontent by the simple expedient of appropriating the revenues of the Established Church in Ireland to secular purposes, or to the payment of the Roman Catholic clergy. These extreme propositions, however, were dropped for the present; and the measure brought before Parliament, and passed in the Session of 1833, followed the principle of giving up a part in order to save the whole. Its principal provisions were, the abolition of the obnoxious impost called *Church-cess,* and the suppression of ten bishoprics, the revenues of which were to be applied to the purposes for which the Church-cess had been collected. This measure, which many excellent Churchmen regarded as one of sacrilegious spoliation, received a decided, though a qualified support from Bishop Blomfield. There were some of its details to which he strongly objected; but some such measure, he contended, had become absolutely necessary from the present state of the Irish Church, in which tithes had become for the time extinct; and the principle of the bill he regarded as conservative rather than destructive. For several years, he thought, it had been evident to most persons, that the time would come when the number of Irish bishops must be reduced. No doubt, to his practical mind, there was much weight in the fact that while England, with at least eight millions of her people professing to belong to the Established Church, had but twenty-six Archbishops and Bishops, the Irish Church possessed twenty-two, though her members numbered no more than a million. In the course of the debate the Duke of Newcastle took occasion to rebuke the bench of Bishops for looking too much to consequences, and too little to principles; and in allusion to the Bishop of London's conduct on the Reform Bill, hinted that he had lately "collated himself to the office of high priest in the temple of expediency." In reply, the Bishop said that he did not hesitate to assert, with Paley, that there were cases in which expediency might be our guide; and with regard to the office which the Duke had conferred upon him, he had no objection to receive the investiture even at hands so little qualified to bestow it as those of his Grace.

One main reason by which the Bishop justified his support of the measure in question, was his hope and belief that it would be final. But the history of Irish Church Temporalities was not destined to end here. It is needless to detail the dissensions on this and kindred subjects which drove Lord Grey from office, after the loss of some of his ablest colleagues, broke up the first administration of Lord Melbourne, gave a brief tenure of power to Sir Robert Peel, and finally replaced Lord Melbourne as Premier, in the position which he continued to hold for six years. Thrice in three successive years during this period the subject was brought before the House of Lords. First, in 1834, a Commission, consisting only of laymen, was appointed to inquire into the revenues of the Irish Church—a measure to which Bishop Blomfield offered a strong, but unsuccessful resistance. This was immediately followed by the introduction of a bill substituting for tithes a land-tax payable to the Crown, which, through the vacillation of the Government (Lord Melbourne's) and the perseverance of O'Connell, was rendered still more unfavourable to the Church than it was originally intended to be. This bill Bishop Blomfield opposed as a violation of the pledges of finality given by the Government when introducing the measure of the previous session, and as putting a bonus into the pockets of the landlords at the expense of the Church; and it was thrown out in the House of Lords by 189 to 122. In the following year, when a combination of Whig and Irish members on the same subject had restored the former party to office, after the short administration of Sir Robert Peel, the bill was again introduced into Parliament, but with the addition of clauses which suppressed all benefices in parishes where there were less than fifty Protestants, and reduced the incomes of all livings to £300 a-year; and of an "appropriation clause," as it was called, enacting that the surplus revenues of the Irish Church should be applied to the purposes of general education. On this occasion Bishop Blomfield delivered a speech which extorted the admiration of his political opponents (especially, it is said, of Lord Lansdowne), and which was certainly one of the most powerful of his parliamentary speeches. He declared that no necessity existed for this bill which did not exist in 1833, when the measures proposed were declared to be final; except such a necessity as an honest and constitutional statesman would not be forward to avow: alluding to the alliance between the Whigs and O'Connell, which had brought them into office in 1835 pledged to the "appropriation clause," which in 1834 they had strenuously resisted.

"Let us see," he said, "whether besides this, any other necessity for the measure can be alleged. It is said that it is necessary to pacify Ireland. Would to God, my lords, that some plan could be devised for the pacification of that unhappy country! Which of your lordships would not consent to sacrifice much for such an object? What is here meant by pacification? Look, my lords, at the nature of the intended process. It does not deal with the country at large; it is intended to pacify it parish by parish; and how? To appease religious discord, the bane of that land. And what remedy does the bill supply? No doubt a very effectual one. In order to quiet the Roman Catholics it will exterminate the Protestants, and then all will be quiet; *Ubi solitudinem faciunt, pacem appellant* .... Pacify the Roman Catholics! Have we not abundant and melancholy proof of the utter futility of such efforts as these, in the way of pacification? Has any such device, produced though it may have been under the happiest auspices, and with the most flattering promises, in any degree succeeded? Has not each of them, in its turn, signally and lamentably failed? My lords, it has been unhappily characteristic of all the measures hitherto adopted for the quieting of Ireland, that in none of them has been the principle, or property, of finality. Every succeeding measure has been but the stepping-stone to another. But I am wrong: in the bill before us, my lords, there *is* a principle of finality; a very discernible germ at least of something final and conclusive; the seed of extermination and destruction. I speak the fullest conviction of my heart, when I declare to your lordships, unwilling as I am to prophesy, that if you pass this bill into a law, you will as effectually pass sentence of extinction upon the Church of Ireland, as if you were to embody in one of its clauses a distinct enactment, that from the year of our Lord 1840—no matter what precise year, but certainly at no very distant date—the Protestant Church of Ireland shall for ever cease and determine... Pacify the Roman Catholics of Ireland! And do your lordships still think that they are to be pacified? Or if they are, are you prepared for the consummation of that object, desirable as it is, to sacrifice upon the altars of their hatred and ambition the holocaust of a Protestant Church?"

After eulogizing the character and conduct of the Irish clergy, and ridiculing the notion that the surest way to increase a clergyman's usefulness is to diminish his income, he declared his conviction that the proposed measure would exterminate Protestantism in Ireland; and that, though the fate of the Church of England was not necessarily bound up with that of her Irish sister, yet an act of spoliation against the one would be necessarily an encouragement to the enemies of the other. He concluded his speech with the following words:—

"My lords, I have evinced on more than one occasion, that I am not indisposed to adopt any well-considered measures of salutary and real reform. Least of all am I indisposed to their adoption with respect to that institution in which the dearest and best interests of the country are involved. But to a measure such as this, of direct spoliation, I will never give my consent. Your lordships will do me the justice to admit, that I have not been accustomed, in the debates of this House, to use stronger language than the nature of the subject on which I have been speaking seemed to justify. But if there be terms in the English tongue more expressive and emphatic than others, I would gladly employ them on this occasion, while I implore your lordships, by all that you hold sacred, by the gratitude you owe to that Church from which you have imbibed your Christian principles and knowledge; in whose consolations, I trust, you delight—and may you all experience their efficacy at the closing hour of your existence—not to give your consent to a measure which will destroy the Protestant Church of Ireland, without benefiting the poor Roman Catholic population; which will starve the meritorious dispensers of God's truth, without adding to the real comforts of those who are engaged in diffusing religious knowledge under a different form—a measure, of which it is not too much to say, that it commences with spoliation and sacrilege, and must end in ruin and confusion."

The .result of the debate was that all the obnoxious clauses were struck out of the bill, and it was then dropped by the ministry.

A third and last time, in 1836, the same measure reappeared and met with the same fate; but on that occasion Bishop Blomfield was too ill to be present in Parliament. He had, however, already done good service in the cause; and it is owing to his vigorous opposition, as one among the obstacles which prevented it, that the destruction of the temporalities of the Irish Church has, at least, been deferred for more than a quarter of a century.

We now return to 1834, in which year Bishop Blomfield delivered his second Charge to the clergy of his diocese. It was the misfortune of the circumstances of that time, that they compelled those who had the interests of the Church of England at heart, to dwell more upon her title to the endowments which she possessed, and less upon her moral and spiritual aspect, than they were naturally inclined to do. When every act of the Church, as represented by her clergy, was looked upon with the jealousy not of friends anxious for her reputation, but of foes rejoicing in the hopes of her disgrace; when no artifice nor falsehood was spared to prejudice her in the eyes of the people, by "the Ecclesiastical Knowledge Society," and other associations of the more rancorous Nonconformists; when Mr. Binney, a well-known dissenting minister, declared that the Established Church "is a great national evil; is an obstacle to the progress of truth and godliness in the land, and *destroys more souls than it saves;*" when a document, circulated among those least able to ascertain the falsehood of its assertions, stated as the income of each bishop *the sum total of the value of all the preferments in his gift,* in addition to the revenues of the see itself; by which means the Archbishop of Canterbury was represented as receiving £70,000, and the Bishop of Durham £91,000 a year, and even Llandaff, not worth £1,000 a year, was invested with the liberal income of £13,000;—when such was the position of the Church in England towards her enemies, it was her claims as an establishment which required to be put forward the most prominently. It is on these, accordingly, that the Bishop mainly insists in this Charge. After remarking upon the spirit of innovation now abroad, and the increasing bitterness and unfairness of some, though not all, of the dissenting body, he proceeds to show that the Church has a just claim to her endowments, which, so far from being excessively large, are quite inadequate to the purposes for which they were intended; the deficiency of churches and clergymen in large towns being a patent fact. But at the same time he expresses his opinion that Church reform, in the sense of a redistribution of Church revenues, is highly to be desired:—

"It is undoubtedly incumbent upon us, to do all in our power to render the Established Church efficient in the highest possible degree; and if any changes can be made in the actual distribution of its resources, which would have a clear and unquestionable tendency to increase its usefulness, and which are not inconsistent with the fundamental principles of its polity, we ought surely to carry them into effect, even if it be at the expense of some of those ornamental parts of the system, which have their uses, and those by no means unimportant; yet not so important as that they should be suffered to stand in the way of improvements, calculated to enhance and give lustre to the true beauty of the Church—the beauty of its holy usefulness."

It seems from these words that the Bishop was already prepared for the step which was afterwards the most unpopular of those recommended by the Ecclesiastical Commissioners—the reduction of the cathedral establishments. But that he was not prepared to go further in altering the management of Church property than those changes which have eventually been made, is clear from the following sentence:—

"It will only be step by step that we can advance towards the wished-for consummation (the improvement of small benefices), unless we are prepared to hazard the fearful experiment of fusing the whole mass of ecclesiastical property in the crucible of reform, in order to produce that which, even if it were brought about by gentle means, would be most detrimental to the interests of religion—a perfect equality of preferment."

Other points are also touched upon in this Charge: such as the gradual extinction of pluralities; the National system of education, and the improvements of which it was susceptible; the office of rural deans, which he said he had revived with good effect in the preceding year; and the proposed alterations in the Liturgy, for which, though not denying some to be desirable, he thought the present times of agitation no fitting opportunity; adopting as his own the opinion of John Newton, expressed nearly forty years before: "As to our Liturgy, I am far from thinking it incapable of amendment; though, when I consider the temper and spirit of the present times, I dare not wish that the improvement of it should be attempted, lest the remedy should be worse than the disease." On the subject last mentioned, he had thus expressed himself to Archdeacon Lyall:—

"LONDON, *Nov.* 21, 1833.

"MY DEAR ARCHDEACON,—I am much disposed to concur with you in thinking, that whatever improvements might be suggested in the formularies of our Church (and I think that of some they are clearly susceptible), the present is not a proper time for raising the question; and that is one reason why I deprecate the proposed Association [projected at Oxford to resist reform in the Liturgy, but never brought into operation], as being calculated to bring into direct collision those who hold opposite opinions on this subject. The improvements of which the Liturgy is susceptible, are not, in my judgment, of such a kind as to render it the positive duty of those who think them such, to insist upon them as indispensable, at the risk of the Church's peace and safety. I have, therefore, uniformly deprecated the agitation of this question in times of unsettledness and danger; but I think nothing is more likely to *force* us upon the discussion of it, than the measures now in progress. I have never yet expressed in public any opinion on the subject; and I would gladly be spared the necessity of doing so; but if I am compelled to it, I must speak the truth. In the *Articles* of our Church I have never been inclined to admit any change, and am now less inclined than ever; nor can I make up my mind to consent to a new translation of the Scriptures, of which poor Bishop Lloyd was desirous, and which many are still anxious to have. I confess that the crude propositions, which have been thrown out within the last two or three years for the alteration of the Liturgy, have made me very doubtful about meddling with it at all. And yet, surely, there is very little in the changes which Berens suggested, that would not be an improvement. I think there has been, and is, so little reason to apprehend any attempt of importance to alter the Liturgy, that the question might have been suffered to rest for the next few years at least; and there was, I think, something like a pretty general understanding to that effect, when the Association stood forward and broke the truce. I believe you are much mistaken as to the difficulty of carrying through the House of Lords a proposal for a Commission to revise the Liturgy. And it is because I do not believe that there *would* be any difficulty, that I would fain prevent the question from being brought forward. The public mind, whether in or out of the Church, is not in a proper state for the consideration of the subject. Why then should the Association *insist* upon its being kept in sight?"

On presenting a copy of his Charge of 1834 to the eminent Nonconformist, Dr. Pye Smith, the Bishop received the following acknowledgment:—

"MY LORD,—I beg to return my thanks for your lordship's kindness in presenting me with your late Charge to the clergy of your diocese, which I have read with much interest, and the sincerest wish and prayer that its great objects, in the best quality and the highest degree of the religious cultivation of our country, may be attained in the most perfect manner. For this, our only sure resource is in the grace and power of our Divine Saviour: and, if we seek more and more to resemble Him in spirit and conversation, our reliance will meet His effectual support.

There are a few observations and implications respecting Dissenters which, I am persuaded, have arisen from mistake. But I have not time, nor could I be so vain as to intrude upon your lordship's time, for any noticing of them. It is one of the unhappy effects of controversy, which yet is necessary in this state of trial and purifying, that it acts as the tides and storms do upon some coasts, throwing up rows of sand-hills, barren in themselves and preventing enlarged views. To such more just and comprehensive views, however, by the Divine blessing and mercy, we hope to attain. There is much misunderstanding on both sides. Let us more fervently pray that God may give light and Christian love to all."

On the question of Church reform in general, Bishop Blomfield had now to show in his place in Parliament, in answer to the attacks to which the Church was exposed, that though by no means indisposed to salutary changes, he could meet resolutely the bigotry and misrepresentation which were rife on the subject. To the peers who descanted upon the abuses existing in the Establishment, he replied that the heads of the Church, so far from desiring to retain these abuses, had long been consulting how they might best be removed. Sometimes he employed a sharper weapon of defence. When Lord King, descanting upon the enormous wealth of the Church, declared "that it was not to be endured that deans and chapters, registrars, and all the other rubbish of cathedrals should take so much; he would only say, get you gone, give place to honest men;" and ended by moving for a return of the cathedral bodies who enjoyed the great tithes of small benefices; the Bishop threatened a motion to include *lay* impropriators in the returns; and Lord King had to withdraw his motion. And when Lord Tavistock, the heir of Woburn Abbey, spoke of the abuses of non-residence and pluralities, he replied:—

"Pluralities are an abuse which we have inherited from the Papal dominion, and their continuance has been rendered absolutely necessary by the continuance of one of the greatest abuses possible—that of impropriations. No one can have a clearer perception of what I mean than the noble marquis. I hope that he will not take me to be offensive, when I say that it is impossible to do away with pluralities without doing away with impropriations; that it is impossible to ensure competent instruction for each parish throughout the country, unless the means requisite for that purpose are provided; and I know no means of doing that, except those which might be devised, if the great impropriators were to come forward and contribute their share towards the accomplishment of the desired object. That, indeed, would be a real reform."

Indeed, in effecting such reforms within the Church as he was then competent to accomplish, the Bishop already, in 1834, began to find some of those difficulties, and to meet with some of that unpopularity which beset him as an Ecclesiastical Commissioner a few years later. The reader of Sydney Smith's 'Letters to Archdeacon Singleton' may remember that in the third letter he speaks of the living of Edmonton as "a parish which the Bishop of London has the greatest desire to divide into little bits," and that in the first letter he relates some particulars of this division, which it seems the Bishop was not able to effect, owing to the opposition of the Dean and Chapter of St. Paul's, of which body Sydney Smith was a member. The Canon probably did not recollect a letter which the Bishop had written to him on this subject in answer to one which has not been preserved, but in which Sydney Smith seems to have applied the *argumentum ad hominem*, with what success may be judged from the Bishop's reply:—

"LONDON HOUSE, *May* 3, 1834.

"MY DEAR SIR,—The parallel, or rather contrast, which you have drawn is a very good argument for dividing the see of London, but none whatever against dividing the vicarage of Edmonton; and I still hope that you may, upon further consideration, be as willing to consent to one of these partitions as I am to facilitate the other. Whether I should readily acquiesce in a new arrangement during my own incumbency is a question which I need not at present determine; but you appear to have overlooked the consideration that no diminution of Mr. Warren's income will take place, because the proposed division would not be carried into operation till the next avoidance. No individual could suffer by such a measure, unless it be the incumbent of Edmonton *in posse*, or the individual who expects to nominate his friend to the vicarage, which, in case of a division, would be only a poor pittance of £1,300 per annum.

If you are of opinion that the district of Winchmore Hill will be as well provided for, in respect of pastoral superintendence, by placing there a Curate with from £40 to £100 for his stipend, arising from the precarious source of pew rents (for the Vicar is not bound to pay a farthing), as by entrusting it to an incumbent minister with £300 per annum, all I can say is, that I should be glad to hear your reasons, which, whatever they may be, I shall expect to hold good for the maintenance of pluralities to any extent.

You say that there has been no complaint of any neglect of duty at Winchmore Hill. But there *has* been a complaint of the inadequacy of the stipend, and it was only at my earnest request that Mr. ——, who, at the time when he made the complaint, received only £40 per annum from the pew rents, consented to remain for a time at his post. That there has been no complaint of neglect of duty proves that the clergyman has been faithful, not that he is competently provided for. The Canons of St. Paul's, London, may not, perhaps, '*see* the evil' which the Curate of St. Paul's, Winchmore Hill, *feels*.

With respect to your remaining argument, I would remind you that the pastoral care which a vicar does, or ought to, exercise over the individual members of his flock, is so different in kind from that which a bishop has to exercise over the clergymen of his diocese, that no fair reasoner would seek for an analogy between the two.

You see that I have written to you very freely, and I have done so because you have set me a most encouraging example. In conclusion, I can only say that you have my full and free permission to urge the expediency of dividing the larger bishoprics, and of abolishing cathedral sinecures, as earnestly and as sincerely as I have urged, and shall continue to urge, the propriety of dividing the vicarage of Edmonton. Nay more, if you will assist *me* in the one project, I may, perhaps, give *you* a helping hand in the other, if both of us are not spared all trouble on such subjects."

In the same year Bishop Blomfield published two sermons, which had been preached at the consecration of various churches, 'on the uses of a standing Ministry and an Established Church.' In these he insisted upon the duty of the State to promote and maintain religion, and showed that the Established Church keeps Christianity alive in places, and under circumstances which, without her, would lose it altogether. He illustrated the evils which result from the absence of religious establishments by the example of America, where the spiritual wants of millions scattered over the thinly peopled States were supplied only by the desultory visits of itinerant preachers, and by the short-lived stimulus of revivals.

On the position of the Church towards the Dissenters, the necessity of reform, the extent to which such reform could safely be carried, and other topics of interest which came into prominent notice during the period to which this chapter refers, the opinions of Bishop Blomfield may be gathered from the following letters:—

Answer to a Memorial on Church Reform—An acting Convocation not desirable.

"LONDON, *Jan.* 22, 1833.

"REV. AND DEAR SIR,—It is only within the last few days that I have received your letter, dated the 9th of January, accompanying a memorial which has been addressed to me by eleven clergymen of my diocese, yourself one of the number, on the subject of Church Reform.

The memorial states that you are desirous of making known through me, as your Diocesan, the sentiments which you entertain upon that important subject; but in your letter you inform me that it is your intention to adopt a much more effectual method of giving publicity to your sentiments, by printing the memorial, without asking my opinion as to the expediency of such a proceeding.

I am also informed that, together with the memorial, you are about to print 'a petition to his Majesty to appoint a Convocation,' which has been transmitted to his Majesty not through me, as your Diocesan, but through the Secretary of State.

Of that petition I have not been favoured with a copy; but I presume that it prays his Majesty not to *appoint* a Convocation (for a Convocation has been actually summoned, by virtue of the King's writ, to assemble on the 30th instant), but to empower that body so assembled to deliberate upon such matters as may be submitted to it, touching the good of the Church.

I am much inclined to doubt whether it be expedient to revive the ancient functions of Convocation under its present constitution; but if this should be done, or if in any other way the subjects referred to in your memorial should come under the consideration of a body duly authorised to entertain them, it will be necessary that I should enter into the discussion of them unfettered by any previous expressions of my opinion upon particular measures of reform. I should therefore use great reserve in answering a memorial addressed to me by the clergy at large of my diocese, assembled by competent authority for the purpose of making known to me their deliberate opinions upon these important and difficult questions. You will not, I hope, take it amiss, if I practise at least an equal degree of caution, in replying to a communication made to me by a small number of the clergy, especially when I am informed that the public are to be made acquainted with it.

I shall therefore content myself with assuring you of my earnest desire to promote all such measures of improvement as may be likely, under the Divine blessing, to give increased efficiency to the Established Church, as a chosen and honoured instrument for imparting to the people of this country the truths and consolations of the Gospel, and for upholding the honour of God's holy Name. Whatever measures shall be proved to have a clear and indisputable tendency to these great ends will, I hope, be adopted, from an honest desire to make the Establishment what it is intended to be. But I need hardly remind you that this desire may be entertained by many who differ as to the best method of securing its accomplishment.

I thank you sincerely for the assurance of your prayers. We stand, indeed, greatly in need of mutual intercession to Him, whose cause we have in hand, for a more than ordinary measure of His grace at this trying season, that we may be guided to desire and to attempt that which is best, not for ourselves personally, but for His Church and for the eternal interests of our brethren."

Henry Drummond, Esq. to the Bishop of London, on the supposed gifts of Tongues.

"ALBURY PARK, *Sept.* 14, 1833.

"MY DEAR LORD,—The propriety of making known to your lordship the truth of what God is now doing in His Church has often crossed my mind, but I could not perceive that any duty pointed positively the one way or the other. Recent circumstances, however, have brought your lordship in direct contact with the subject; and, in now sending you a copy of a narrative of what has taken place here, I beg you to pardon me if I offend in doing so, or in having withheld it so long. The theory of the question is ably stated in a work entitled, 'General Delusions of Christians on the ways of God's Revealing Himself,' published by Seeley, and also in 'Boys' (?) Suppressed Evidence.' The best work on the other side, though partly of theory and partly of fact, is that by Goode; all the other statements which I have seen are pure falsehoods, especially in the *Record* newspaper. It is needless [useless?] to deny that every feeling, and all *primâ facie* reasoning drawn from the experience of anything that has occurred since the days of the Apostles, is against it, and that therefore we come to the consideration of the case with a load of 1,800 years of prejudice on our minds; but there is some consolation in the reflection that your lordship has ability to separate what is sound from what is unsound in the argument, and courage to follow what you believe to be right; nevertheless, I must not be unfaithful to God or to you, by concealing my conviction that to make any human being receive a truth of God, whether he be learned or an idiot, requires a power as omnipotent as that which raised Jesus from the dead...."

The Bishop of London to Henry Drummond, Esq.

"FULHAM, *Sept.* 26, 1833.

".... I thank you for the statement which you have been so good as to send me; and you will not be offended if I say, that I lament the circumstances which it details. With respect to the special gifts of the Holy Spirit, to which you and others lay claim, I think it sufficient to observe, that as every man appears to be the sole judge of his own inspiration, and no one pretends to afford to others any sure test by which they may try his spirit, neither I nor any other person can be justly censured as incredulous, if we withhold our assent. With regard to the occurrence alluded to in your letter, as having brought me more directly in contact with the subject, I have, as a ruler of the Church, a very plain rule to guide me—'Let all things be done decently and in order;' 'God is not the author of confusion, but of peace.' That He may be pleased to guide us both into the way of truth, which is the way of peace, is the sincere prayer of, &c. &c."

The Rev. John Clayton[1] *to the Bishop of London, on the feeling of moderate Dissenters towards the Church.*

"CHAPEL HOUSE, POULTRY, *Jan.* 20, 1834.

".... Permit me to assure your lordship that not only are there many hundreds of the citizens by whom I am immediately surrounded, but a large mass of both minis-

[1] Formerly minister of the Poultry Chapel.

ters and their people in London and in the country, who totally disapprove of the violent and pugnacious procedures which a few vehement partisans now adopt and pursue; and we hope that we shall not be confounded with those, whose tempers are our dishonour, and some of their measures injurious to their true interests. Your lordship would justly dispute my sincerity, if I did not avow my preference for a liberal and catholic Congregationalism; but in so doing, I should be unjust to myself, were I not also to add, that as I enjoy the right of private judgment, and can peacefully pursue my official course, I cheerfully yield the same right to others, and quietly leave them to manage their own religious economy.

That there are some irksome pressures on Dissenters, and which are felt more powerfully in the country than in the metropolis, your lordship is well aware, and I rely on the wisdom, candour, and sound patriotism of the administration, and on the known principles of our beloved Sovereign, for their gradual mitigation and ultimate removal."

The Bishop of London to the Rev. J. Clayton, in answer to the last.

"FULHAM, *Jan.* 31, 1834.

"DEAR SIR,—I beg to thank you for your letter of the 20th inst., and to express the pleasure which I received from the sentiments therein contained. That pleasure, however, is not mingled with any feeling of surprise; because the experience of some years has taught me to appreciate the candour of your mind, and the moderation of your views. You may be assured that even if I had not heard from you on the subject, I should not have imagined that you were in any degree answerable for the violent, and I must add, unchristian proceedings to which you refer, and of which I am persuaded that a very large part of the Dissenting body by no means approve.

Christian charity and moderation apart, it surprises me that the parties, who are now holding such intemperate and threatening language, do not perceive the impolicy and imprudence of their proceedings. Whatever they may think, they are very far from being strong enough to carry any violent measures into effect; and their attempt to do so, frustrated as assuredly it will be, will render more difficult the attainment of those objects, which they might with much greater reason set themselves to obtain. Such conduct is equally embarrassing to the friends of moderation, both amongst Churchmen and Dissenters; and to the former more especially, it renders it exceedingly difficult to persevere in a course of conciliation.

I hope I shall never be so unjust, as to confound the more candid and peaceable part of the Dissenting body with its violent and noisy champions. But there are many men, and moderate ones too, who will ask the question, If the more respectable portion of the Dissenters disapprove of the calumnies and invectives against the Established Church which are issued by the Ecclesiastical Knowledge Society, and Dr. Bennett or Mr. Binney, &c., why do they not disavow them? The public in general suppose these gentlemen to be the acknowledged, if not the official organs of the general body of the Dissenters. I am very much afraid, that a war is beginning between the Dissenters and the Church, into which the latter will have been driven by measures of which it is impossible that the Christian public should approve; and although I have not the least doubt, but that the issue of the conflict will be honourable and advantageous to the Church, I grieve to think, that the great gulf between us will be widened by the efforts of the combatants; and that the cause of Christian charity will suffer.

May the Lord avert such an issue, and disappoint my forebodings! This is a prayer in which I am sure you will heartily join with,

Dear sir,

Your faithful servant,

C. J. LONDON."

It was at this time, when a member of the Poor Law Board, and subsequently of the Ecclesiastical Commission, that Bishop Blomfield had greater opportunities than at any former period of his life for displaying his powers as a man of business, and disproving the assertion of Fuller, the Church historian, that spiritual men are generally left-handed in secular affairs. His clear head, accurate knowledge, and rapid despatch of business, drew from the laymen who were associated with him at this time a sincere tribute of admiration. One of them, Mr. N. W. Senior, writes thus to the editor:—

"Your father's services, first in the Poor Law Commission and afterwards in carrying the Poor Laws' Amendment Bill, cannot be too highly estimated. During the two years that the Commission was at work, he was present at all our meetings, never fewer than once a week, often more numerous. He brought to them great knowledge both of principles and of details, unwearied attention, and, what was equally important, undaunted courage. Much that we had to propose was opposed to the interests, and more to the prejudices, of powerful bodies and individuals. But your father was undeterred by the invidiousness of the task which he had imposed on himself.

I do not believe that we could have agreed to our Report, in the form in which it was presented, or have carried the bill, as it was carried, through the House of Lords, if the courage and authority of your father and of the late Bishop Sumner had not supported us."

Indeed, even the duties which lay more immediately within his province as Bishop of London, becoming as they did every year more and more burdensome and complicated, required for their proper fulfilment not only piety and zeal, but method and order, a knowledge of ecclesiastical law, a retentive memory of persons and events, readiness as a public speaker, promptness in counsel and quickness in action: and all these Bishop Blomfield possessed in no common measure. One who has long occupied, usefully and honourably, a less onerous position on the Episcopal Bench, is said to have expressed, at the meeting of a religious society, a sentiment alike creditable to him who uttered it, and deserved by him of whom it was uttered. "When," said he, "I look round upon this vast city, with its ever-increasing population, and consider the almost superhuman efforts which must be required to meet its spiritual needs, my first thought is, that I am thankful that *I* am not Bishop of London: my second (turning to Bishop Blomfield) is, that I am thankful that *you are.*"

CHAPTER VIII.

EARLY STEPS TOWARDS CHURCH REFORM—ORIGIN AND PROGRESS OF THE ECCLESIASTICAL COMMISSION—LORD MELBOURNE'S CHURCH-RATE BILL—THE BISHOP AND THE PREMIER—PUBLIC DISLIKE OF THE COMMISSION—SYDNEY SMITH—HOW REGARDED BY BISHOP BLOMFIELD—THE BISHOP'S CONNEXION WITH THE COMMISSION—ITS RESULTS.

WE now approach a period in the life of Bishop Blomfield during which it was his lot to incur, in the discharge of what he conceived to be his duty, the hostility, not of the enemies, but of the friends of that Church with which one of his opponents considered him to be more identified than any living man.[1] The subject of Church Reform, in the sense of a better distribution of ecclesiastical revenues and duties, the prevention or diminution of pluralities and non-residence, and the augmentation of poor benefices and endowment of new ones, was one which, in common with all who noted the signs of the times, he had long been accustomed to consider, and which the agitation of Parlia-

[1] "When the Church of England is mentioned, it will only mean *Charles James of London*, who will enjoy a greater power than has ever been possessed by any Churchman since the days of Laud, and will become the *Church of England here upon earth.*"—*Sydney Smith's First Letter to Archdeacon Singleton.*

mentary Reform, in 1831-32, and the unpopularity of the Church thereupon ensuing, had brought into special prominence. In 1832 Bishop Blomfield thus expressed his sentiments on the subject to Archbishop Howley:—

"LONDON, *Dec.* 11, 1832.

"MY DEAR LORD ARCHBISHOP,—I have been prevented by the pressure of business from carrying into effect my intention of writing to your Grace on the subject of your letter to Lord Grey; although, in point of fact, I could certainly have found time to do so before, had I considered that I should have very little to say. The truth is, that as to the principal point which is touched upon in your letter, there is little, if any, difference between us.

I have long been convinced of, and have for some time past been urging, the necessity of a mixed commission of clergymen and laymen to consider what measures should be adopted in the way of Church reform, whether as to the establishment of a consistent scheme of discipline, or the arrangement of ecclesiastical property. Whether this commission should be permanent, and be invested with the power of initiating all legislative measures affecting the Church in its spiritual character, or in its secular provisions, or in both, I am not quite prepared to say; but that as things now are, the Church is governed in an indirect, and in some respects a merely conventional manner, cannot be denied.

There are some matters which will not wait for the investigation and deliberation of a commission, especially the question of a commutation of tithes, which must be settled at once, if it is to be settled at all[1] in

[1] This was not in fact done till 1836, when the Tithe Commutation Act now in force was passed.

any other way than that of spoliation; but I do not see how the final determination of the questions concerning pluralities, and cathedral establishments, involving as they do so many complicated interests, can be made, with any prospect of a wise and equitable decision, except through the medium of a commission. At the same time some general principles may be agreed upon, and should be declared at once, as those upon which such commission is to proceed. This would satisfy all reasonable persons, and the unreasonable it is useless attempting to satisfy.

Parliament (*i.e.* the House of Commons) would probably be jealous of any distinct body legislating, even only initiatively, on Church matters; for they may be expected to be tenacious of their own privilege in this respect precisely in the degree in which they are unfit to exercise it. But we have a right to demand, either a convocation (which we do not wish for), or something which shall possess all the advantages of a convocation without the evils which were found to result from it under its old constitution. How to secure the good and to exclude the evil will be no easy problem: nevertheless we *must* attempt the solution of it; it is impossible that the Church (in so far as it is of human institution) can go on as it is.

Never was there any order so well instituted, but that in long tract of time there will be a bending and declining from its primitive perfection, and a necessity of reducing it to its first principles."

The first public step taken in the matter was the appointment by the Government of Lord Grey of a Commission to collect statistics, as to the existing condition of the revenues and patronage of the Church. Of this Commission, which was renewed in 1833, and again in 1834, Bishop Blomfield was a member. The result of its labours was a series of tables, on the authority of which subsequent measures were based, and which amply proved the unequal distribution of the revenues of the Church, and the extreme poverty of many of its benefices; there being 4,883 which did not possess an income of 200*l.* a year. This Commission was not expected, or indeed empowered, to make any *suggestions*, being only a commission of inquiry; but the Bishop had probably already, in his own mind, arrived at the conclusion which he afterwards maintained—that the principal source from which the deficiency of the endowments of the Church could be made up, must be found in those cathedral preferments to which no duties at all, or only duties of the lightest kind, were attached. It appears, moreover, that at an early period in the progress of the question, he had proposed to Lord Grey to make use of this source of income in the case of his own cathedral: for, in 1836, he writes to Mr. William Cotton, of the Bank of England :—

"I stated to Lord Grey, and authorized you to state, that I was willing to give up the whole of my sinecure patronage in St. Paul's, amounting altogether to more than £10,000 per annum, for the purpose of endowing new churches in the populous and destitute parts of London. This was long before any commission for Church reform had been proposed."

The whole subject was frequently talked over by him with the Archbishop of Canterbury; and on several occasions he stated in the House of Lords that it was receiving the attention of the heads of the Church. The Archbishop himself stated, in 1836, that he had long been aware of the necessity of taking some vigorous measures for the correction of the abuses which had crept into the Church, and for the removal of these anomalies, which had long lessened its efficiency; that the first step which he had taken, on being called to the Primacy, was to confer with the Duke of Wellington, then at the head of the Government, on the subject; and that he had a bill in preparation, when a change of Ministry took place, which stopped for a time his proceedings. The political excitement of 1832, it was thought, though proving the necessity of change, rendered it undesirable to propose any comprehensive measure at the moment: and beyond the inquiries above mentioned, no further public step was taken. But the temporary feelings of hostility to the Church soon subsided; and when Sir Robert Peel succeeded to office, towards the close of 1834, one of his first acts was the appointment of a new Commission, which was empowered to extend the inquiries previously made, and to found upon them proposals for promoting the efficiency of the Church—partly by a re-arrangement of dioceses and equalization of episcopal incomes, but principally by the augmentation of poor benefices, and by adding to the number of the parochial clergy. This body was generally known as the Ecclesiastical Commission. No want of confidence in the Commissioners—among whom, besides the Bishop of London, were the two Archbishops and the Bishops of Lincoln and Gloucester—was expressed at the time; on the contrary, they seemed to meet with general approval.

Sir Robert Peel, writing to Bishop Blomfield in 1838, after the receipt of the Bishop's Charge, in which he had related the early history of the Commission, speaks thus:—

"I read the Charge, I need hardly say, with great attention, and can entirely confirm the correctness of the statement made with regard to the original appointment of the Church Commission, and the objects contemplated by it.

When I came into office in 1834, the public mind had been very much excited by the demands for Church reform, proceeding from very high authorities—carrying with them great weight, not only from official station in some instances (a Divinity Professor at Oxford, for example), but from their known attachment to the best interests of the Church. I wished inquiry to precede reformation—inquiry to be conducted exclusively by those who were believed by the public and by the Church to be sincere friends to the Establishment.

There appeared to be general satisfaction with this course of proceeding: the prospect of improvement, to be calmly and deliberately made, seemed to satisfy the friends of the Church, and to silence foolish and ignorant opponents. And then, *because* this result was produced—*because* the heat and excitement died away, in the confidence that the Church would undertake the task of reformation—it was discovered that there was no need for reform at all, and that any practical proceeding, of any nature whatever, towards it ought to be vehemently opposed. I have some communications on the necessity and advantage of Church reform (when it was at a distance), which surprise me, now that I refer to them, at the excessive scruples of the authors of them. The conduct of the Government in not keeping good faith partly justifies them."

The subsequent history of the Commission may be told in the words of Bishop Blomfield's Charge, just referred to:—

"Upon Sir Robert Peel's retirement from office (April, 1835), the proceedings of the Commission were for a time suspended; but as soon as Lord Melbourne had settled the new Administration, he made known to the Archbishop the wish of the Government that the Commission should be renewed, with the change of those Commissioners only who had been members of the late Administration [Lords Melbourne, Lansdowne and John Russell taking the places of Sir Robert Peel and his colleagues]. Before the other Commissioners acceded to this proposal, they required a pledge from the Prime Minister, that they should be suffered to proceed on the same principles, and with the same views, which had been originally contemplated; and that no measure affecting the property of the Church should be introduced into Parliament, with the consent or sanction of the Government, except such as should consist with their recommendations. That pledge was given. Without it, the other members of the Commission would certainly have declined continuing to act; but having received it, they did not consider themselves at liberty to retire from the performance of the task which they had undertaken—the object of their appointment being unchanged, and the principles upon which they had up to that time proceeded being distinctly recognised by the Government, as those by which their future deliberations were to be shaped. The new Commission was accordingly issued, and the inquiries which had been for a short time suspended, were renewed."

The deliberations of the new Commission, adds the Bishop, went on for some time with perfect unanimity. It was at this time, by an Act passed in 1836, not without strong opposition in the House of Commons, that the Commission was constituted—what it still remains—a body politic and corporate, with power to hold real property, to receive episcopal and capitular incomes, and to frame schemes for ecclesiastical purposes, which, when ratified by Orders in Council, were to have the force of law. The constitution, however, of the Commission is not the same now as it was in 1836; since, by an Act of 1840, all the bishops and many other persons were added to its members.

Thus the deliberations of the Commission proceeded for some time. The Bishop writes to Bishop Monk, Nov. 28, 1836:—

"…. We have been sitting every day, except Sunday, from the 15th inst. inclusive, and have now adjourned. … We have settled the Plurality and Residence Bill without any material alteration; and the only point for further consideration in the Dean and Chapter Bill is that of the Chapter Patronage, which we think must be modified, but the precise mode of doing it is not yet settled."

But early in 1837 the relations of the Episcopal Commissioners to the Government of Lord Melbourne assumed a different character, in consequence of the ministerial proposition to abolish Church Rates, and to pay the expenses which had been met by that impost out of the incomes of Deans and Chapters. "This," says the Bishop in his Charge, "being regarded as a distinct and unequivocal violation of the pledge given by the Government to the Commissioners who had consented to resume their office in the new Commission, they announced to the Prime Minister that they could no longer continue to take part in measures, the very ground of which was taken away by the proceedings of the Government in the House of Commons. Their Fourth [Fifth] Report, which had been agreed to, was never signed;[1] and they are therefore, strictly speaking, not answerable for the Bill grounded upon that Report, which has since been brought into Parliament, but with some important additions, at variance with the Report itself and with the principles which its framers had kept steadily in view." The obnoxious measure of the Government was dropped, partly owing to the strong opposition of the Bishops.

The following extracts from letters to the Bishop of Gloucester will illustrate the progress of events at this time:—

"*Jan.* 12, 1837.

"…. There must be a Board very soon, at which it is very desirable the Bishops should be present, Lord John having some schemes which must be stoutly resisted. I rather anticipate a complete break-up of the Commission on the subject of Church Rates."

"*March* 15, 1837.

"…. The letter [a protest against the Church Rate Bill], signed by all the Episcopal Commissioners, Lord Harrowby, Sir H. Jenner, and Mr. Hobhouse, was sent to Lord Melbourne, and, as I hear, took him by surprise. He has, however, merely acknowledged the receipt of it in a letter to the Archbishop…. We decline concurring in any further recommendations while this measure is pending, as Commissioners of Inquiry; but we must go on as Ecclesiastical Commissioners under the Act of last Session, to carry into effect the provisions of that Act."

[1] The draft of the Fifth Report has this note appended to it: "This Report was not signed when the Commission expired by reason of the demise of the Crown."

"*April* 3, 1837.

". . . . The Church Rate Bill is put off till the 23d inst., in contemplation of some such break-up as I have mentioned; Ministers being desirous of getting rid of the question with which they have so unwisely embarrassed themselves. The two Archbishops and I have agreed upon a letter to Lord John, to the effect that as to the Pluralities Bill there will be no difficulty, it having been agreed upon by the Commission; and that as to any Bill relating to Cathedral Churches, &c., the Commissioners will, no doubt, be disposed to concur in any measure intended to carry into effect the recommendations of the Fifth Report, agreed to, but not signed, provided that no other change is to be made in the tenure or distribution of Church property than those which the Commission has recommended."

It was during the progress of this Church Rate Bill, while the measure was under discussion in the House of Commons, that Bishop Blomfield had one of his most successful engagements with Lord Melbourne in the other House. The Archbishop of Canterbury having taken occasion, when presenting petitions against the abolition of Church Rates, to protest against the proposed Bill, and to exonerate the Bishops on the Commission from the charge of having approved it, the Premier retorted upon the Primate with no little acrimony, denouncing the Episcopal Bench as "ministers of peace, banded together to prevent the passing of a measure of peace," and insinuating that the Archbishop was put forward by some "who had more guile and entertained deeper designs than himself." No sooner had Lord Melbourne ceased than the Bishop of London rose. "And so," exclaimed he, "because a body of men, speaking the sentiments of the clergy, who are so deeply interested in this question, and the sentiments of the laity, who feel their interests on this subject to be identified with those of the clergy, come forward and protest, mildly and respectfully, against the spoliation of the Church, we are to be denounced with more than ordinary vehemence by the King's Prime Minister, and to be told that we are unmindful of the peace of the community, because we designate this measure as a sacrilegious act of spoliation! And so, when the Prime Minister tells us that a sacrifice is to be made to secure religious peace and harmony, we, the Bishops of the Church of England, are not to complain of it, because the only sacrifice to be made is the sacrifice of that Protestant Church of which we are the superior ministers! . . . Peace!" cried the Bishop—"produce peace! Does not the noble viscount know that this measure never can produce peace? Is he so blind to the experience of the past, as not to see that peace will never follow concession made so absolutely at the expense of one party alone? Measure after measure have we passed to conciliate Ireland, and always under the promise that they would remove contention and produce peace; and have they not all been made the substrata for further agitation? Have we not, I would ask your lordships, the confession of those who are most prominent in promoting the abolition of Church Rates—is it not their boast and triumph that this measure is only valuable to them as a first instalment? Has not an influential member of their body, at a large public meeting of Protestant Dissenters held in this metropolis, said, 'Only one step at a time; let us not meddle with other matters, for they are not relevant.' 'Not relevant!' said a Dissenting minister from Scotland, 'what do you mean? Does not this measure lead to the abolition of tithe as a necessary consequence?' The reply to this question was, 'Be prudent; only one step at a time.' Can we, then, either talk or think of peace as a result of this measure of sacrilegious spoliation?" He went on to say that the scheme of the Government had been unanimously declared by the Ecclesiastical Commissioners to be impracticable and inexpedient.

But the Whig Government was not the only quarter from which the Commission met with difficulty and opposition. Many Churchmen of the High Conservative school considered its very existence a deadly blow to the Church; others thought its constitution inimical to their interests. The amiable Joshua Watson "did not cease to regret that the composition of the board had been such as to exclude the greater portion of the Bishops, and to embody such an unequal proportion of the lay element." "Assuredly," he said of it long afterwards, "it ought on every account to have had much more of an ecclesiastical character in its first concoction, especially when it is considered that all its recommendations were to be referred to secular decision."[1] This, however, was but a mild resistance. A more formidable opposition was aroused by the recommendation contained in the Second Report of the Commissioners, that the deficiency of churches and clergymen in populous districts should be made up by reducing the cathedral establishments, and applying to this purpose the revenues of about 360 prebends which it was proposed to suppress; while a portion of the patronage of the Chapters, thus reduced

[1] Life, by Archdeacon Churton, vol. ii. p. 19.

in number, was to be transferred to the bishops of the respective dioceses. This sweeping proposition naturally met with very strong opposition, which eventually had the effect of considerably modifying it. The capitular bodies saw themselves stripped of half their glory, and no small part of their patronage; and they lifted up their voices and cried aloud. They drew beautiful pictures of the useful purposes which, certainly, cathedral bodies might have fulfilled, but which it was equally certain that, as a rule, they had not fulfilled. They represented the Commission as a body in which a few bishops had had it all their own way, and had decided matters entirely for their own selfish interests: petitions and memorials began to flood the tables of the Commissioners; and a shower of pamphlets darkened the ecclesiastical atmosphere.

Conspicuous among the defenders of the cathedrals on this occasion, was a champion whose early combats, under the blue and yellow standard of the North, had been in a cause the reverse of Conservative. Sydney Smith's 'Letters to Archdeacon Singleton,' the first of which was published at the beginning of 1837, will probably continue to be read for their racy humour, long after the particular occasion which gave rise to them has ceased to excite any interest. He selects Bishop Blomfield, the most prominent among the Commissioners, as the main subject of his attack.

"The original Commission (says he), excluding the Ministers of State and the Archbishops, was the Bishop of London, diluted with some watery additions."[1] "You have probably seen Sydney Smith's letter," wrote the

[1] Note to original edition of First Letter.

Bishop to Dr. Monk, "which is less *funny* than I had expected. I don't think the Chapters will be very proud of their advocate. He makes me out to be a sort of Dragon of Wantley."

His description of the Bishop as "a man of very great ability, humane, placable, generous, munificent; very agreeable, but not to be trusted with great interests where calmness and judgment are required," and as having "an ungovernable passion for business and a constitutional impetuosity;" and his application of Hermann's criticism on Blomfield's Æschylus, "we find a great arbitrariness of proceeding, and much boldness of innovation, guided by no sure principle," to the Bishop's dealings with the cathedrals—all this was happily put; and the defence of the "prizes and blanks" system, the sketches of the characters of Lord Melbourne and Lord John Russell, and the picture of the country clergyman, "with a second-rate wife, dusty and deliquescent, and four parochial children, full of catechism and bread-and-butter, driving in one of those Shem-Ham-and-Japhet buggies, made on Mount Ararat soon after the subsidence of the waters," are all very good reading. But when he described the propositions of the Commission as "the most awful confiscations ever known in England;" when he declared that on the tombs of the Commissioner Bishops it would be written, "that under their auspices, and by their counsels, the destruction of the English Church began," and that, now "the Church is gone, and what remains is not life, but sickness, spasm, and struggle"—he spoiled his own case by exaggeration; and when he insinuated that Bishop Blomfield's motive in proposing a change in the arrangement of St. Paul's, was the hope of securing to himself additional patronage, he lent the weight of his name to an accusation, which a better acquaintance with the object of his censure would have made him glad to retract, and which was, moreover, contradicted by the plain facts of the case; since the Bishop had resigned the patronage of sinecure dignities to the value of more than £10,000 a year.

Though the Bishop himself was justly offended at much that was contained in these Letters, no one had a keener appreciation of their humour; especially the admirable apologue in the first Letter, of the Bishops eating the dinner of the Deans and Chapters. The communications which passed between Sydney Smith and the Bishop, while these matters were pending, were always of a friendly character. Perhaps the members of the cathedral bodies would not have been very well pleased with their champion if they could have known the terms in which he wrote of them behind their backs to Bishop Blomfield:—

"*Jan.* 13, 1838.

"....I think the best reason for destroying the cathedrals is the abominable trash and nonsense they have all published since the beginning of the dispute. It is not unlikely that they may endeavour to preserve all the resident stalls in cathedrals; and, perhaps, by the assistance of the dissident Bishops and the Tories in the Lords, they may do it. But they are a miserable lot, and I should think their courage would fail. They have not the elements of sedition in them: if one Bishop was to come in his pontificals and *charge* them they would all run away, and then thank him for his charge and beg him to publish it. As far as I am concerned,

I want only justice; but if I am compelled to fight for justice [this was before the publication of the third Letter], I will avail myself of all collateral topics. I would have done less than the Commission has recommended, as I stated in my last Letter; but there may be, on this topic, a hundred minds among a hundred men."

A saying of Sydney Smith's has been preserved, humorously illustrative of the view which he took of Bishop Blomfield's character. The Bishop had been bitten by a dog in the calf of the leg, and, fearing possible hydrophobia in consequence, he went, with characteristic promptitude, to have the injured piece of flesh cut out by a surgeon before he returned home. Two or three on whom he called were not at home; but, at last, the operation was effected by the eminent surgeon, Mr. Keate. The same evening the Bishop was to have dined with a party where Sydney Smith was a guest. Just before dinner, a note arrived, saying that he was unable to keep his engagement, a dog having rushed out from the crowd and bitten him in the leg. When this note was read aloud to the company, Sydney Smith's comment was, "*I should like to hear the dog's account of the story.*"

When this accident occurred to him, Bishop Blomfield happened to be walking with Dr. D'Oyly, the Rector of Lambeth. A lady of strong Protestant principles, mistaking Dr. *D'Oyly* for Dr. *Doyle*, said that she considered it was a judgment upon the Bishop for keeping such company.

In writing to a friend of the Bishop's, Sydney Smith once said, "The only fault I find with the Bishop of

London is, that he does not ask me to dinner." It is remembered that when he *was* invited, he proved less amusing than had been expected. Perhaps he was experiencing that comparative degree of nervousness which he once described: "When I am afraid of my neighbour at dinner, I always crumble my bread; I crumble my bread a good deal when I sit next the Bishop of London; but when I sit next the Archbishop of Canterbury, I crumble my bread with both hands."

To one who had so much humour of his own as Bishop Blomfield, the humour of Sydney Smith could not fail to be a source of great delight and amusement. He used to relate, with especial glee, his saying, when the Dean and Chapter of St. Paul's were discussing the plan of a wooden pavement round the cathedral, that they had only got to *lay their heads together*, and the thing would be done at once.

But with the manner in which Sydney Smith sometimes indulged his humour, and the subjects on which he occasionally exercised it, Bishop Blomfield could not help finding fault. He wrote of the Memoir by Lady Holland:—

"It is impossible for any one to read it, without receiving a far deeper impression of his extraordinary talents and great goodness of heart, than could have been caused by his conversational powers, great as they were. At the same time, I cannot help regretting that his exuberant wit was wont to overflow upon the Church, of which he was a dignitary and beneficed clergyman. The Church, like all other institutions, suffers from the weaknesses and errors of human nature; but the correctives which they require should be administered in a spirit of seriousness and charity, and especially when the office of physician is undertaken by one of her own ministers. Take the instance of Bishops, who, like most other men, do not always embody in their own persons and conduct the *beau idéal* of Episcopacy. But there have been a great many, and there are still, I hope, some, who are faithful to the requirements of their vocation; and therefore Bishops ought not to be spoken of, as a body, in terms implying a sweeping condemnation of the class.

But, objectionable as I deem this habit of censuring or ridiculing the clergy (always spoken of as *parsons*), and especially the Bishops, I find still greater fault with the use of Scripture incidents and phrases in speaking of trivial or ludicrous things. This, although not proceeding from any want of respect for the Word of God in the speaker or writer himself, has a direct tendency to impair, in those who hear or read it, that deep reverence for Holy Scripture, which every clergyman should endeavour to encourage and excite in the minds of those with whom he converses. I once took the liberty of writing a letter to Sydney Smith, remonstrating with him as a friend upon his indulgence of this habit. He took my remonstrance very kindly, and wrote me an explanatory and defensive answer, which, I believe, I have among my papers, although I cannot now lay my hands upon it."

It is not known that Bishop Blomfield ever allowed himself to transgress the rule which he here lays down, with regard to quotations from Scripture. Yet he would occasionally himself point a remark with a phrase borrowed from the Bible. When a friend of the Bishop's was once interceding with him on behalf of a clergyman who was constantly in debt, and had more than once been insolvent, but who was a man of talents and eloquence, he concluded his eulogium by saying, "In fact, my lord, he is quite a St. Paul." "Yes," replied the Bishop drily, "*In prisons oft.*" And when, at the consecration of a church, where the choral parts of the service had been a failure, the incumbent asked him what he had thought of the music, he replied, "Well, at least, it was according to Scriptural precedent: '*The singers went before, the minstrels followed after.*'"

To return to the subject of the Ecclesiastical Commission. It is well known that the principal recommendations of the Commissioners, though delayed by the pressure of the Radicals upon Lord John Russell, eventually became law, by Acts passed in 1836, 1838, and 1840. A few remarks upon Bishop Blomfield's connexion with the Commission seem to be called for before we leave this subject. He was undoubtedly the life and soul of the body. We have seen that Sydney Smith, as well as the public in general, so regarded him; and his brother Commissioners were hardly less ready to attribute to him the same prominence. "Till Blomfield comes," said Archbishop Vernon-Harcourt, "we all sit and mend our pens and talk about the weather." It is no less certain that this connexion brought upon him more unpopularity than he had to encounter at any period of his life, except, perhaps, in the controversy which ensued upon his Charge of 1842. "We knew from the first," he said, "that we were undertaking an invidious and unpopular task."[1] On the one hand, a large body of Churchmen regarded him as a rash innovator, who, in order to gratify a crotchet, or satisfy a clamour which had ceased to be heard,

[1] Speech in the House of Lords, July 30, 1840.

would not hesitate to play at nine-pins with ecclesiastical dignities venerable with the prestige of centuries; on the other, the enemies of the Established Church looked upon his proposed reforms as mere shufflings of the cards, from which no advantage would accrue to *them*. For some he did too little, for others too much. The cathedral bodies opposed him because he touched them in their interests; many who had no personal interest concerned, thought him ambitiously covetous of power or selfishly greedy of gain. Tories disliked him because he was acting with Whig statesmen, and Radicals because, though bent on reforming, he was also bent on preserving the Established Church.

The first answer to these various charges is to be found in the fact (already briefly mentioned in his own words) that the changes proposed by the Ecclesiastical Commission had been thought expedient, if not necessary, by the Bishop *long before* the appointment of that Commission, and before any popular clamour on the subject. He writes, in 1838:—

"My own opinion with respect to the correctness of these principles [laid down by the Commissioners] and the propriety of our recommendations as to their main features, remains wholly unchanged by all that has been said and written on the subject; and I believe I may say the same as to the other Commissioners. As to myself, it was not likely that I should be easily driven from an opinion which I have held *for many years*, and which was not hastily or uninquiringly taken up. I think it not improbable that the vehement resistance which is made to our proposals (a resistance which I believe not to have been by any means spontaneous on the part of the great body of the clergy, but excited by the grossest misrepresentation of the constitution, powers, aims, and proceedings of the Commission,) may prevent the execution of our plans. I shall yield reluctantly to the pressure of that resistance, because I shall yield against the convictions of my reason, and the suggestions of my conscience. I must adhere while I can to counsels which, in the depths of my heart, I believe to be such as are best calculated, all things considered, to uphold and strengthen the Church of this realm."

It may be observed, in the next place, that few, probably, would now deny that the evils resulting to the Church from the deficient supply of parochial churches and clergymen, or, as the Bishop called it, "the appalling amount of spiritual destitution," far more than counterbalanced the harm that could be done by diminishing the ancient establishments of cathedrals. His words, when defending the "Ecclesiastical Duties and Revenues Bill" of 1840, are striking on this head:—

"No person has more ample opportunities of witnessing the spiritual destitution of the country, nor more frequent occasion to deplore it, than I have as Bishop of the diocese in which this vast metropolis is situate. Weekly, almost daily, is brought under my notice some instance of the evil which results from the present state of things. I am continually brought into contact, in the discharge of my official duties, with vast masses of my fellow-creatures living without God in the world. I traverse the streets of this crowded city with deep and solemn thoughts of the spiritual condition of its inhabitants. I pass the magnificent church which crowns the metropolis, and is consecrated to the noblest of objects, the glory of God, and I ask of myself in what degree it answers that object. I see there a dean, and three residentiaries, with incomes amounting in the aggregate to between £10,000 and £12,000 a year. I see, too, connected with the cathedral, twenty-nine clergymen, whose offices are all but sinecures, with an annual income of about £12,000 at the present moment, and likely to be very much larger after the lapse of a few years. I proceed a mile or two to the east and north-east, and find myself in the midst of an immense population, in the most wretched state of destitution and neglect, artisans, mechanics, labourers, beggars, thieves, to the number of at least 300,000. I find there, upon an average, about one church and one clergyman for every 8,000 or 10,000 souls; in some districts a much smaller amount of spiritual provision: in one parish, for instance, only one church and one clergyman for 40,000 people. I naturally look back to the vast endowments of St. Paul's, a part of them drawn from these very districts, and consider whether some portion of them may not be applied to remedy or alleviate these enormous evils. No, I am told, you may not touch St. Paul's. It is an ancient corporation, which must be maintained in its integrity. Not a stall can be spared. The duties performed there are too important to admit of any diminution of the number of those who perform them. One sermon is preached every Sunday by a residentiary, and another by a clergyman appointed by the Bishop, and paid by the Corporation of London; while the non-residentiaries either preach an occasional sermon on saints' days, or pay a minor canon for preaching it. And yet if the principle of perfect integrity, as to numbers and property, is to be maintained, as the opponents of this measure assert, not a farthing must be taken from those splendid endowments, for which so little duty is performed, to furnish spiritual food to some of the thousands of miserable destitute souls that are perishing of famine in the neighbourhood of this abundance."

On this subject Bishop Blomfield never altered his opinions. On no occasion did he seem to be so much pleased with his own success in debate as by the speech of which a part has just been quoted, and in which he had replied to the Bishop of Exeter, who had attacked the Dean and Chapters Bill with considerable acrimony. A clergyman observed to him when the debate was over, "I saw that you and the Bishop of Exeter were lying in wait for each other." "Yes," replied he; "and I think I gave him as good as he brought." Archdeacon Sinclair had once occasion to visit him, at the time when these measures were being discussed, and when he was confined by temporary illness to his bed. He explained to Mr. Sinclair his reasons for the course he had taken, and defended himself from the charges which had been brought against him; then suddenly raising himself in his bed, he exclaimed with strong emotion, "They now blame me for these measures, but they will hereafter confess that those very measures have been the saving of the Church." He would often point to the new districts created in London—the endowment, for instance, however inadequate, of ten new churches in Bethnal Green out of the revenues of the suppressed prebends of St. Paul's—in proof of the greater good which the cathedral endowments were doing by their new application. He did not live to witness in the increased usefulness and efficiency of the cathedrals themselves—in the restorations of Ely and Lichfield, the resuscitation of Llandaff from its ruins, the "special services" at St. Paul's, at Westminster, and elsewhere, and the "choral festivals" at Lichfield and Peterborough—a proof that those ancient foundations gained rather than lost by a diminution in the number of their canons and prebendaries.

It is another question, and one which admits of much more doubt, how far the particular mode in which these endowments were applied, under the guidance of Bishop Blomfield, to the purposes of his own diocese, was a wise one. His object was to divide London into districts of moderate size, ecclesiastically separate from each other. He considered that "the glory of our Established Church, and the secret of its efficiency and usefulness, is the division of the country into parishes and districts of manageable size, each with its church, its pastor, its schools, its local charities."[1] If subsequent experience has tended to show that the problem which was before him could not be satisfactorily solved in this manner, and that possibly parishes of larger size, and therefore better endowed, each with its chapels of ease and staff of curates, might have met the exigencies of the case better than the multiplication of distinct incumbencies with miserable endowments, it must be remembered that the question was one which had to be dealt with summarily in some way or other, and that, being a new one, there was no preceding experience to show how it might best be treated.

Lastly, the connexion of Bishop Blomfield with the Commission may suggest the wider question, How far has the Ecclesiastical Commission deserved the confidence of the Church? It will not be attempted to answer this question here; it is to be hoped that the subject will some day be taken up by competent hands. But with regard to the subject of this memoir, it may

[1] Speech quoted above.

be remarked that it was only during the more palmy and promising days of the Commission that he was the prime mover of its designs; in its subsequent decline and fall he took a much less prominent part. It was begun under good auspices, being the child of the Government, not of Lord Melbourne, but of Sir Robert Peel, whose party were universally regarded as the firm friends of the Established Church. It found a precedent in that Commission which in the reigns of Henry VIII. and Edward VI. undertook to reform the ecclesiastical laws; and it was received at first with almost general applause. But when it touched vested interests, it became unpopular; and when it began to betray the inherent weakness of human things; when it was found parsimonious where it was expected to be liberal, and liberal where it might well have been parsimonious; when the bills of solicitors and the palaces of bishops swallowed up the hopes of lean and houseless incumbents, it came to be looked upon only as a melancholy illustration of the truth—

> "Omnia fatis
> In pejus ruere, ac retro sublapsa referri."

Still, while we point to what the Ecclesiastical Commission has failed to do, it would be fair to remember what it has actually done. By equalizing the incomes of bishops, it has made translations unnecessary, and has set free for the benefit of the parochial clergy benefices and dignities previously held in commendam; by the re-arrangement of dioceses, it has made efficient episcopal superintendence a possibility; and, in the instances of Manchester and Ripon, it has at least established the principle, that increase of population requires increase of bishops. It has almost entirely removed the crying evils of pluralities and non-residence; and if its main objects, the increased provision for the pastoral superintendence and religious instruction of the people, has not been attained to anything like the extent which its projectors and original members anticipated, still what has been effected in this way is by no means inconsiderable. In the course of twenty-five years, a sum of £108,500 has been added to the annual incomes of the parochial clergy, representing, if capitalized, a sum of more than three millions sterling; and this has been so apportioned, that while 1,100 existing benefices have been augmented, 288 new districts have been formed, with an aggregate income of £37,640, and an aggregate population of 922,692; the Commission also supplying in many cases benefactions for churches and parsonage houses. The moral and religious influence which is represented by these figures is no small thing. Lastly, the Commission has done what it has done without taxing one class of the clergy for the support of another,[1] without diverting Church revenues in the slightest degree from their proper objects, without appealing for aid to an unwilling legislation, and without diminishing the usefulness and true dignity of the establishments which it has remodelled; and it has not only not checked, but has very remarkably stimulated, the liberality of private Churchmen for the objects at which it has professed to aim. It is hardly too much to say that Bishop Blomfield's noble scheme for building fifty new churches

[1] This plan was proposed by Dr. Burton and others in 1836–7.

in London, which will be noticed in the next chapter, could hardly have been carried out, if it had not been for the existence of this body to assist and systematize and perpetuate his efforts. What Sydney Smith called the Bishop's "ungovernable passion for business" would have been overtasked, and half his plans defeated, if the substantial aid of the Commission had not been at hand.

CHAPTER IX.

SPIRITUAL DESTITUTION OF LONDON—SCHEME FOR BUILDING FIFTY NEW CHURCHES—HOW RECEIVED BY THE PUBLIC AND THE PRESS—CHURCH-BUILDING IN BETHNAL GREEN—ITS RESULTS—REVIEW OF THE METROPOLIS CHURCHES FUND AND ITS SUCCESS—BISHOP BLOMFIELD AS A CHURCH-BUILDER—HIS ILLNESS IN 1836.

WHILE Bishop Blomfield had been busily engaged on the work of the Ecclesiastical Commission, he had not neglected other schemes of usefulness, in which he could effect permanent good for the Church without the use of means disliked by many of her friends. One of the most glaring evils which met him in his diocese, was the miserably inadequate provision of churches and clergymen for the rapidly increasing population of London. Scattered efforts were made from time to time to meet this deficiency, both by private individuals and by grants of public money distributed through the Church Building Commissioners. But as all which had thus been effected was quite insufficient to supply the religious wants of London, and as it became more and more evident that no assistance for Church purposes could be expected in future from the House of Commons, the Bishop determined to make a special appeal to the liberality of Churchmen for the work. Accordingly, in April, 1836, he issued "Proposals for the creation of a fund to be applied to the building and endowment of additional churches in the metropolis." He began by availing himself of the statement contained in the Second Report of the Church Commissioners, recently laid before Parliament:—

"The most prominent of those defects which cripple the energies of the Established Church, and circumscribe its usefulness, is the want of churches and ministers in the large towns and populous districts of the kingdom. The growth of the population has been so rapid as to outrun the means possessed by the Establishment of meeting its spiritual wants; and the result has been, that a vast proportion of the people are left destitute of the opportunities of public worship and Christian instruction, even when every allowance is made for the exertions of those religious bodies which are not in connexion with the Established Church."

The Commissioners then proceed to give some figures, showing that in London and its suburbs there were four parishes with an aggregate population of 166,000, church-room for only 8,200, and eleven clergymen; and thirty-four parishes with a population of 1,137,000, and church-room only for 101,682; while many of the chapels which contributed to swell the amount of church-room in these districts, having no districts assigned to them, were unavailable for purposes of pastoral visitation.

"The evils (said the Bishop) which flow from this state of things, and which must continue to increase, unless some remedy be speedily applied, are such as cannot be contemplated without grief by those who desire to bring into the fold of a scriptural Church the thousands who are now destitute of pastoral care and instruction; nor without the most serious apprehension, when it is considered, in how great a degree the stability and prosperity of a country are dependent upon the principles and habits of those classes which form the basis of the social fabric.

It is a work of prudence, not less than of charity, to impart to the multitudes who are now scarcely acquainted even with the first principles of Christianity, a knowledge of its duties and consolations, its motives and restraints; and the most hopeful method of effecting this, is to send more labourers into the Lord's harvest; to increase the number of churches and clergymen; to bring home to the very doors and hearths of the most ignorant and neglected of the population, the ordinances, the solemnities, the decencies, and the charities of our Apostolical Church; to divide the moral wilderness of this vast city into manageable districts, each with its place of worship, its schools, and its local institutions.

It is to this work that I earnestly entreat the prompt and liberal assistance of the Christian public. The examples of Glasgow and Manchester, where large sums have already been raised within the last year for a similar object, forbid me to entertain any doubt as to the success of this appeal. If this object be important anywhere, it is surely *most* important with reference to the metropolis; and I cannot forbear from indulging a sanguine hope, that an effort will be made for its attainment, commensurate with the breadth and depth of the evil which it is intended to cure. It is an object in which not merely the inhabitants of this great city, but the people of the empire at large, are interested; for the influence of the metropolis upon all the towns of the kingdom, and upon the springs of the Government itself, is every day increasing. My desire and hope is, that by means of donations, much higher in amount than those which are usually given as annual subscriptions, or for temporary objects, a very large fund may forthwith be raised, for the purpose of building or purchasing, and partly endowing, at least fifty new churches or chapels, in the most populous part of the metropolis and its suburbs.....

Upon the whole, I appeal, with no inconsiderable degree of confidence, to the humanity, as well as to the Christian charity of my countrymen, to furnish the means, not merely of commencing, but of carrying on far towards its accomplishment, under the blessing of God, this most important work; the work of evangelizing thousands and hundreds of thousands of their poor brethren; of reclaiming them from practical heathenism; of imparting to them the Word and Sacraments of God, through the ministry of His Church; of placing them under the guidance and teaching of men rightly appointed to the office, and duly qualified for its discharge; of gathering them together into Christian neighbourhoods, each round its centre of knowledge and godliness; of giving increased efficiency, and therefore increased stability, to our Church; and so promoting at once the cause of social order and true religion, and bringing down a blessing from Him who is the author of peace, and lover of concord, and the giver of national as well as individual prosperity."

While thus appealing to private liberality, the Bishop added that he by no means relinquished the claim which he considered the people to have upon the Government of the country, for supplying their religious needs through the Established Church; although he was not very sanguine as to the success of an appeal to Parliament for aid in the work. He suggested that an additional duty of 2*d.* per ton on coals imported into London, while it would be scarcely felt by the consumer, would produce a sum sufficient to provide many additional churches. For endowments, he looked principally to the property of the prebendal stalls in St. Paul's Cathedral, the suppression of which, as they should become vacant, had already been recommended by the Ecclesiastical Commissioners.

Scarcely had sufficient time elapsed for these "Proposals" to make any great impression on the public mind, when the Bishop was seized by an attack of illness, so violent as to prevent him for some time from doing active business. He attempted, indeed, to resume his work soon after the first attack; but this attempt was followed by a relapse, and he was forbidden by his physicians to attend to more business than was absolutely necessary for two or three months. He was sufficiently recovered, however, in July, to summon a meeting at London House of persons interested in his scheme, and anxious to forward it. A committee was formed, and rules drawn up for the management of the proposed fund, and the proceedings of this meeting were shortly afterwards made public, accompanied by a second letter or statement from the Bishop.

"A great effort," said he, "is required; great as men are now accustomed to measure the requirements of Christian charity. And yet are there not hundreds of persons who could give to the cause of Christ and of His Church their thousand pounds each, without sacrificing one of their comforts or enjoyments? And are there not multitudes whom we have a *right* to call upon, even for such a sacrifice, if it be requisite, in order to rescue so many of their fellow-creatures from the miseries of irreligion and vice, and to prevent the further growth of an evil which threatens our national peace and safety? The duty of contributing to this object is especially incumbent upon all those persons who are *the proprietors of land and houses* in the metropolis; and upon those who have been enabled, by the local advantages which it affords to business of various kinds, to realize a competent share of worldly goods.

An earnest appeal is respectfully but confidently made, to all the inhabitants of London and its suburbs, who possess the means of doing good; but especially to the *owners of large property in the metropolis;* to the great *companies and commercial establishments;* to the *merchants, bankers, and opulent tradesmen,* to lend prompt and effectual aid to the promotion of an object of such paramount importance; and to set an example to the great towns and populous districts of the empire, which cannot fail to exert a salutary influence upon its religious and moral state."

When Dr. Chalmers, the great instrument of Church extension in Scotland, was told of this scheme of Bishop Blomfield's, he was astonished at the boldness of the project.

"The Bishop's scheme," he said, "is on too grand a scale: advise him to be more moderate in his views: let him show the effect of the parochial system in one great parish, and he may then proceed by degrees to other parishes; but if he insists upon expatiating over the whole metropolis by building fifty churches at once, his whole scheme will be nothing more than a devout imagination, impossible to be realized."

The result, however, of the Bishop's appeal showed that he had not altogether misplaced his confidence in making it. The list of subscriptions included the names of all parties in the Church, and showed some sums which corresponded to the Bishop's description of "donations much higher in amount than those which are usually given as annual subscriptions, or for temporary objects." The mercantile firms and companies did not in general contribute according to their means and duties; but many private individuals gave very largely to the general or to special funds. The Bishop's own first donation was £2,000; two ladies gave anonymously £5,000 each; a brother and sister £3,000 each; "Commercial Prosperity," £2,000; "A Successful Emigrant," £1,000; Dr. Pusey and the Rev. C. P. Golightly, £1,000 each. Two months after the first publication of the scheme, the subscriptions reached £74,000; at the end of the year 1836 they exceeded £106,000. This was encouragement enough to begin the work at once, and the consecration of Christ Church, St. Pancras, in the summer of 1837, built entirely by the Metropolis Churches Fund, was the first-fruits of the Bishop's benevolent scheme.

An incident, which in an embellished form made a good story for the newspapers, belongs to this period in the Bishop's life. The Duke of Wellington had received a letter from the well-known horticulturist, Mr. Loudon, containing an inquiry about some famous beeches growing in his Grace's grounds at Strathfieldsaye. The Duke, mistaking the signature *J. C. Loudon* for *C. J. London*, sent his reply to Bishop Blomfield. By substituting the Duke's *breeches* for the Duke's *beeches*, the newspapers amused their readers for some time with this story; nor was it ever publicly contradicted, though Mr. Loudon, the author of the original letter, explained to the Bishop his share in the matter. The public did not know the sequel to the real story, which the Bishop himself used to relate. On receiving the Duke's letter, he wrote to say that there must be some mistake, as the only letter he had addressed to his Grace for some time past was one requesting a subscription to the scheme for building new churches in London, *and to this letter he had not had the honour of receiving any reply.*

It was, perhaps, hardly to be expected that Bishop Blomfield should be able to originate and set going so important a work for the good of the Church, without offering some handle for cavil. This was found in the fact that, by the advice of those most interested, and at the special request of many subscribers, the patronage of most of the new churches was vested in the Bishop. "Who," asked the *Times*, "is to have the patronage of all the new churches about to be built by *public contribution* within the diocese of London? It is clearly too much to put into the hands of one man." .... "The Bishop of London must not, we tell him frankly, think for a moment of appropriating so vast a property as the patronage of the new churches to himself and his see; he must cast the idea from him in an instant, if he ever harboured it, as the 'accursed thing,' or he will create a confusion in the metropolis, of which no one can foresee the issue." Such expressions could only arise from ignorance of the laborious nature of the new incumbencies, and the poverty of their probable endowments. But, besides this, the Bishop had resigned, or was prepared to resign, patronage far more valuable than that of the new churches could possibly be. Besides resigning all his sinecure patronage in St. Paul's Cathedral, "I am willing," he wrote to Mr. William Cotton, "to give up country livings for the Brazenose livings in London, an exchange clearly to my disadvantage, under any circumstances, looking at the question as one of patronage merely. . . . . A part of my patronage as Bishop of London will be given up to the Bishop of Rochester when he takes his new diocese, and I shall thus lose twenty-nine pieces of preferment, worth more than £10,000 per annum, with *no* duty attached to them, and several benefices with cure of souls. So that even if those new churches were of any value as pieces of preferment (which they are not), the Bishop of London must be a loser, and not a gainer, were he to receive them in exchange for what he gives up. Add to this, that the proposition which assigns the patronage of them to the Bishop was not mine, but was in a measure forced upon me; a large number of the subscribers having given their money expressly upon that condition."

The liberality excited in the first instance in the cause of church building in London was due, perhaps, as much to the novel and striking character of the Bishop's appeal as to the merits of the case itself. At all events, as the novelty wore off, the subscriptions decreased, and in the third year of the establishment of the fund they amounted to no more than £5,600. This diminution suggested to the promoters of the scheme the idea of creating *local* funds, and thereby exciting a livelier interest in the wants of particular districts. Hence arose several associations for church extension in different parts of London, attended by differing measures of success. Among the instances of parishes which owe their improvement to these efforts, the most remarkable, perhaps, is that of Bethnal Green. "The parish of St. Matthew, Bethnal Green," said the first appeal made on its behalf, in 1839, "containing a population of more than 70,000 souls, was lately a rural district, and contained the country-houses of many wealthy merchants. Now it is inhabited by a large manufacturing population, many of them the descendants of those who, on the revocation of the Edict of Nantes, left their country rather than abjure their Protestant faith, and many who have been driven from their habitations by late improvements in London. This growing population has been left without any adequate addition of churches, schools, or clergymen; and the parish has become the resort of persons who, from abject poverty or vicious habits, desire to live secluded from observation. It is scarcely possible to imagine an equal amount of population, in a Christian country, more destitute of the means of religious and moral instruction; and this, too, in the immediate vicinity of a city which has been abundantly supplied with churches by the piety and wisdom of our ancestors, and which owes no inconsiderable part of its wealth to the industry of the artisans and labourers who are congregated in the district of Bethnal Green." At that time the parish had but two churches, one chapel belonging to the Episcopal Society for the Conversion of Jews, five clergymen, and one national school; and the committee who issued the appeal just quoted stated that it would be necessary to create ten new districts in addition to the two already existing, each with its church, schools, and parsonage house; and that for this purpose a sum of £75,000 would be required. By the Christian liberality of many benevolent persons, and especially of Mr. William Cotton, the first promoter of the work, whose name deserves to be mentioned with all honour, the undertaking prospered in the hand of its friends to at least as great an extent as they had hoped. Within a year from the beginning of the movement more than £45,000 had been contributed; and within eleven years the last of the ten proposed churches was consecrated, and Bethnal Green, instead of two churches, possessed twelve, each commemorating in its name one of the apostles of Christ. Other religious means had followed in quick succession; there were, in 1853, ten parish schools instead of two, twenty-two clergymen in the place of three, eleven parsonages where there had been but one, six thousand children in the schools instead of nine hundred and fifty, and ten Scripture readers, nineteen pupil teachers, one hundred and twenty-nine district visitors, and two hundred and forty-four Sunday-school teachers, where these aids had before been quite unknown.

It was hardly to be expected, however, that so good and great a work should completely answer all the expectations of its promoters. There were many discouraging circumstances in Bethnal Green, from first to last. Although, in addition to the sums already mentioned, the parish obtained from the Ecclesiastical Commissioners grants amounting altogether to £50,000 for endowments, yet this was only sufficient to provide a very meagre pittance for the new incumbents, which the district was too poor to increase materially by way of pew-rents. Hence it was not always easy for the Bishop to find clergymen who by means, ability, and character were well fitted to take charge of the new churches. Moreover, the poverty of the parish was the cause of perpetual difficulties as to the repairs of the churches, and the expenses connected with them. Lastly, though the schools were crowded as soon as built, the older generation, which had grown up in a time of neglect, were slow to avail themselves of the means of worship provided for them in the churches; so that, judged only by this test, the experiment would appear to have been only very partially successful. But there are other ways, besides the attendance in churches, in which the success of a moral and religious work may be tested; and in these the results of what was done in Bethnal Green were of quicker growth. When the churchwardens presented to Bishop Blomfield a congratulatory testimonial, on the completion of the last of the ten new churches, in 1850, they said:—

"My Lord, it has been significantly said, that the churches of Bethnal Green have not answered. We are here to testify that they do answer; we see it in the good order, the improved moral and religious habits of the people; and we believe it will never be known until the last great day, when all things shall be revealed, how vast is the amount of good you have effected in the building and endowment of these churches."

When the Committee made their "final appeal" in 1853, they could point to the facts that the annual number of baptisms had increased, in ten years, from 768 to 2,030; that provident funds and other kindred institutions, conducted by the clergy, were receiving from the poor more than £2,000 a year; and that the character of the population had shown so great an advance, that while the poor-rates had been, in 1839, £15,000, they were reduced, in 1853, to £14,000, although the population had increased from 70,000 to 90,000.

Before the erection of the new churches, Bethnal Green was the resort of the worst characters, and the frequent scene of disgraceful riots. On the spot now occupied by St. Thomas's Church, with its schools and parsonage house, and by the model lodging-houses which the munificence of Miss Burdett Coutts has erected for the labouring population, were situated the notorious "Nova Scotia Gardens," in which resided the infamous "burkers," May, Bishop, and Williams, who procured subjects for dissection by secret assassination, and were convicted of the murder of a friendless Italian boy in 1826; after which time the place was known in the neighbourhood as "Burkers' Hole." When Mr. Norris, rector of the adjoining parish of South Hackney, sent his curate, the present Archdeacon Sinclair, to preach a charity sermon in the old church of Bethnal Green, soon after serious riots had occurred there, he suggested to him as appropriate texts, "The fear of the Lord is not in this place; they will slay me for my wife's sake;" and, "Take heed lest ye be devoured one of another."

The change in the character of the people was strikingly shown in their altered manner of receiving Mr. Cotton's benevolent scheme. When it was first started, the persons who went round to collect subscriptions for it were met with jeers and insults; and when the first stone of the first new church was to be laid, the people, regarding the movement as an unwarrantable intrusion, assembled in crowds to jeer and scoff; and an infuriated bull was wantonly let loose to disturb the procession. But when the first stone of the ninth church was laid, the temper of the people had entirely changed; thousands lined the street, decently attired in their Sunday clothes, and showing every mark of respect, and the working men bowed and took off their hats as the procession passed.

Other districts of the metropolis followed the example set by Mr. Cotton in Bethnal Green; and Islington, St. Pancras, Paddington, and Westminster, all owe their present provision of churches to local associations, which were suggested or stimulated by the Metropolis Churches Fund. In the case of St. Pancras, which, when Mr. Dale accepted the incumbency in 1846, contained a population of 150,000, since largely increased, a scheme of church extension started by him proved so successful that ten new churches had been built and endowed before he resigned his charge in 1860. This scheme was superintended and energetically aided by Bishop Blomfield. In 1847 he pleaded the cause of church extension in the pulpit of the mother church of St. Pancras with such effect, that a collection of 500*l.* was made at the time, and the income of the local Church Building Society, which had been only 300*l.* in the previous year, rose to upwards of 3,000*l.*, which increased, in 1848, to 7,000*l.* The Bishop further aided the work by his influence with the Ecclesiastical Commission, and by the readiness with which he counselled the vicar in every emergency, and strengthened his hands in every difficulty. "If," says Mr. Dale, "I were to state in detail the services rendered by the Bishop to the cause of church extension in St. Pancras, I should be compelled to enter into the special circumstances of every church which was built and consecrated during the remaining years of his active episcopate."

Bishop Blomfield himself, in his Charge of 1846, thus spoke of the success of the new churches in general:—

"We are told that the new churches are not more than half filled; and that the spiritually destitute, for whose good they have been erected, refuse to avail themselves of the remedy provided for them. Now, I would observe, in the first place, that the statement is by no means generally true; that many of our new churches are extremely well attended; and that where this is not the case, it may be accounted for, without supposing either that the scheme itself is faulty, or that the agents by whom it is carried out are incompetent or unfaithful. For I would remark, in the second place, that the promoters of this plan were not so unreasonable as to expect, that the good effect which they confidently anticipated as likely to result from it, would be everywhere, or indeed *anywhere, all at once*, perceptible. In neighbourhoods where there existed a comparatively educated and well-informed population, feeling the want of the Church's teaching and ordinances, and desiring to have that want supplied, it was to be expected that when a church should have been built, it would be well attended. And such has been the case. But in these great and populous parishes, where the mass of the people had been left almost entirely without the benefits of pastoral superintendence, or religious instruction of any kind, their physical and social condition being mostly on a level with their spiritual, it would have been perfectly marvellous, if our new churches had been all at once, or even within a few years, filled with worshippers. In such districts as these, the work to be done by the Church is of a strictly missionary kind. The people are to be taught the very first rudiments of Christianity; and before even that can be done, they must be brought to a knowledge of Christianity itself, as a fact. The religious sense is to be awakened in them; and the obstacles which oppose themselves to the efforts of the clergy in such a work are even greater, in some respects, than those which are encountered by the missionary in heathen lands. The change to be effected in this case must be gradual, and will be wrought chiefly through the medium of the rising generation. The school must train up a congregation for the church; while, at the same time, the influence of religious instruction will, in many instances, find its way through the children to the parents. We have, therefore, been especially careful, in such districts, to provide *schools* as well as *churches*, and schools *before* churches, where both could not be reared at one and the same time; and the good resulting from our efforts is to be measured by the effect of this joint provision, and not merely by the number of persons who have, up to the present time, availed themselves of the increased facilities of attending public worship."

From the same Charge may be quoted the retrospect of the work which the Bishop took, and his view of that which still remained to be done:—

"Ten years have now elapsed since I called the attention of the public to the religious destitution of London, by putting forth proposals for raising a fund to be applied to the building and endowment of additional churches. . . . . For the ready, and in some instances almost unprecedented liberality with which that appeal was answered, I am deeply thankful to Him from whom all good designs and all works of piety and charity proceed. . . . . Provision has thus been made for the erection of sixty-three new churches, of which forty-four are completed, ten are in course of erection, two are about to be commenced, and seven, for which grants have been voted, will, it is hoped, before long be put in hand. These churches will contain altogether about 65,000 persons, and will furnish the means of attending divine worship once in the day to 130,000. It makes the total number of persons accommodated at any one time in church 205,000, out of a population (omitting the smaller parishes) of 1,380,000; and supposing, what we by no means admit, that it is enough for each person to attend divine service once in the day, 410,000 only have an opportunity of doing so, while 970,000 are wholly unprovided for, as far as the Church is concerned. This is with reference to the metropolis at the time when the proposals were put forth. But in the meanwhile it has continued to increase at the rate of 30,000 per annum; and therefore another 200,000, at least, must be added to the number of those who require some provision to be made for even their imperfect participation in the privileges of Church-membership.

It has been calculated that the number who can be accommodated in all the different places of worship, of whatever denomination, in the metropolis, amounts to somewhere about 500,000. I believe it to fall far short of that amount, and that the number allowed in that estimate for the contents of Dissenting places of worship is much too large. The population itself being more than 2,000,000, an addition of 400 new churches, each to contain 1,000 persons, would not be sufficient to meet the actual exigencies of the case.

It is fearful to think, and yet I see not how we can escape the conclusion, that more than a million of souls in this vast aggregate of human beings are unprovided with the means of grace; and that, for want of them, thousands and thousands are suffered to pass every year into the eternal world, *in the gall of bitterness and the bond of iniquity*, having no share in the comforts, or privileges, or hopes of the Gospel. Is not this a case in which the resources of the State might be equally and profitably employed, if not to do all that is wanted, yet at least to aid the pious and charitable endeavours of private Christians? As Luther told the magistrates of Germany, that if they desired the strength and prosperity of the country, they would, in addition to all the money laid out upon walls and dykes and munitions of war, pay a few schoolmasters to teach the rising generation; so may we with truth remind *our* rulers, that if but a tithe of the outlay which is annually voted for gaols, and penitentiaries, and convict emigration, were expended upon churches and schools, it would provide that which in due time would obviate, in great measure, the necessity of such a costly machinery of punishment and reformation.

But we cannot afford to wait for the re-awakened liberality of the legislature. The Church must endeavour, by her own unassisted energies, to *lengthen her cords*, and *strengthen her stakes*, and to gather into her fold those who are now *scattered abroad as sheep having no shepherd*. A fresh subscription has been opened for continuing the good work which has been so successfully carried on to a certain point; and I earnestly entreat you, my reverend brethren, to urge upon your wealthier parishioners the claims of the Metropolis Churches Fund. Remind them, that the want which it is intended to supply, is in great measure occasioned by those very causes which augment their own resources, or contribute to their pleasures. The labourers and artisans who form the bulk of that population whom we desire to bring under the Church's teaching and care, minister to *their* wealth and comfort. Liberal as have been the contributions to our fund, we cannot dissemble the fact, that it has been raised chiefly by large donations from a few; and that many, whose connexion with the metropolis is a source of profit, or an occasion of pleasure, have not yet thrown their offerings into the treasury of the Lord's House. There are not a few members of our Church, whose incomes, derived from the successful pursuit of commerce in this great city, are so large, that they might annually build and endow a church, without abridging themselves of a single comfort or even luxury.

> 'Ego vectigalia magna
> Divitiasque habeo tribus amplas regibus. Ergo
> Quod *superat*, non est melius quo insumere possis?
> Cur eget indignus quisquam, te divite? *Quare*
> *Templa ruunt antiqua Deûm?* Cur, improbe, caræ
> Non aliquid patriæ tanto emetiris acervo?'
> HOR. *Sat.* II. ii. 100.'

The Metropolis Churches Fund continued to exist till 1854, up to which time it had received altogether about £266,000; while the whole expense of managing this large sum, during eighteen years, had only been £5,100, or less than two per cent.; and £23,000 had been realized from interest on sums subscribed, and other similar sources. Then, having done its work, the fund was merged in the London Diocesan Church Building Society, which is still in operation.

When, at the close of his episcopate, Bishop Blomfield received a complimentary address from this society, he said, in the course of his reply:—

"I have been thought by some persons to have been wrong in urging forward the building of new churches, rather than the multiplying of the parochial clergy;

but I did so as a means to an end. I considered that to build a new church in a district where the means of public worship were wanting was a sure way of increasing the number of clergymen in the district, and that it would be a centre from which would radiate all around, not only the light of Gospel truth, but the warmth of Christian charity, in the various benevolent institutions of schools, visiting-societies, dispensaries, &c., which never fail to follow closely upon the erection of an additional church. A remarkable proof," adds the Bishop, "of the justness of my views in this matter is to be found in the present state of the great parish of Bethnal Green, compared with the condition, both religious and social, in which it was before the erection of its ten new churches."

Bishop Blomfield's own contributions to the work of church building in London were characteristically munificent. From 1836 to 1854 he contributed £6,200 to the Metropolis Churches Fund; £1,000 to the Westminster Spiritual Aid Fund; the same for a church in St. James's, Westminster; £2,000 for churches in Paddington; £750 to the Bethnal Green Churches Fund; besides building and endowing a church at a cost of about £7,000 in Hammersmith, and besides his contributions to individual churches, seldom less than £50 to each, and in some cases as much as £200.

On the whole, Bishop Blomfield's scheme for church building in London was the most successful of his works, and the one by which he will be best remembered when many undertakings, to which he devoted much time and attention, and which did much good in their day, shall have been long forgotten. The time at which it was first broached was a happy one; falling in as it did with the revived zeal among Churchmen, which had recently been stimulated by external attacks, and preceding by some years the internal disturbances of which that zeal was partly the cause. It was also a work for which the sagacity and business habits of the Bishop eminently suited him; and to which he could invite the assistance of the influential laity by arguments of which they could hardly deny the force and cogency. The scheme encountered, as all other benevolent schemes must encounter, many checks and hindrances; and it was not taken up by the mass of wealthy inhabitants of London with anything like the readiness which its importance, and even necessity, required. Yet a great and permanent work was effected by the Bishop's influence and example; and it was no small thing that, when he resigned the care of his diocese, he should be able to point to nearly 200 churches consecrated in it during his incumbency.

Nor have Churchmen been slow to acknowledge what have been well called "the almost superhuman exertions of Bishop Blomfield, whose name will never be forgotten for this among other good works, that he early saw where the Church's weakness lay, and when exercising the guidance of the diocese did his best to remove it."[1] Differently judged as he has been by different men on other subjects, his wisdom, his labours, and his munificence on *this* point have rarely been questioned. And if that which, when it was first proposed, appeared to be so vast an undertaking, that many excellent persons thought it impossible to be realized, has yet, when accomplished, proved by no

[1] Quarterly Review, Jan. 1861.

means sufficient to cope with the evils which it was intended to meet; if it be true that "thousands and tens of thousands of human beings are living, as for years they have lived, in Shoreditch, in Bethnal Green, in Stepney, in Islington, aye, and in Marylebone, St. George's, Hanover Square, and St. James's also, for whose souls no one appears to care, and to whom the great truths of the Gospel are practically as little known as if the land of their birth were a heathen land, and not the great bulwark of Protestant Christianity;"[1] if other means besides those devised by Bishop Blomfield for his diocese, have been found necessary to effect the objects which he had at heart, and even these have in some measure failed of their end: yet honour is none the less due to him who first originated this great Christian work, who first opened the eyes of the wealthier inhabitants of London to the startling fact, that they were allowing to grow up around them, at their very doors, an immense population to whom all that sanctifies, that elevates, that cheers human life, must of necessity, unless a speedy remedy were found, be almost unknown.

It has been mentioned that the works upon which Bishop Blomfield was engaged in 1836, were temporarily interrupted by a serious illness. Prayers were offered up for his recovery in most of the churches of the diocese, and in some Dissenting meeting-houses. During this illness, in his hours of enforced idleness, his mind would often revert, as it always did under similar circumstances, to the classical studies of his earlier life; and he amused himself by turning the greater

[1] Quarterly Review, Jan. 1861.

part of Gray's "Elegy in a Country Churchyard" into Latin verse. But the subject that was uppermost in his thoughts was his scheme for building fifty new churches; and when he could not write, he dictated many letters on this subject. Soon after his first attack, when well enough to go out for a drive with his wife, one of the carriage-horses was seized with a fit. The Bishop jumped out and held the wheel of the carriage, to prevent its backing into a gravel-pit; and this exertion was followed by a relapse, which left him for some time perfectly helpless.

On his recovery from this illness, in the autumn of the same year, he was gratified by receiving from the archdeacons and clergy of the diocese, an address acknowledging his labours as their Bishop, and congratulating him on his restoration to health. The President and Fellows of Sion College, in a separate address of the same nature, ventured to remonstrate with him on the excessive labour which he underwent in the discharge of his duties, and to suggest to him that in future he should be more sparing of himself. In his reply, the Bishop said:—

"With respect to my personal welfare, I am deeply sensible of the kindness which has prompted your advice, that for the future I should spare myself somewhat more than I have hitherto done. Indeed, reverend brethren, I feel it to be a duty, not inconsistent with that which I owe to the great Head of the Church, to set a certain limit to my exertions; but while I listen to the suggestions of prudence, I trust that I may never lose sight of the sacred obligation which binds me to set an example of diligence and faithfulness to my fellow-labourers, 'neither to count my life dear to myself, so that I may finish my course with joy, and the ministry which I have received of the Lord Jesus, to testify the Gospel of the grace of God.'

Let us, reverend and dear brethren, mutually encourage and intercede for one another, and pray that in this day of trial our strength may be proportioned to the exigencies of the Church; and however disheartening may be, in some respects, the aspect of the times, let us be confident, looking to the holiness of our cause, and the might of our God, that in due time we shall reap, if we faint not."

CHAPTER X.

ACCESSION OF QUEEN VICTORIA—NATIONAL EDUCATION—SERMON FOR THE NATIONAL SOCIETY—GOVERNMENT MEASURES ON EDUCATION—OPPOSED BY BISHOP BLOMFIELD IN PARLIAMENT—THE NATIONAL SOCIETY AND THE GOVERNMENT—THE MANAGEMENT CLAUSES—BISHOP BLOMFIELD AND THE EDUCATION CONTROVERSY IN 1850.

THE year 1837 was marked by the death of William IV. and the accession of the present Sovereign. On the 16th of July Bishop Blomfield preached at the Chapel Royal before the new Queen; and at her coronation, in June, 1838, it devolved upon him, at the request of the Archbishop of York, (whose proper duty it is,) to preach the sermon, as he had done on a similar occasion before; and the publication of this sermon was shortly followed by that of another, preached at St. James's, Westminster, on "the duty of prayer and intercession for our rulers."

"To obey our governors," says the Bishop, "to honour them, to defend them with our lives and fortunes, is not enough. We must pray for them. *I exhort that, first of all, supplications, prayers, intercessions, and giving of thanks, be made for all men.* This is the general direction; and then the apostle specifies more particularly, as having a special claim to benefit of this rule, *kings, and all that are in authority.* And surely, my brethren, they have special need of our prayers.... Look at the nature of their trust, as compared with those of the other members of Christ's household. There is but one class of responsibilities which can be thought to exceed or equal theirs in sacredness or importance: those of the commissioned ambassadors of Christ, the dispensers of His holy Word and Sacraments: but if we reflect in how great a degree the efficacy even of *their* ministrations may depend upon the Christian faithfulness of the powers that be; that the prosperity and growth of true religion must of necessity be most materially promoted or impeded by the influence and example of those who are in authority; that the Church is specially commended, as to its worldly means of efficiency, to the fostering care and protection of *kings* as its *nursing fathers*, and *queens* as its *nursing mothers;* we shall see reason to doubt whether, with reference at least to the present interests of society, the office of a Christian *minister* be as important as that of a Christian *sovereign*. The conduct of the one may influence, for good or evil, the principles and conduct of a small section of the community;... but still the good or evil which any individual steward of *the manifold grace of God* can occasion to others by his mode of dispensing it, is very insignificant, compared with the consequences which result to a whole people from the piety and wisdom, or from the sins and follies, of their rulers."

The question of National Education was one which, about this time, began to occupy a more prominent place in parliamentary discussions, and in the minds of reflecting men in general, than it had hitherto done. Bishop Blomfield on every occasion strenuously upheld the claims of the Established Church to be the educator of the people; and he looked to the National Society, which had now existed for about a quarter of a century, as the principal assistant of the Church in this work. To this Society he gave throughout his life his contributions and his counsels; and not many months before his death (June, 1856) he bore this testimony to the value of its services:—

"Of the National Society it is but justice to say that the great educational movement, which for nearly half a century has been pursuing its steady course, and diffusing more and more from year to year the blessings of civilization and religious truth throughout the land, originated in a great degree with that Society, and has ever since, under Providence, been sustained by its influence. . . . And, above all, the Society, as our Church at large can testify, has been essentially instrumental in connecting sound religious principle inseparably with useful knowledge in the education of the people. The Society has, by God's help, contributed to resist successfully the multiplied attempts of philosophical or political theorists to introduce their systems of merely secular teaching, or of a religious teaching so restricted and so generalised as to be comparatively inoperative."[1]

But schemes of education very unlike those of which the Bishop approved were now being set on foot, and were known to find favour with many of the most influential members of Lord Melbourne's government, which had remained in office after the accession of the Queen. The agitation for changes in this respect was carried on principally by an association called the "Central Society of Education," which advocated a system entirely secular, and one which should not even permit any instruction in religion in any schools under its care.[2] Against these schemes Bishop Blomfield

[1] Letter to the Secretary of the National Society, June, 1856.

[2] A celebrated lecturer of those times insisted that it was of no consequence whatever what were the religious opinions of the teachers

uttered his protest on one or two occasions, in the first parliament which met under the new reign; declaring his belief that a system of education altogether detached from the Scriptures, by whomsoever it might be advocated, would never find favour with the great body of the people of England.

The issuing of a "Queen's Letter" on behalf of the National Society gave him an opportunity, in February, 1838, of preaching and publishing a sermon on the subject of education. In the preface to this Sermon he renewed his protest against the plans of the Central Society, and against the Education Bill lately introduced into the House of Lords by Lord Brougham; while at the same time he defended himself against the charge of disparaging secular knowledge.

"I wish," said he, "not to be misunderstood. I am not prepared to maintain that our present system of national education is perfect, or even very near to perfection; nor am I indisposed to take hints for its extension and improvement from the Central Society, or from any other quarter which may furnish them. In a Charge delivered to the clergy of the diocese of London in the year 1834, I expressed a strong opinion as to the importance of mixing instruction in different branches of useful knowledge with Scriptural reading, to a greater extent than had been generally recognised as necessary in our national schools. But the fundamental principles of the National Society are right; and from *them*, by God's blessing, we will not recede. Reading the Scriptures, and instruction in the Scriptures, according to the

of elementary schools; for he would provide by statute that any schoolmaster or mistress who should utter a single word in school, either for or against religion, should be liable to immediate dismissal.

doctrines of our Church, and the formation of devotional habits in accordance with her offices, are features of the system which, far from relinquishing, we must endeavour to carry out still more fully and effectively; and we will do so, if we are furnished with the means."

He fortifies his opinions by the testimony of M. Cousin, in his recently published work, "On the Education of Holland," who had admitted, almost in spite of himself, not only that religious instruction ought to be given in national schools, but that that instruction ought to be direct and particular. In his Charge to the clergy, in the autumn of the same year, he said:—

"Upon the success of the efforts which are now to be made in behalf of the National Society, will mainly depend the decision of the question, whether the education of the country is to be a religious education, and a Church education, conducted, as it has hitherto been, by the parochial clergy. I trust that you will give no countenance to any scheme, however plausible, which is not calculated to secure these objects."

It was not long before such a scheme as the Bishop seemed to have in his mind was brought before Parliament. He records in his diary, January 22, 1839: "Went with the Archbishop to Lord John Russell about education: asserted the claims of the Church to conduct the education of the people;" and the session of this year was a marked one in the history of national education. For some sessions, Lord Brougham had been in the habit of regularly bringing forward an Education Bill, which he as regularly withdrew; but now the Government determined to propose a measure of its own on the subject. The chief features of the scheme, as disclosed by papers laid upon the table of the House of Commons by Lord John Russell, in February, were, the institution of an Educational Board, consisting of the Presidents of the Council, and five other Privy Councillors, who were to distribute the grants which, amounting to £20,000 a year, had been, since 1834, divided between the National and the British and Foreign Societies; and the establishment of a model or normal school, on a non-exclusive plan, with teachers of various persuasions, different versions of the Bible, and a "rector" of no particular religion. The scheme was the more suspicious, because it corresponded in substance, and almost in words, with the suggestions of the Central Society. The proposed Committee of Council, not requiring an Act to originate it, was established at once; and the Bishop took occasion, in his place in Parliament, to protest against the mixed system of education which it was understood to be about to inaugurate, and which, he said, had "all the vices of the Irish system of education, without the justification, or rather palliation, which might perhaps be found in the very peculiar and unfortunate circumstances of the sister island." "It is supposed, indeed," added he, "that a kind of general religious instruction can be given, which will not trench on peculiar tenets; but religious instruction which is not peculiar, and grounded on the interpretation of the Scriptures, does not, my lords, deserve the name. It gives me great pain to be obliged to speak in this strong language on a system which is believed by its devisers, the Committee of the Privy Council (if it be, indeed, devised by them), to be calculated to promote the best interests of the country; but I cannot help considering that such a system would prove the heaviest blow that has been struck at the religion of the country for many years. You cannot assail a more vital part of the Church, than by attacking her through the means of education. Unless I shall find further discussion rendered unnecessary by the result of the proceedings that may take place in the other House of Parliament, I shall bring the subject forward more distinctly, and more fully; feeling, as I do, that it is the duty of the Church of England to protest against any system of education as entitled to be called 'national,' which is not connected with the Established Church."

No further steps with regard to the Education Bill were taken by the Government till later in the session; but, at the annual meeting of the National Society, May 28th, Bishop Blomfield reiterated, in a speech which was afterwards published, his sentiments on the question. He addressed himself principally to the case of those who upheld, not the entire exclusion of religion from the instruction to be given to the poor, but the introduction of a kind of religious teaching which the Bishop described as "in some cases uniform, even as the barren surface of the desert is uniform; in other cases taught with such vagueness and generality, as to deprive it of those specific qualities, which make it an instrument of sanctification and of truth; or still further, leaving it to the casual and desultory inculcation of teachers, who are to bear no part in the main process of education." "They talk, indeed," said he, "of neutrality in religion—*neutrality in religion!* To be neutral in religion (on the part of a religious teacher) is *treason* against the truth. I repeat it, it is treason against the truth; it is a dishonest betrayal of the sacred trust committed to his hands; because experience proves, if reason did not suggest the conclusion, that those who are brought up, as children, without a decided attachment to some particular form of religion, will grow up without attachment to any religion at all. I say, also, that a religion without a creed, without some recognised and particular creed, is not the religion of common sense; it is not a practical religion; it is not the religion of the Church Catholic, nor of any branch of that Church. . . . . When we contend that instruction in the truths and precepts of Christianity ought to be an essential part of every education intended for the people at large, we mean instruction in the peculiar truths and in the characteristic precepts of Christianity. I say, *peculiar* and *characteristic:* Christianity itself is an eminently peculiar religion—peculiar in its revelations, its precepts, its motives, its promises, and its hopes. Deprive Christianity of what is essentially peculiar to itself, take away the doctrines of man's sinfulness and corruption, the necessity of an atonement to be made by a Divine Saviour, justification through faith in that Saviour, sanctification by the Spirit unto obedience—take away these doctrines, and the doctrines of the sacraments of grace, and what remains? *Not* Christianity! not even a faint adumbration of Christianity; not even the *true* religion of a less perfect dispensation, but a mere *caput mortuum* of Deism, from which, when it has thus been passed through the alembic of a generalising philosophy, you will scarcely and with difficulty extract a few residual grains of cold and spiritless morality, utterly ineffective and useless for the great purposes of right conduct and peace of mind in this life, much more for those of preparation for a better.... Let all the peculiar doctrines of the Bible be blotted out, and the result will be darkness; let this or that doctrine be obliterated, and just in proportion will imperfection and dimness follow. It is only in the perfect combination and blending together of all the rays of heavenly light, beautiful as they severally appear in their separate colours, that we see and feel the brightness and vital warmth of daylight; and if it were possible, by any vast process of refraction, to separate the elementary parts of this light, in their combination so perfect and inimitable, for the purpose of accommodating a fancied preference of certain eyes for certain colours, what would be the result upon created nature? What but universal confusion and utter perplexity, almost equivalent in its effects to Egyptian darkness?" He maintained the right of the clergy to superintend the education of all children whose parents were willing to place them under their care. Not long after the delivery of this speech, Bishop Blomfield had another opportunity of making known his sentiments on the subject of education. The progress of events at this time could hardly be better sketched than in the words of Dr. Biber[1]:—

"On Friday, the 14th of June, 1839, Lord John Russell brought the question before the House of Commons in the form of a vote of £30,000, in the estimates of the year, for educational purposes. The minute of the Com-

[1] 'Bishop Blomfield and his Times,' p. 251.

mittee of Council on Education of the 11th of April, containing the details of the Ministerial scheme, inclusive of the projected normal school, and fully justifying the description given by Bishop Blomfield of its latitudinarian character, had in the meantime been communicated to Parliament; and Lord Stanley, who had taken charge of the question in the Lower House, brought on the discussion on the subject by proposing, as an amendment on the motion for going into committee of supply, an address to the Crown, praying that the obnoxious minute might be rescinded. After a protracted debate, which extended by adjournment over several days, Ministers carried the motion for going into committee of supply by a narrow majority of five, which, in the division on the grant itself, dwindled down to two. The time had now arrived for the episcopate to oppose the Ministerial scheme in the Upper House. A series of resolutions, to be embodied in an address to the Crown, were prepared, and on the 5th of July moved by Archbishop Howley in an unusually crowded House. The speech which Bishop Blomfield addressed to the House on this occasion, in support of the resolutions, was one of the most elaborate and forcible efforts of his parliamentary eloquence. He spoke immediately after Bishop Stanley, of Norwich, who, in endeavouring to vindicate the Ministerial project, had expressed not only a wish 'that all men might be brought to a community of religious sentiment,' but a hope 'that the Church of England might in time become as tolerant in practice as she was in theory.' To this Bishop Blomfield replied by observing, that 'if there was a Church in the whole world which deserved the character of toleration in practice as well as in theory, it was the Church of England. Nay, my lords,' he continued, 'I am by no means sure that she is not more tolerant in practice than in theory; I am not sure that toleration has not been extended, in fact, further than is consistent with the Church's constitution.'"

While acquitting the Ministers who had brought forward the scheme of any sinister motives, the Bishop declared that he believed them to be acting under the advice and from the impulse of another party, whose object was nothing less than the destruction of the Church:—

"That there is such a party in the country," said he, "a party bent upon destroying its best and dearest institutions, is a fact which cannot have escaped the observation of your lordships; a party, not, perhaps, very numerous, certainly not very respectable, but active, sagacious, persevering in their endeavours; constantly at work about the very foundations of the Monarchy and the Church, and knowing perfectly well, that through the medium of the Church the Monarchy may be most successfully assailed; for if the Church falls, my lords, all the other glorious and happy institutions of the country will follow; if ever the Church should be cast down, it will involve the Throne in its ruin."

In proof of this assertion, the Bishop adduced the existence and activity not only of the Central Society of Education, but of a "Society for Promoting Religious Equality," which had for its object the destruction of the Church establishment, and which had declared that, in furtherance of that object, the education question must be immediately settled.

He proceeded to show that the Church was already the educator of more than eleven-twelfths of the whole number of poor children then receiving instruction;

and if it were urged that though the number of children educated in Church schools was great, the education there given was a worthless education, he maintained that this objection really meant that the education was one which gave a prominent place to special religious instruction, not one in which no religion at all, or only a vague and general religion, was taught—plans which had been found, in France and America, utterly valueless for the diminution of crime and the real improvement of the people. He was by no means disposed, he said, to call in question the right or duty of the State to interfere in the matter of education; but he thought that that interference would be better exercised, as it had hitherto been, by the distribution of grants through the Lords of the Treasury, than by the means of such a board as the Ministerial plan proposed to establish.

"How is it possible," he asked, "that four or five political personages, holding office at the pleasure of the Crown, or, more properly speaking, of the House of Commons, whose time and thoughts are of necessity occupied with far different matters, whose habits of life are not likely to have been such as to qualify them for so delicate and difficult an office, should exercise their functions, as superintendents of general education, with all the knowledge and all the discretion requisite for such a task? and what security have we for anything like permanency of principle, or consistency of operation, in such a body? Will they not, of necessity, be acted upon, and moved as puppets, by a few artful and designing persons behind the scenes, who will pull the strings from time to time, and make the Privy Councillors gesticulate, and excite the mirth or the sorrow of the bystanders; and will themselves do all the mischief, without incurring any of the responsibility? If this be not the case—if they are not mere tools in the hands of a party, active but unseen—there is yet an alternative. The functions which they cannot perform themselves, they will delegate to their secretary, who will thus become the sole arbiter and director of popular education. And what security have we that that secretary *shall* be a member of the Established Church; that he will not be a Socinian, or a Roman Catholic; nay, what security have we for his being a Christian? My lords, I would not speak disrespectfully of any of Her Majesty's Privy Councillors, and I hope I may not have given offence by the comparison which I have made; but it is forced upon me by the symptoms which, I think, I have already discovered of this fantoccini process, in the recent movements of the Committee of Privy Council."

The State, he maintained, had delegated its functions, in the matter of educating the poor, to the Church; and those functions the Church must continue to claim the right of exercising, at least, over the children of her own communion. Not that it was impossible to educate together the children of Churchmen and Dissenters, without compromising the principles of the former:—"I have myself had the principal direction of a large national school, in which children of every denomination, Jews not excluded, were receiving education. I know that it requires judgment and kindness to maintain that state of things; but it *is* possible to avoid giving offence to reasonable Dissenters, without compromising any important principle of the Church; and in the case to which I allude, the Dissenters were content to leave their children in our hands, satisfied in general that the essential truths of their own creeds would be taught in every school which was in connexion with the Church of England." If, however, such a combination were, from whatever causes, found impossible, separate education would be far better than the schemes now proposed.

Such was the substance of Bishop Blomfield's speech upon this occasion; and the result of the debate was, that the Archbishop's motion for an address to the Crown was carried by 229 to 118—nearly two to one—and the Ministerial measure was thus defeated. The address was taken by the peers in procession to Buckingham Palace, where, of course, it met with an unfavourable reply.

"I have to thank you," wrote a lay peer to the Bishop, "for a copy of one of the most eloquent and effective speeches that I ever heard in Parliament. Notwithstanding the coldness of its reception, the address has had an excellent effect in the country. I was surprised to hear at Coventry that the discussions about the Church and about education, in Parliament, had called out in that place many good Churchmen who had before been intimidated, and that in effect the Church was making great progress there. I hope your speech will have great circulation. You have attained the difficult art of saying enough and not too much upon each subject."

It is not necessary to give a detailed account of all the fluctuations of the educational controversy, between the claims of the National Society on the one hand, and the efforts of the Whig Government, on the other, to lessen the legitimate influence of the Church; until the passing of the Concordat, which has lasted, without any alteration, ever since. Bishop Blomfield agreed with the Committee of the National Society in the view which they took of the effects likely to arise from the Government inspection, as at first proposed; and he concurred with Archbishop Howley in recommending the clergy to refuse the Government grants until the plan of an inspection unsanctioned by and unconnected with the Church should be modified; a recommendation which was very generally followed. But when the opposition thus offered by the Church had induced the Committee of Council to make considerable modifications, and so remove the most objectionable features of their plan of inspection, he could not share in the apprehensions of those who dreaded the admission of Government inspectors into their schools, even when sanctioned by the archbishops, each for his own province; for, said they, "*the archbishops themselves may become unfriendly to the Church*, and dangers innumerable lurk within the scheme of archiepiscopal concurrence."

He wrote thus to a clergyman interested in the question:—

"FULHAM, *Nov.* 6, 1839.

". . . . My opinions as to the proper course to be pursued by the clergy with respect to the acceptance or non-acceptance of the money offered by the Committee of Privy Council, is in exact accordance with that which is entertained by the Committee of the National Society, and which has been made public in Mr. Sinclair's[1]

[1] The Rev. John Sinclair, then recently appointed Secretary to the Society, now Archdeacon of Middlesex, whose services in the cause of

letter. I fully believe that the evils which are therein represented as likely to follow from admitting the principle of a Government inspection, will be the result of such admission."

But a few weeks later he wrote thus:—

"After having consented for some years, as a member of the National Society, to accept a portion of the Treasury grants, and after having declared in Parliament that we should have been contented to go on receiving money from the Government on the same conditions, I cannot now, with any regard to consistency, pledge myself to the principle of not receiving pecuniary aid from the State for our national schools, under any circumstances whatever. Upon this point I cannot give way. If the Government would grant us money, and be content, as they ought to be, with an inspection authorized by the Church, we should act very preposterously, I think, if we were to refuse their proffered assistance.

I should not object to a resolution of the following tenor: 'That this Society will not sanction the principle of receiving any pecuniary assistance from the Government for the establishment or maintenance of schools, the grant of which shall be held to confer upon the Government the right to exercise any inspection or control without the sanction of the constituted authorities of the Church.'"

The agreement between the Church and the State as to the inspection of schools, which was entered into not many months after the date of the letter last quoted, was a great relief, not only to those clergymen who

education are well known, and to whom the writer is indebted for valuable assistance in this part of the Bishop's life.

were now enabled to share the benefits of the Government grant without scruple, but also to the mind of Bishop Blomfield, who, with the Archbishop, had undertaken the responsibility of advising the National Society, first to break off, and afterwards to renew, its connexion with the State. In the compromise which was effected, he had not carried with him some of the older supporters of the Society. Mr. Joshua Watson, for instance, whose maxim with regard to the Committee of Council was *Delenda est Carthago*, resigned the treasurership of the Society rather than sign his name to the receipt of a Government grant of £5,000 for St. Mark's Training College. *Timuit Danaos et dona ferentes.*

Meantime, Bishop Blomfield did not neglect other means of forwarding the cause of education. At one time he made a considerable effort to establish in London what would now be called *middle* schools, in connexion with the Church. He wrote to Joshua Watson in 1838:—

"I have finally determined upon a Metropolitan or Diocesan Society for the purpose of establishing schools for the ten-pounders, which I do not think it will be advisable to connect with the National Society, for this reason, amongst others, that the character of superiority which I wish these schools to possess, would be impaired by their alliance with a purely *charitable* society."

A "central school" of the kind here described was, in fact, established in Rose Street, Soho, and existed for several years; but not fully answering the expectations of its promoters, it was abandoned.

But he was enabled to effect something in the same direction, when, in 1839, following out a suggestion of the Committee of the National Society, he established the London Diocesan Board of Education. This body was not intended to supersede the National Society, but to act as its auxiliary in the metropolis. Its objects were, to examine schools not inspected by the Government, to pay monitors and pupil-teachers, and to establish superior schools of the kind just described. The Diocesan Board was not supported by very liberal contributions, nor were its operations so extensive as the Bishop perhaps expected they would be; partly because the compact eventually made between the Church and the Committee of Council has rendered its superintendence less necessary. But it has been ably officered by such men as Mr. F. C. Cook, Mr. Burgess, and the late Mr. Shergold Boone; and it has aided the cause of education of London, under the guidance of Bishop Blomfield, in two principal ways—by encouraging the foundation of "collegiate" schools for the middle classes in London, some of which have been very successful; and by assisting the schools of poor parishes in reaching the standard required by Government as a condition of its grants. Since the institution of the London Diocesan Board, similar boards have been established in other dioceses, with the best effects.

To the system of mixed education established in Ireland Bishop Blomfield was always strenuously opposed; and on several occasions, in the House of Lords, he expressed his disapproval of it, and defended those Protestant clergymen who refused to assent to it, from the charges of ignorance and bigotry liberally bestowed upon them. He declared not only that it was unscriptural and irreligious, but that it failed of its chief object—the conciliation of the Roman Catholics; and he trusted that on attempt might ever be made to introduce a similar system into England.

Another part of the controversy on National Education in which Bishop Blomfield took an active part had reference to what were called the "management clauses" in the trust-deeds of National Schools. Up to 1839 no definite plan of management had been insisted on by the National Society in schools which it took into union; and in many trust-deeds no sufficient provision was made for the superintendence of the clergy, the natural guardians of the education of the poor. The Committee of Council, observing perhaps these omissions, proposed to the Society a form to be used for the trust-deeds of schools, in which the clerical element was deliberately ignored in the management. This aroused the Society to contend for a distinct recognition of the clergy as school-managers; and the controversy with the Committee of Council, after lasting for some years, was eventually settled, in 1847, under the administration of Lord John Russell, and the plan which still holds good was agreed upon. This plan Bishop Blomfield supported in his place in Parliament.

In this case, however, as in that of inspection, there were some Churchmen who considered that the Society had not contended strenuously enough for the rights of the Church, and that it would have been better not to enter into negotiations at all. Bishop Blomfield, on the other hand, contended that it would be folly in the Society to decline a compromise which, though not all that could be desired, was on the whole favourable to the Church; and that to declare such a compromise impracticable would be to give a great triumph to the opponents of the existing system, and the advocates of school-rates and mixed education. In the Committee of the Society these arguments prevailed; but there was still a small but active body of remonstrants among its members, who at length, in 1851, determined to bring this protracted controversy to a definite issue. The note of war was sounded by Mr. (now Archdeacon) Denison, who gave notice that, at the annual meeting of the Society on the 4th of June, he should move as a resolution—"That this meeting deeply regrets that her Majesty's Government continue to disallow the equitable claims of members of the Church of England: that those founders of Church-schools who see fit to place the management of their schools solely in the clergyman of the parish and the bishop of the diocese, should not on that account be excluded from State assistance towards the building of their schools." When the day arrived, the meeting was crowded by clergy and laity, and was presided over by the Archbishop of Canterbury. Bishop Blomfield, among others, was present; and this, the last occasion of his taking a prominent part in the question of education, was not the least remarkable. The speech of Mr. Denison in support of his resolution (which was seconded by Mr. Beresford Hope) was accompanied and followed by a confused and stormy wrangle rather than debate. On the opposite side Sir John Pakington moved as an amendment, "That the cause of sound religious education and the interests of the Church demand, at the present juncture, the friendly cooperation of the National Society and the Committee of Council; and this meeting, satisfied that such cooperation must be for the advantage of the National Society, as well as of the Church at large, desires to deprecate any renewal of the agitation which has characterised the recent meetings of the Society, and to express its earnest hope that the two bodies may act cordially together." This amendment seemed likely to be carried; but when the meeting drew at length to a close, and the president was about to put the amendment to the vote, the Bishop of London rose and said, that though aware that he was acting somewhat irregularly, yet, deprecating as he had done, in common with the Committee of the Society, such discussions as had just taken place, he should now venture to interpose.

"I earnestly recommend," said he, "to the present meeting to reject *both the amendment and the resolution*. I speak as a member—I hope not an inactive member—of the Committee to whom, by the tenor of the charter, is confided the exclusive administration of the funds of the Society, and the direction of its operations; and I am sure I speak the sentiments of the Committee at large, as well as from the depth of my own feelings, when I say that if a triumph be afforded to either of the parties who have moved the resolution or the amendment, the operations of the Committee will be gravely and seriously compromised. Gentlemen, and my reverend brethren in particular, I earnestly implore you to put a stop to these proceedings; for I believe that by doing so you will effectually put a stop to all further discussions of this kind. It is only in this room, and on these annual occasions, that I deprecate such discussions. I trust, therefore, that you will put a stop to these discussions by distinctly negativing both the resolution and the amendment."

Upon this proposition being made, Sir John Pakington, with the instinct of a parliamentary tactician, withdrew his amendment; but Mr. Denison refusing to follow this example, his resolution was rejected, on a show of hands, by a considerable majority.

Thus, by his weight and influence as the "*vir pietate gravis*," Bishop Blomfield was enabled to put an end to a contest which was looked upon as a pitched battle between the High Church party on one side, and the combined forces of the Low Church and the moderates or liberals on the other. And if by this course he displeased the friends of Mr. Denison, he might have the satisfaction of knowing that he was equally far from contenting the extreme section of the opposite party. The *Record* complained "that matters had been so arranged after the usual policy of the Bishop of London, that there should be no triumph for the cause of Protestant education," and feared that the "leaven of Tractarianism" would not yet be "purged out" from the National Society. "And if not," continued the Evangelical organ, "the good done is, after all, more specious than real. For the modified Puseyism practised by the Bishop of London is more dangerous, as being more specious, than the other, and is nearly as much removed from the truth and simplicity of the Gospel. It is a mere deception to imagine or to set forth that it is the very Gospel of Jesus Christ, which converts the heart and saves the soul."

CHAPTER XI.

THE COLONIAL CHURCH IN 1840—BISHOP BLOMFIELD'S APPEAL FOR NEW BISHOPRICS—ITS RESULTS—THE BISHOP'S REVIEW OF THEM IN A MISSIONARY SERMON—THE JERUSALEM BISHOPRIC—BISHOP BLOMFIELD AND THE CHEVALIER BUNSEN—THE AMERICAN AND SCOTCH CHURCHES—ADMINISTRATION OF SIR ROBERT PEEL.

WE have now reached a time at which we have to view Bishop Blomfield in a new character, as a promoter of the Church's efficiency, not only in our own country, but through the world at large. The inadequate support given by England to the work of missions among the heathen was an evil which he lamented in common with all zealous Churchmen; but the unsatisfactory condition of the Church in many of our colonies and dependencies, owing in great measure to their having no bishops of their own, was brought home to him more strongly than to any other member of the English Church. For, by immemorial custom, a jurisdiction had always been claimed and exercised by the Bishop of London, not only over foreign chaplains in Europe, but over all English clergymen, wheresoever officiating, who had no bishop of their own.[1] This jurisdiction, indeed, holds good to

[1] "The care of it [the Church of England] as an Episcopal Church is supposed to be in the Bishop of London. How he comes to be charged with this care I will not now inquire; but sure I am that the care is improperly lodged: for a Bishop to live at one end of the

this day in cases for which provision has not otherwise been made; and it is said that one of the first letters received by Bishop Blomfield's successor was from a clergyman on the further side of America, complaining of the little attention which his lordship paid to that part of his diocese. Such an authority was necessarily vague and shadowy, easily eluded, and resting on no definite law or precedent: but such as it was, the Bishop of London was compelled to exercise it, and to decide the questions which came before him as well as he could without any means of inquiring personally into the facts which formed the subjects of the appeals made to him. At the time of Bishop Blomfield's translation to London there existed only five colonial bishoprics; those of Nova Scotia, Quebec, Calcutta, Jamaica, and Barbados; and all not included in these belonged to him. Before 1840 the sees of Australia, Madras, Bombay, Newfoundland, and Toronto were added to the number; but as in all these cases, except the first, no new sees were founded, but existing ones subdivided, the area still left without any episcopal authority of its own was but little lessened in extent.

That which had been hitherto done towards supplying the religious wants of the colonies had been done chiefly through the two Church Societies; but of these the Propagation Society could at no time attract very large contributions; and of the constitution of the Church

world, and his Church at another, must make the office very uncomfortable to the Bishop, and, in a great measure, useless to the people. .... For these reasons I did apply to the King, as soon as I was Bishop of London, to have two or three bishops appointed for the plantations, to reside there."—*Bishop Sherlock to Dr. Doddridge*, 1751, *in Hawkins's 'Documents relative to Colonial Bishoprics,'* 1855.

Missionary Society the Bishop had never yet approved, believing it to be framed in a spirit hostile to episcopal government. He wrote to Bishop Wilson, of Calcutta, in 1839:—

"…. I am truly glad to learn that the Church Missionary Society has at length made arrangements which are satisfactory to you. How greatly I wish that the Society would put itself on such a footing that all the bishops could cordially join it, and that then the two great Societies should go on with equal steps, the one taking care of our own colonies, the other evangelizing the heathen."

And to a clergyman about the same time:—

"…. I have been prevented from joining the Church Missionary Society, partly because it was at one time made a party matter, and acted in seeming opposition to the Society for the Propagation of the Gospel, and still more because I objected to its constitution, and because the spirit which seemed to animate its Committee was, or appeared to be, hostile to episcopal government, with reference to its operations in the East and West Indies.

The former of these objections does not now exist to the same degree as formerly; and the latter has been somewhat lessened by the result of the communications which have taken place between the Committee and the Bishops of Calcutta and Barbados. But the regulations of the Society as to its missionaries in the colonial dioceses are not what the regulations of a *Church* Society ought to be; and such as they are, they are set at nought by the Colonial Committee of the Society, and rendered, if not wholly inoperative, yet much less efficient than I presume they were intended to be."

It was not till 1841, when certain alterations were made at his suggestion in the rules of this Society, with a view to placing its missionaries more completely under episcopal superintendence, that Bishop Blomfield consented to join it.

The Societies, moreover, if they had been able and willing, could not of themselves have supplied the particular want which the Bishop had now in view. Under these circumstances, he determined to make a public appeal on behalf of a work which should put an end to the anomalous condition of the Church in the colonies, and give her an efficiency which she had never hitherto possessed. Accordingly, in April, 1840, he published a "Letter to the Archbishop of Canterbury upon the formation of a Fund for Endowing Additional Bishoprics in the Colonies."

"The time," said he, "appears to me to have arrived, at which a great effort is required on the part of the Church of England, to impart the full benefits of her apostolical government and discipline, as well as of her doctrines and ordinances, to those distant provinces of the British empire, where, if the Christian religion is professed at all, it is left to depend for its continuance, under the blessing of its Divine Head, upon the energies of individual piety and zeal, without being enshrined in the sanctuary of a rightly constituted Church, the only sure and trustworthy instrument of its perpetuation and efficiency.

The duty incumbent upon the government of a Christian country, of making provision for the spiritual wants of its colonies, a duty recognized and fulfilled by those states which have maintained their communion with the Church of Rome, was felt at far too late a period by the rulers of this Protestant country, and has at no time been completely and effectually carried out. At present it is openly called in question by a large proportion of the members of one branch of our Legislature; and there does not appear to be much hope of our obtaining, at the present moment, in the actual state of the public revenue, any considerable aid from the national resources, for the purpose of planting and maintaining the Church of this country in its colonies. In the meantime, those colonies are rapidly increasing in extent and population, and the want of some effectual provision for the preservation of their Christianity is augmented, just in proportion as the chance of supplying it seems to be diminished.

Every year's experience tends to prove, and the opinion is rapidly gaining ground, that in our endeavours to provide for our colonists that which, in the first instance, they have not the means of providing for themselves, the ministrations and opportunities of our holy religion, it is not enough that we send out *with* them, or *amongst* them, a certain number of missionaries; and that we contribute to build a certain number of churches and schools. No doubt, even this provision will be productive of much good; but if we desire the good to be complete, permanent, and growing with the Church's growth, we must plant the Church among them in all its integrity. Each colony must have, not only its parochial, or district pastors, but its chief pastor, to watch over and guide and direct the whole. *An episcopal Church without a bishop is a contradiction in terms*. . . .

The difference between our past labours in the work of erecting colonial churches, and those which are now called for, must be this: that whereas we formerly began by sending out a few individual missionaries, to occupy detached and independent fields of labour—unconnected with one another by their relation to a common oversight in the execution of their task, although deriving their spiritual authority from a common origin—and then, after an interval of many years, placing them under the guidance and control of bishops; we should now, after having supplied the wants of those older colonies, which are still destitute of the benefit of episcopal government, take care to let every new colony enjoy that blessing from the very first."

To supply the deficiency, the Bishop said that he looked neither to the Home Government, nor to the colonies themselves, some of which had not the means, and others not the inclination to supply it. His recent experience of the "Canada Clergy Reserves Bill," which proposed to alienate the endowments of the Episcopal Church in that colony, and against which he had protested, and had assisted in modifying its most obnoxious clauses,[1] must have taught him, that aid from either of these quarters could no longer be expected. Resources must be found in the voluntary liberality of Churchmen, creating a fund which might be administered, according to the principles so long acted on by the Society for the Propagation of the Gospel, through the Archbishops and Bishops of the English Church. Large endowments could not be expected; but it might be hoped that they would afterwards be augmented by the colonists themselves. Such, he contended, was the imperative duty of the Church of England to her colonies, if she would not see the place which she ought to occupy, filled by other Churches.

This letter, of which Bishop Broughton, the first Australian bishop, said, "It is most admirable, and will entitle his name to veneration in this hemisphere

[1] He spoke on the subject in the House of Lords, April 7, 1840, and on other occasions.

as long as the sun and moon shall endure,"[1] had a remarkable effect in stimulating the exertions of Churchmen in the extension of the colonial episcopate.

In furtherance of the object, in the spring of the following year, 1841, a public meeting was held, by the invitation of the Primate, at Willis's Rooms, of which the newspapers record, "the rooms were more crowded than upon any occasion of which we have been witnesses for many years." At this meeting, in moving the resolution "that the Church of England, in endeavouring to discharge her unquestionable duty of providing for the religious wants of her members in foreign lands, is bound to proceed upon her own principles of apostolical order and discipline," Bishop Blomfield dwelt upon the evils resulting from the absence of episcopal government, in accordance with the old axiom, *Ecclesia est in Episcopo;* and showed how the presence of Protestant bishops was desired by the colonists themselves, while at the same time the Roman Catholic Church, less backward than the English, was planting new sees of her own throughout the world. The list of subscriptions announced at the meeting showed that the work had already been taken up in earnest. The Christian Knowledge Society had voted £10,000 for the purpose; the Propagation Society £5,000 (to which it soon afterwards added £2,500); the Church Missionary Society £600 a year for New Zealand; the Queen Dowager gave £2,000; the Archbishop of Canterbury, and the Bishop of London, £1,000 each. In subsequent years many individuals

[1] Churton's Life of Watson, vol. ii. p. 128.

have come forward in the same cause with great munificence; especially Miss Burdett Coutts, who has endowed three colonial bishoprics at her own sole charge.

The meeting at Willis's Rooms was followed by a council of prelates at Lambeth, which issued a declaration, signed afterwards by the entire body of English and Irish bishops, setting forth the necessity of erecting additional bishoprics in the colonies, and announcing the intention of the bishops to take charge of the fund for that purpose, as requested. The first result of the plan was the creation of the see of New Zealand; which was soon afterwards followed by that of Gibraltar, for the superintendence of English congregations on the shores of the Mediterranean.

Bishop Blomfield also aided the work in 1842, by addressing a letter to his clergy recommending the fund as an object for collections in their churches; an appeal which produced in the diocese upwards of £8,000; and on St. Bartholomew's Day in that year, it fell to his lot, owing to the illness of Archbishop Howley, to consecrate with his own hands no less than five colonial bishops, four of whom were appointed to dioceses owing their erection to the movement which he had himself originated.

Altogether, the increase of the colonial episcopate, to which the influence and example of Bishop Blomfield gave the first impulse, has been one of the most remarkable instances of vitality and energy which the Church of England has shown during the last twenty years. Instead of ten bishops, scattered at vast intervals over three-fourths of the habitable globe, and leaving immense tracts of country almost without the possibility of episcopal supervision, she now numbers beyond the shores of our own island, forty-three bishops, placed with more or less regularity at the chief centres of colonization, India being now the only country in which the staff of bishops bears no sort of proportion to the wants of the Church. Instead of a Church belying her own constitution, and incapable of administering her own ordinances, she now presents to the world the appearance of one governed according to her own principles by men invested with the highest order of the Christian ministry, and, in many cases, with truly apostolic zeal and wisdom; of one which assists and systematises, and supplements the labours of the lower order of her servants by the authority and the counsel of the higher. And, lastly, she has now begun to send out her bishops, not only to the scattered members of her own communion, but to the native converts who are willing to receive the faith of Christ according to her teaching, and through her ministers.

Bishop Blomfield himself, in a sermon, the substance of which was preached on more than one occasion before the great missionary societies, reviews the work of the Colonial Bishoprics Fund in a passage which, as it refers to a subject in which he was so deeply interested, may properly be quoted at length:—

"We do not wonder that some zealous and fervid minds, struck by the fearful contrast between the actual state of the Christian world in this respect, and that which ought to characterise the Lord's people, should have been led to expect some special interposition of Divine power, some extraordinary operation of the Holy Spirit, to counteract the effect of man's apathy and sinfulness, and to hasten the coming of the Lord's kingdom. And it would be presumptuous to deny that this, after all, may be the method to which God will resort for the completion of His designs of mercy. It may be, that if the ordinary influences of the Holy Spirit in the Church are unimproved and neglected by His servants, the Lord Himself shall come, and all the saints with Him; and '*by fire and by sword will the Lord plead with all flesh;*' He will make '*bare His holy arm in the eyes of all the nations; and all the ends of the earth shall see the salvation of our God.*'

But the possibility of such a consummation is no reason why we should slacken our exertions to carry forward the Church's work; the progress of which may depend, in what degree we know not, upon those exertions, put forth in undoubting reliance upon the Spirit who helpeth all our infirmities, and crowned by Him with such a measure of success as may seem good to Him: '*not by might, nor by power, but by My Spirit, saith the Lord of Hosts.*'

An entire trust in the power of that Holy Spirit to accomplish His own purposes by no means excludes the necessity, nor exempts us from the duty, of using all the instrumental means which He has provided in His Church. The neglect or misuse of them, if they are of Divine appointment, cannot be consistent with His will, even if it could by possibility hasten the display of His power in the conversion of the world. But let us never forget that they are only instrumental; and that in the faithful use of them we shall be most likely to succeed, when we place our dependence, not upon them, nor upon any subordinate agency, but upon '*the blessed and only Potentate,*' whose we are, and in whose might alone we can triumph. It deserves our serious consideration, whether, in the fervour of a newly-kindled zeal for the cause of Christ, and under the excitement of new undertakings, having in view such unspeakably interesting objects, we have not been insensibly led to think too much of the grandeur and efficacy of the means employed by us; and to magnify the instruments, instead of looking humbly and hopefully to the Hand which alone can wield them with success. We think and speak so much of the machinery which we set to work, our apparatus of societies and missionaries, and churches, and schools, that we are apt to ascribe to them an efficacy not their own; and to forget how utterly worthless and inefficient they are, without the direct intervention of God Himself. Let us rest assured, that the more humbly we think of ourselves, and of our exertions and labours, even in the holiest cause, the more surely we may calculate upon success, and the less will be our disappointment, if success should be withholden from us.

I have already observed, that the possibility, which cannot be denied, of God's having reserved the complete establishment of His kingdom upon earth for a special and manifest interposition of His own power, is not a sufficient reason why we should relax our endeavours to hasten that blessed consummation. But of one thing we should be thoroughly persuaded; that if those endeavours are to be in any measure successful, it can only be by the direct and continued influences of His Holy Spirit. No power but His can take away the veil from the hearts of those benighted millions, who are blinded, not only by the delusions of a polytheism, which throws the charm of voluptuousness over the dark intricacies of superstition, but by the deceitful perplexities of a subtle and refined philosophy. I allude more particularly to that vast field of missionary labour which is opened to us in our Eastern empire. With some of the less civilized of the heathen tribes the missionary's task may seem to be more promising. The simplicity of the Gospel may be more likely to find access to their untutored, and, in one sense, unperverted minds; but neither in their case will anything effectual be done in the way of conversion, without the unceasing aid of the Holy Spirit, nor, consequently, without a strong and lively faith in the certainty of that aid, leading to earnest prayer, that the Lord will accomplish the number of His elect and hasten His kingdom.

But singleness of purpose, and earnestness in prayer, indispensable as they are to the success of every effort to extend the limits of the Redeemer's kingdom, must be accompanied by the faithful use of those instruments and means which He Himself has appointed for the conversion of the world. '*The sword of the Spirit which is the Word of God,*' must be taken from the Church's armoury, and wielded by those who are specially ordained to that work. If, as St. Paul declares, while speaking of his mission to '*preach among the Gentiles the unsearchable riches of Christ,*' it is God's intention that not only unto them but '*unto the principalities and powers in heavenly places, might be known by the Church the manifold wisdom of God,*' it is clearly our duty to work in and by the Church, in our endeavour to communicate the blessedness of that knowledge to the heathen. And as the Church's office of teaching is specially committed to the ministry, we must employ that ministry in its completeness and integrity, as we believe it to have been constituted by the Apostles, '*for the perfecting of the saints for the edifying of the body of Christ.*' It can hardly be questioned, that the slow and uncertain progress of evangelization in some parts of the world, the failure and abandonment of missions, have been, in some measure, occasioned by the individual and desultory nature of those missionary enterprises, which have had no connexion with what we believe to be a divinely-appointed order of Church government, and have wanted its authority, its restraints, its sympathies, and its supports. We are warranted in this supposition, not only by the consideration, that if there be an order of Church government having the stamp of apostolical authority, its absence must be an impediment to the preaching of the Gospel to the heathen, but by the increased measure of success in that work, which has followed the establishment of Colonial Bishoprics.

Compare the time, when four clergymen only of the Church of England were found in the whole continent of America, and not one bishop in any of our Colonial possessions (for such was the case at the end of the seventeenth century), with the present era of the Church's awakened energies. In the United States thirty-two bishops, and one thousand five hundred and fifty-seven clergy; in our own Colonies and dependencies, where, at the close of the eighteenth century, only two bishoprics had been erected, and where twelve years ago there were but eight, we can now count with gladness twenty-four, and can look with confident hope to a speedy increase of that number. We may not rest satisfied till all the members of our Church, in whatever quarter of the globe they may have fixed their households, shall be within reach of all the means of grace to which that membership entitles them, and enjoy the benefits of apostolical order and discipline, as well as that of scriptural teaching. Although the Society for the Propagation of the Gospel cannot claim the exclusive praise of establishing the Colonial churches in their integrity, it suggested, encouraged, and assisted the undertaking; and the Colonial Bishoprics' Fund may justly be accounted an offset, God be praised, a flourishing offset, from this parent stock. And, truly, it rejoices one's heart to see the mutual inter-dependence and co-operation of the two. If the Society provides a maintenance for the clergy of an infant Church, the Bishop to whom its oversight is committed, speedily multiplies the numbers of those clergymen, in some instances three and four fold; builds churches and schools, founds colleges, forms Church societies, completes the machinery by which the Church may best work out the purposes of her institution, gives to it an impulse, which no other moving power could impart, and directs its movements with an authority, superior to all human laws, as to its essence, while it conforms to them in all things not contrary to the law of Christ.

The enlargement of the Church follows rapidly upon its perfect organization. In the extension of the Colonial episcopate, we have the surest pledge of success in our increased efforts to provide the means of edification and grace for our brethren who are of the household of faith, and to cause the light of the world to shine upon those heathen tribes who are connected with us, whether by conquest or by commerce. In the lands where the Society for tho Propagation of the Gospel has laboured, where, a century and a half ago, there were scarcely a dozen clergymen of the Church of England, there are now two thousand seven hundred and fifty under the government of fifty-seven bishops, dispensing the Word of God and the sacraments of His grace to three millions of souls in communion with a reformed Episcopal Church.

Again, let us turn our eyes with thankfulness and hope to New Zealand, and the Polynesian World, where the Church, which now exists there in the integrity of its apostolical constitution, was founded and built up by the Church Missionary Society; and let us rejoice in the success of its labours, pursuing as it does the same holy objects by the same legitimate means. A similar blessing has been vouchsafed to that branch of the Church in Africa, which has long been fostered by the maternal care of the Church Missionary Society, under circumstances of great difficulty and trial. If there be any part of the heathen world which in an especial degree deserves our sympathy, and to which we are pre-eminently bound to impart the privileges of the Gospel and the Church, it is surely that country, of whose children we were so long the guilty oppressors. What cause for thanksgiving to Him, '*who hath made of one blood all nations of men,*' is to be found in the thought, that He has not only blessed our labours by bringing many of those neglected and persecuted people to the knowledge of a Saviour; but that, from among a race who were despised as incapable of intellectual exertion and acquirement, He has raised up men, well qualified, even in point of knowledge, to communicate to others the saving truths which they themselves have embraced, and to become preachers of the Gospel to their brethren according to the flesh. I speak this the more feelingly, as having been myself privileged to admit to the holy order of priesthood, after due examination, more than one native of Africa; and to send them forth into the Lord's vineyard, strong in the faith of Christ, armed with the knowledge of His Word, and animated by all the sympathies of brotherhood toward the objects of their missionary labours.

In these events, as also in the open exertion of our influence as a nation, for the protection of Christians from the cruelty of unbelieving persecutors; in the gradual loosening of the great fabric of Mahomedan superstition; in the spirit of inquiry which has been awakened among God's ancient people; in the sudden growth of the Church in some districts of our Indian Empire; in the opening made for the Gospel by our recent alliance with the vast Empire of China; we discern enough to excite our hopes, and to encourage us to perseverance; streaks of light in the horizon of that darkness which still shrouds so large a portion of the world; harbingers, we humbly trust, of a coming, though perhaps distant day, when '*the glory of the Lord shall be seen*' upon the people; '*and the Gentiles shall come to His light, and kings to the brightness of His rising.*' It may still be reserved for our Church—I devoutly and soberly believe that it is reserved for her—to be, in a sense subordinate to the prerogative of her glorified Head, the Light of the world; I believe that unto her, imperfect as she may be, '*is this grace given, that*' she '*should preach among the Gentiles the unsearchable riches of Christ.*'

But let us not forget that the success of great exertions will be the condemnation of future inactivity. Indeed, we have great need to be careful not to indulge in feelings of exultation, as though we had done the whole of our duty. While we praise God for what He has graciously enabled us to do in His cause, let us humbly and sorrowfully confess, how much more we ought to have done; and pray that He will open the eyes of all His servants to the real nature and extent of their Christian responsibility; that the inhabitants of a country so favoured with worldly blessings, and opportunities of good, and especially the members of a Church so providentially reformed and protected, may turn an attentive ear to the cry which may well be imagined to go forth from millions of benighted heathens, objects like themselves of Redeeming Love, but perishing for want of some to seek and to save them.

If ever there was a time, when the servants of Jesus Christ could innocently stand aloof from the work of evangelizing the world, *this* surely is not the time. But this *is* a time, if ever there has been a time, since the first uttering of the awful sentence, when the lukewarm disciple of the Saviour may well be reminded of those words, of fearful application to every neglected opportunity of advancing the cause of His Gospel; *'He that is not with Me is against Me, and he that gathereth not with Me, scattereth.'*"

To show that Bishop Blomfield took an almost equal interest in the more directly missionary work of the Church, as well as in her extension in the Colonies, a few words may be quoted from another sermon on a kindred subject:—

"We do not lay this matter to heart as we ought. We are not sufficiently alive to the progress of that spiritual dispensation, which must embrace the whole habitable globe; nor consider that if God condescends to employ us as instruments in the accomplishment of His purposes, its final establishment will be hastened by our diligence, or retarded by our coldness and neglect. How large a portion of that world, which is one day to be covered with the knowledge of the glory of the Lord as the waters cover the sea, is still in darkness and the shadow of death! How many of those nations, for whom the Son of God shed His precious blood, and to whom He commanded His disciples to preach the Gospel of life, are still aliens from the Christian commonwealth, strangers to the covenant of promise, and living without God in the world! Scarcely more than one-fourth part of the whole population of the earth profess the religion of Jesus Christ. How infinitely more important are these considerations than those of the petty movements and intrigues of international policy; or even than the great revolutions which disturb the established order of human government. And when will men learn to regard even these, with reference to their bearing upon the final object of all God's providential dispensations, the consolidating of all earthly empires into one great spiritual dominion, when '*all the kingdoms of the world*' shall '*become the kingdoms of our Lord, and of His Christ.*'"

Side by side with the establishment of the Colonial Bishoprics' Fund, another scheme was now occupying the attention of Bishop Blomfield, which at the time seemed likely to be of almost equal importance to the Church. King Frederick William IV. of Prussia, who succeeded to the throne in 1840, was well known for his attachment to the Church and constitution of England, and for his desire to promote the cause of religion throughout the world. He had conceived the idea of uniting with the Church of England in the creation of a bishopric which should have its seat at Jerusalem, where no Protestant communion had as yet a representative, hoping by this means both to assist the conversion of the Jews, and to obtain the advantages of episcopal superintendence for his own subjects in Palestine. Such at least are the objects set forth in the authoritative statement of proceedings afterwards published.

"... In making this proposal, his Majesty had in view not only the great advantages to be derived from its adoption, with reference to the conversion of the Jews, but also the spiritual superintendence and care of such of his own subjects as might be disposed to take up their abode in Palestine, and to join themselves to the Church so formed at Jerusalem. There is reason to expect that a considerable number of German as well as English Christians will be attracted to the Holy Land by the influence of strong religious feelings.

The immediate objects for which this bishopric has been founded, will appear from the following statement. Its ultimate results cannot be with certainty predicted; but we may reasonably hope that, under the Divine blessing, it may lead the way to an essential unity of discipline, as well as of doctrine, between our own Church and the less perfectly constituted of the Protestant Churches of Europe, and that, too, not by the way of Rome; while it may be the means of establishing relations of amity between the United Church of England and Ireland, and the ancient Churches of the East, strengthening them against the encroachments of the See of Rome, and preparing the way for their purification, in some cases from serious errors, in others from those imperfections which now materially impede their efficiency as witnesses and dispensers of Gospel truth and grace. In the meantime, the spectacle of a Church, freed from those errors and imperfections, planted in the Holy City, and holding a pure faith in the unity of the Spirit, and in the bond of peace, will naturally attract the notice of the Jewish nation throughout the world, and will centralize, as it were, the desultory efforts which are making for their conversion.

While the Church of Rome is continually, and at this very moment, labouring to pervert the members of the Eastern Churches, and to bring them under the dominion of the Pope, sparing no arts nor intrigues, hesitating at no misrepresentations, sowing dissension and disorder amongst an ill-informed people, and asserting that jurisdiction over them which the ancient Churches of the East have always strenuously resisted, the two great Protestant Powers of Europe will have planted a Church in the midst of them, the Bishop of which is specially charged not to encroach upon the spiritual rights and liberties of those Churches, but to confine himself to the care of those over whom *they* cannot rightfully claim any jurisdiction, and to maintain with them a friendly intercourse of good offices, assisting them, so far as they may desire such assistance, in the work of Christian education; and presenting to their observation, but not forcing upon their acceptance, the pattern of a Church essentially scriptural in doctrine, and apostolical in discipline."

In order to effect his object, the king, in 1841, sent over to England the Chevalier Bunsen as a special envoy, with directions to communicate on the subject of the bishopric, both with the Government, and with the Archbishop of Canterbury, and the Bishop of London. It was at this time that Bishop Blomfield began a friendly and familiar intercourse with Bunsen, which lasted during the long subsequent stay of the latter as ambassador to the English court. In the later writings of this eminent man there were many things of which the Bishop disapproved; but Bunsen possessed in so high a degree the art of showing to those into whose society he was thrown that side of his mind in which he sympathized with them, not that in which he differed from them, and he had so intelligent an appreciation of all the peculiar excellencies of the English Church and nation, that the Bishop felt no difficulty in their intercourse.

From the Government, which, after Midsummer, 1841, was that of Sir Robert Peel, the Chevalier Bunsen met with no opposition to the scheme; and by Archbishop Howley, though with his characteristic caution, and by Bishop Blomfield, it was well received. It was agreed that the King of Prussia should nominate to the bishopric alternately with the Crown of England, and that he should furnish half the endowment, the rest being provided by voluntary contributions in England; that the Bishop should have jurisdiction over English congregations in Syria and Palestine, and over such others as might place themselves under his authority; that he should maintain friendly relations with the orthodox Greek and other Eastern communions, and that he should ordain, if occasion required, natives of Germany, who were to subscribe both to the Thirty-nine Articles and to the Confession of Augsburg. The only opposition which the plan encountered was from the High-Church party, who looked with dislike and suspicion upon any display of friendly feeling towards an un-episcopal Church, such as that of Prussia, or as the document already quoted delicately expressed it, a "less perfectly constituted Church." These objections, however, were not allowed to frustrate the scheme, and before the close of 1841 the new Bishop was consecrated by the Archbishop of Canterbury.

Nor did Bishop Blomfield see cause afterwards to regret the part which he had taken in this matter. In 1842, when the King of Prussia visited this country as sponsor to the infant Prince of Wales, he was present at a service at St. Paul's Cathedral, at which the Bishop of London preached the sermon. In this sermon the following passage occurs:—

"The Church of England is especially qualified to

undertake the charitable work of bringing the ancient people of God into the fold and family of his dear Son, and of restoring to them the enjoyment of their spiritual birthright and inheritance. It is, surely, at once a strong encouragement to her to persevere in that work of charity, and an omen, under the Divine blessing, of her success, when the heart of a mighty sovereign, bound to her only by the bands of Christian love, is stirred up to assist her in the work, and to recognise her as an instrument providentially ordained for its accomplishment, and possessing authority to send forth labourers into the Lord's harvest-field, wheresoever it may seem to be ripening for the sickle of the Evangelist; that Sovereign being the ruler over a great nation, which, we firmly believe, is indebted, like our own, for its power and glory, to the blessing of God attending its emancipation from the spiritual bondage of Rome, and its continued maintenance of the Reformed Religion; himself descended from a house which numbered among its princes the firmest adherents and most strenuous defenders of the Reformation."

And, speaking of those who would exalt unduly the privileges of our own Church, he says:—

"Let them not think, nor speak, more uncharitably of other national churches than the fathers of our own have spoken; but, contented with and thankful for their own undoubted privileges, let them present to others, in the faithful use of those privileges, and in the exercise of Christian charity, a proof that our belief is catholic, and our discipline apostolic."

That the scheme of the Jerusalem bishopric has failed to produce the results which its projectors anticipated from it, whether in converting the Jews, conciliating the Eastern Christians, or drawing together the Churches of England and Germany, is to be attributed rather to the deficiencies of the agents employed than to any inherent viciousness in the project itself. Both the Bishops selected for this difficult post have been men singularly unfitted for the work; and so it has come to pass that a design, from which men not over-sanguine, nor wanting in foresight, hoped for such large fruits, has become "an offence to the East, and a by-word in the West."[1]

A more successful, though less imposing measure in which Bishop Blomfield bore a part at this time, was the partial removal of the disabilities imposed upon clergymen ordained in the Episcopal churches of Scotland and America. By an Act passed in 1840, intercommunion was so far established between those churches and that of England, that their clergy were allowed to officiate under licence from English Bishops, though for only two Sundays together.

And here it may be proper to mention, that in the schism attempted a few years afterwards in the Scotch Episcopal Church, when two or three clergymen renounced their allegiance to the Scotch bishops, and rendered it to the English, who neither would nor could accept it, Bishop Blomfield always wrote and acted on the side of order. Clergymen calling themselves episcopalian, but under the jurisdiction of no Bishop, presented an anomaly which he could not tolerate. He wrote to Bishop Russell of Glasgow in 1844:—

[1] Biber, p. 293.

"My opinion as to the obligation which binds an English clergyman desirous of officiating in Scotland, to seek for authority to do so at the hands of the Bishop in whose diocese he officiates, and to pay him canonical obedience, has long been known in that country, and I retain that opinion unchanged.

As to the jurisdiction which, it appears, some persons suppose me to possess, as Bishop of London, over English clergymen residing in Scotland, I absolutely disclaim it. Were I to pretend to any such jurisdiction, I should be intruding into a province which does not belong to me; and any attempt to exercise it could be productive only of schism and confusion. If I possessed any authority over —— or ——, I should exert it for the purpose of inducing them to return to the spiritual allegiance which they owe, while in Scotland, to the Fathers of the Church in that country. The duty of paying that allegiance I urged very strongly upon —— when he quitted my diocese. The refusal of it must lead to disorder, and to a weakening of the Church, at a time when all her energies are needed to resist the assaults of those who are equally hostile to the Scotch and English branches of Christ's Holy Catholic Church, as possessing the apostolical inheritance of Episcopacy."

In the session of 1841, the question of removing the restrictions from marriages of affinity was mooted in the House of Lords by Lord Wharncliffe. Bishop Blomfield spoke strongly against any alteration in the law of marriage; maintaining that marriage with a wife's sister, which was the object really in view, was contrary to Scripture, to the ancient laws of the Catholic Church, and to the feelings of the nation at large; and that the question had best be left as it was settled by Lord

Lyndhurst's Act in 1835. On this subject the Bishop never changed his opinion; indeed, in 1851 he stated that his objection to such marriages, on the scriptural ground, was even more decided than it had been in 1841.

Shortly afterwards, the admission of Jews to municipal corporations was a subject of debate in the Lords. The Government measure for removing their disabilities was supported by the recently appointed Bishop Thirlwall; on the other side, Bishop Blomfield delivered a speech of which Bishop Copleston wrote thus:—

"The Bishop of London, *qui nil molitur inepte*, was great on this occasion, as he always is; but no report can do him justice; it is always below the truth."[1]

The bill was lost by ninety-eight to sixty-four.

The same year witnessed a change of administration very pleasing to Bishop Blomfield. The Government of Lord Melbourne, which had only escaped annihilation by a not very creditable manœuvre in 1839, received its final death-blow after the assembling of a new parliament, in August 1841; and Sir Robert Peel succeeded to office. With this great statesman Bishop Blomfield always maintained the most friendly relations. It has been the policy of some subsequent Prime Ministers to act on ecclesiastical matters, without consulting, or even in opposition to, the Heads of the Church. But this was by no means Sir Robert Peel's method of acting. On all appointments to important Church dignities, and on all matters affecting the interests of the Church, he consulted the Archbishop, or the Bishop of London, and, as far as possible, acted in concert with them. In

[1] Memoir of Bishop Copleston, p. 178.

1843 he entrusted to Bishop Blomfield the task of carrying through the House of Lords his Church Endowment-bill; without doubt, one of the most important, and, on the whole, one of the most beneficial measures which any statesman in recent times has obtained for the Church; establishing, as it does, the principle that the cure of souls, not the material church, is the great essential of the parochial system.

Thus Bishop Blomfield was able to feel for some years that, instead of perpetually resisting the Government of the day as the champion of the Church, he could act with them for its good. An enemy once called him "an ecclesiastical Peel;" and he would probably have accepted as a compliment this intended reproach. In high principle, in calmness of judgment, in readiness to yield cherished opinions to the necessities of the times, the mind of the Bishop resembled not a little that of the Minister. Of the public acts of Peel he always spoke in terms of praise. He defended the part which Sir Robert had taken in establishing the Ecclesiastical Commission. He said that there could be no doubt of his disinterestedness; that he had seen for many years such a tendency in the country towards a more popular form of government as none but enthusiasts could expect to check; and that he had endeavoured to guide and direct the movement, to prevent its being hasty, and to secure its being effected by those who were friendly to the Church and the Monarchy. He thought that his principal fault, as a Minister, was his backwardness in communicating freely with those most nearly associated with him.

Sir Robert thus replied to the Bishop's congratulations on his accession to office :—

"WHITEHALL, *Sept.* 17, 1841.

"MY DEAR BISHOP OF LONDON,—I will avail myself of the first opportunity in my power of calling upon you, should you be prevented leaving home for some days to come.[1] This, however, I sincerely hope will not be the case.

I thank you cordially for the good wishes you express for my success in the arduous and harassing undertaking in which the force of circumstances and a sense of public duty have compelled me to engage, and I fervently join in your prayer that it may please Almighty God todirect and favour me."

[1] The Bishop being ill at the time.

END OF VOL. I.

CPSIA information can be obtained
at www.ICGtesting.com
Printed in the USA
LVHW100441110522
718424LV00003B/183

9 783375 007478